Along the Road

A Becker Family Novel

Pat Wahler

Evergreen Tree Press

Cottleville, MO

Book Layout © 2017 BookDesignTemplates.com
Book Formatting by Jeanne Felfe
Editing by Joy Editing
Cover design by Jenny Quinlan, Historical Editorial

Names: Wahler, Pat, author.
Title: Along the road : a Becker family novel / Pat Wahler.
Description: Cottleville, MO : Evergreen Tree Press, 2020. | Series: A Becker family novel, bk. 2.
Identifiers: LCCN 2019921138 (print) | ISBN 978-1-7323876-4-5 (paperback) | ISBN 978-1-7323876-5-2 (ebook)
Subjects: LCSH: Man-woman relationships--Fiction. | Life change events--Fiction. | Entertainment industry--Fiction. | Nashville (Tenn.)--Fiction. | Tennessee--Fiction. | Romance fiction. | BISAC: FICTION / Romance / Contemporary. | FICTION / Romance / Clean & Wholesome. | FICTION / Romance / Romantic Comedy. | FICTION / Women. | GSAFD: Love stories. | Humorous fiction.
Classification: LCC PS3623.A35646 A4 2020 (print) | LCC PS3623.A35646 (ebook) | DDC 813/.6--dc23.
First edition: February 2020
Printed in the United States of America

Praise for *Along the Road*
(A Becker Family Novel, Book 2)

"A beautifully crafted story with characters and scenes that will speak strongly to readers."
—Ruffina Oserio for *Readers' Favorite*

"Features excellent dialogue, great writing, and a good plot. Pat Wahler combines suspense with humor to create scenes that capture the reader's attention."
—Romuald Dzemo for *Readers' Favorite*

"Readers who enjoy wholesome romances with a splash of drama will love this novel."
—Peggy Jo Wipf for *Readers' Favorite*

Praise for *On a City Street*
(A Becker Family Novel, Book 1)

"Wahler provides a heart-warming roller coaster of emotions and sparks…and who doesn't love puppies?"
—Jeanne Felfe, author of *Bridge to Us*

"I found it really hard to put the book down and loved the twist ending."
—Trudi LoPreto for *Readers' Favorite*

"A delightful read for fans of contemporary romance with a touch of real-life angst."
—Louanne Piccolo for *Readers' Favorite*

Praise for *I am Mrs. Jesse James*

"A vivid, moving tale of the woman behind the man of myth and legend. This is a book not to be missed!"
—Nicole Evelina, *USA Today* bestselling author

"*I am Mrs. Jesse James* tackles the Jesse James story from a new and heartbreaking perspective."   —*Missouri Life*

"This is a fantastically researched historical piece that many readers will enjoy, even if the historical genre is not their first choice."   —*InD'tale Magazine*

Praise for *Let Your Heart Be Light: A Celebration of Christmas*

"The stories are short and engaging...A fun and enjoyable read, especially around Christmas time."
—Gisela Dixon for *Readers' Favorite*

"*Let Your Heart Be Light* is rich and sweet and will warm your heart."
—Donna Duly Volkenannt, winner of the 2012 Erma Bombeck Global Humor Award

To Mom and Dad with love. How I miss you!

Chapter One

Mother's hand trembled as she placed her cell phone on the table. Kat thought it might be smart to walk away from the squabble she knew was brewing. But a mere second later, astonishment pinned her feet to the floor.

At the corner of her mother's eyes, she noticed a web of fine lines. When did that happen? Without a doubt, Mother could be melodramatic, but she couldn't counterfeit creases. They made her look…old. The realization dumped a hefty dollop of extra guilt on her head. It was as if her parent had suddenly turned into someone else. A faint whiff of Chanel No. 5 snapped Kat back into reality. *Let the face-off begin.*

Stage one of Mother's agitation had been brow-raising shock. Stage two a phone call to Daddy. And stage three? What had previously been only a turn of phrase—and a completely old-fashioned one at that—segued into reality. Right in the middle of their family's marble-floored foyer, her mother stood poised like an alabaster sculpture come to life, wringing her hands in distress.

"Kathryn, I'm worried about you. This entire idea seems most ill-advised. We don't know anyone in Nashville, and it's not safe for a young girl to go traipsing off alone to unfamiliar places." Each fear she voiced bounced off walls towering more than twenty feet tall, creating a strangely hollow sound.

Stage four: exaggeration? "Mother think about it. I'm hardly a child. I'll be twenty-four in a few days. Besides, Nashville isn't some far-off scary place like, say, Afghanistan."

Her mother's hand rose and massaged her temple. "What about college? Have you forgotten? You promised you'd finish your degree."

"I plan on registering at Belmont University as soon as I get settled. I've already checked into classes." It wasn't a total lie. She'd heard about the school through a friend, though Kat knew better than to push her mother over the edge by confessing.

"Two semesters, darling. It's all you need. Why don't you continue here at KU? Then, after you complete whatever program you choose—you'll be better prepared to decide on your future."

Kat sensed the hint of accusation over how she'd spent her time at Kansas University as clearly as she heard the dirge of annoyance—seasoned with disappointment. Today was not her first time at this rodeo. *Yes, I got your message. A Becker is expected to be a whiz kid, not a goof-off.*

Her mother's little white poodle trotted into the foyer. His muzzle dripped from a visit to the water dish, and his tail waved in a blur of delight. Kat bent to scoop Louie into her arms and ruffled the curls on his head. The effort to hold her tongue fizzled away.

"Please don't give me another chorus of I-told-you-so. It isn't a crime to switch majors or take a break from school. Lots of people finish on a five-year plan these days. No big deal." Louie applied an array of supportive slurps to Kat's fingers. "For once, why can't you be happy for me? The moment you and Daddy have been waiting for is here. I finally figured things out."

"First of all, darling, I didn't say I told you so. Second, I think we're already on the six-year plan. In any event, your father and I certainly didn't want things to work out this way."

"But guess what? They have. So come on, Elise, chill." The sassy use of her mother's name was meant to make her smile, but it didn't work. Kat placed Louie back on the floor and lit the foyer with a neon-bright smile. No such luck there either.

Her mother started to say something but must have thought better of it, pausing for a long moment before she spoke. "Your father will be home soon. He wants to discuss this with you. Meanwhile, I have work to do, so you and I will talk in more detail later." She pivoted to ascend the wide curving flight of stairs. Even in such an obvious state of displeasure, she glided away with a straight back, regal as a queen. Louie, the court jester, followed in a funny hop from step to step, fast as his short legs would carry him.

Kat huffed out a breath. She hadn't expected cartwheels of joy from Mother, especially after last year when her older sister had dealt with a broken engagement by leaving town. Their mother had been horrified at the idea of a young woman living alone near a sketchy area of downtown St. Louis, but in the end, it all worked out. Carolyn not only found a new job she loved, but also a soul mate in the process. She and her hot new fiancé had no intention of leaving St. Louis for a return to Kansas City anytime soon.

How awesome would it be to find a love like Carolyn's? Her sister's hunky knight-in-shining-armor had actually gone to one knee and proposed in front of the entire family. On Christmas Day. Kat had never before heard her calm and composed sibling screech like a teenager at a rock concert. Or witnessed her mother's look of complete bewilderment. The entire scenario had Kat pursing her mouth together so she wouldn't giggle. She had to hand it to Carolyn. She'd taken charge of her own life. Kat intended to do the same, and she knew it wouldn't happen in the suburbs of Kansas City.

The enormous foyer mirror caught her eye and she made a face. Humidity had a way of creating a cosmic explosion of each strand on her head. She tangled fingers through her strawberry-blonde curls to shove them away from her face. Once upon a time, she used to long for straight, smooth, serious-woman hair like Carolyn's. Yet despite oils and balms and elixirs—plus a flatiron that scorched her hair so badly it smelled skunky for days—her decidedly feral locks refused to cooperate. She'd given up trying to tame her mane. What did it matter? Look at Dolly Parton. No one's hair poufed bigger than Dolly's, but that fact hadn't held her back.

Kat meandered to the kitchen where her brown tabby, Charlie Daniels—named for the singer—lay in a splash of sunlight on the floor. He lifted his head, opened one eye, and meowed. Kat caressed the side of his face until his purrs sounded like rumbles of distant thunder. "How's my baby?" she asked.

When he closed his one open eye, she moved away to let him snooze. Her belly reminded her she hadn't eaten, so she grabbed a yellow apple from a handwoven basket on the counter and crunched into the crisp, tart fruit. Her mother, a champion of many causes, had ordered the basket from Rwanda, in an effort to help fair trade. The basket didn't fit well in the sleek gray-and-cream kitchen décor. Woven with parrot-bright colors of sisal and sweetgrass, it looked like an artsy bohemian had left the token behind to add a touch of color.

Longing for a quiet place to settle, Kat wandered outside to the pool. A breeze rippled sparkles of light across the water. She settled into a chaise lounge, replaying the night before—an evening she'd rank as the most thrilling of her life so far. She'd sure count it among the latest: home at three in the morning only to rise at seven when her yowling cat demanded breakfast. Now her eyelids felt sticky. Could this be a hint of what another birthday would bring? She used to stay sharp on almost no sleep at all.

The sun's warmth lulled her into a decision. She had plenty of time tomorrow to figure out what to pack. At the moment, a nap sounded more appealing. Kat dropped her snack on the side table and stretched out her legs, crossing them at the ankle. Her head bobbed and dipped. She didn't remember another thing until someone touched her shoulder.

"Wake up, sweetie."

Kat's eyes flew open, and she blinked her father's smiling face into view. "Hi, Daddy."

She yawned and grinned at him. He mirrored her smile, and a proud-daughter moment struck her. Tom Becker had to be one of the best-looking men she knew. Ever since middle school, Kat's friends squealed with giddiness whenever her father entered the room. Even with brown hair gone salt-and-pepper, he didn't appear much older than when she was a little girl. Recently, Kat mentioned this observation to her mother, who responded in a slightly resentful tone that men didn't age, they matured.

Daddy sat on the edge of her lounge chair. "Can you explain what in the world you're getting yourself into, young lady? When your mother called, her voice wobbled with every word."

Kat leaned forward, her grogginess replaced by a rush of excitement. "I know she's upset, but I do have a plan. Sort of. I'm going to Nashville as fast as I can get there, which means I'll leave tomorrow."

"You seem in quite a hurry to go. Please tell me, point by point, exactly why."

Lawyer-speak. One of her father's trademarks. She'd grown used to it. "Because I'm going to be a singer and write my own songs. Of all the careers you and Mother have suggested, not one makes my soul dance like this does. You know how much I've always loved music. I never thought about it as anything more than a hobby—until last night."

"You must know there's more to making a living than announcing you want to be a singer or songwriter. Exactly how do you propose to support yourself in the meantime?"

"I can do social media stuff from any place. And if it's okay with you, I'll still take care of your updates." He'd been paying her to oversee the Becker and Harper law firm's media platforms for a while. It wasn't blowing her own horn to say she did a stellar job at it. "Plus I can pick up part-time work somewhere."

He lifted an eyebrow. "What about school? You'll break your mother's heart if you don't finish your education."

"I'll enroll first thing after I find an apartment. I promise." An impish thought made her add, "The college will send you the bills to prove it."

The pump gurgled, and her father glanced toward the pool. His face assumed the unreadable expression of an attorney before closing arguments. Barely breathing, she waited for his verdict. It wasn't like she needed his blessing, yet her father was the one person she didn't want to disappoint. Ever. The pump gurgled again.

He turned to face her. "Are you sure you don't want to think this over?"

"I'm positive, Daddy. This is something I have to do." Her voice rang with every ounce of conviction she could muster.

"My little Kitty-Kat." A pensive look crossed his face in a flash. "You're an adult and certainly old enough to make your own decisions. However, I can't help but point out an observation. In the past, you've had more than your share of…missteps. I trust you'll refrain from doing anything risky or foolish. Above all, your mother and I want you to stay safe."

Kat nodded, and her eyes stung. She looked up to study a wispy cloud just long enough to be sure the tears didn't spill over. "You know I'll be careful."

"All right then. Do what you must." He rubbed his chin. "I don't want you to run short on cash, so I'm putting money in your account as a cushion—no argument. Consider it an early birthday present. And don't be a martyr. Let me know if you need more. Keep it quiet though. With Carolyn in St. Louis and you bound for Nashville, all your mother will have left to worry over is that silly poodle of hers. She's liable to accuse me of being an enabler."

Kat wrapped her arms around her father. Through a lump in her throat, she said, "Thank you, Daddy. Everything's going to work out. I know it will. Anyway, Mother loves you and Louie as much as Carolyn or me. She'll learn to adjust."

"Time will tell, but whatever happens, remember this. If things fail to materialize the way you hope, or if you change your mind, don't let pride get in your way. Come straight back to us and we'll figure it out."

She didn't intend to slink home like some sort of loser, but the gruff comment did remind her how much she'd miss her father, especially summer mornings when they enjoyed a cup of coffee and argued good-naturedly about baseball games. He followed the St. Louis Cardinals. She'd defected to become a fan of the Kansas City Royals. Inspiration had drawn her to the Royals after she briefly dated a brand-new player, who happened to be a total hottie.

An insistent meow caught Kat's attention, and Charlie jumped into her lap. "Who let you out?" she asked, as the cat curled into a knot with a softer purr than before.

"You planning to leave him with us?" Evidently finished with sentiment, her father stood and straightened his shirt collar.

"Heavens no. I'd never go away without my buddy."

"Good. Louie will miss having somebody to pester, but at least you'll have company. Well, I suppose I better smooth things over with your mother. Wish me luck."

She watched him walk away. A daughter couldn't be any more fortunate, and she knew it. Her father's talent for sweet-talking clients often came in handy. If she knew Daddy, he'd soon have Mother resigned to the inevitable, if not enthusiastic over it. Kat's mother meant well, but she tended to practice a parenting style which suffocated more than nurtured. According to her sister, Mother hadn't always been so overbearing, but neither Carolyn nor Kat had a clue of what the heck had turned her salty.

With her feline dozing, Kat felt her own eyes drift shut. Another short nap would be sweet. But instead of counting sheep—what a stupid thing to do—she considered what she ought to take to Nashville. Her guitar and sheets of music, naturally. Clothes. All the paraphernalia required by one rather spoiled cat...

The sound of a guitar riff vibrated the phone in her jeans pocket. She fumbled around to grab it and glanced at the caller ID. Since when did Jenna call instead of text? Kat put the phone to her ear. "Hey, girl, what's up?"

"You did it!" Her friend squealed so loudly Kat had to move the phone six inches away from her head. Jenna's voice still came through abnormally loud and clear.

"I did what?"

"You broke the internet!"

Chapter Two

Kat leaned forward, and Charlie jumped off her lap to stalk toward the house. With his tail straight up, he communicated his supreme displeasure at the interruption.

"Hold on a minute, Jen. Start over and slow down this time. What are you talking about?"

"Trevor T. Ray took a video clip of you singing last night. That's what I'm talking about. He put it on his Facebook page and said you were a cool new talent. Then he told his fans to share the post. Do you know how many followers Trevor T. Ray has?"

"Uh, no." Her pulse sped into overdrive. Trevor T. Ray was the hottest country singer around, and what a break it was for her he'd come into K.C's. Krazy Saloon, where she played acoustic and sang once a month. The money wasn't great, but seeing people get up and dance while she performed sent chills down her spine.

"Let me tell you how many. *Over nine million!*"

"Holy crap. I had no idea he videoed me. Did anyone share it?"

"I'd say at least a half million. Maybe more. It crossed over to Twitter too. Even some of Trevor's famous friends jumped onboard and shared. Who knows how far it'll go!"

Kat pinched her thigh hard. *Ouch!* Yep, she was awake for sure. "Oh, man. What do you think this means?"

"You know damn well what it means. Social proof, for one thing. Take my advice and leverage it while you can, and *please* tell me you're going to Nashville. You won't let your mother talk you out of it, will you?"

"She's not happy." *An understatement.* "But Daddy's on my side. Trevor T. Ray totally convinced me, so I've already made up my mind. After what he said last night, there's no way I'll pass up a chance like this. One way or another, I plan on leaving tomorrow."

"This is so awesome! Much as I'll hate not having you around, you need to ride this wave while it lasts. Trevor must really think you have something special, or he'd never have posted the video."

"All I know is how amazing it was when he told me he liked my sound and that I ought to make a career out of music. He even gave me a card for somebody in Nashville. I don't remember the guy's name, and I'm too stoked to hunt it down now."

"Best. News. Ever. Listen, I have to leave for work, so keep me posted. Fingers crossed for you."

"Thanks, Jen. Talk soon." Kat ended the call and immediately searched for Trever T. Ray's Facebook page. Yep, there was the video. She turned up the volume. He'd captured a little over a minute of her performance, and even though the acoustics weren't the greatest, she didn't sound half bad, thank you very much. She put her cell down.

It had been a one in a million chance, like a lightning strike. Trevor T. Ray had stopped at Krazy's for a beer after he'd finished the final concert of his tour. Of all the places he could have picked—and on a night when she happened to be singing…What were the odds? Almost like it was kismet—her destiny. She'd nearly flipped out when he took a few minutes to talk to her during break. Gray-haired and throaty, he praised her technique and advised her to hustle her fanny straight to Nashville. She knew her mouth must have gaped open like a fish pulled out of water. Completely starstruck, she didn't have enough presence of mind to ask questions. Then Trevor's handler or bodyguard or whoever the big beefy guy was, showed up to tell Trevor they had to go. Dumbfounded, she hadn't even thanked him. No, this experience wasn't a lightning strike at all. More like a Powerball win.

After last night's events, she understood without any doubt what her future held. In the past, arguments with her parents over a career went nowhere. Mostly because she didn't have a clue. She only knew what she didn't want. Now, all uncertainty disappeared. It was as though her fate had arrived and hung up a neon welcome sign.

In all fairness, Mother and Daddy couldn't really be blamed for their frustration. They had a right to be confused. She must have seemed to them like some mythical creature—all show and no substance. They were used to

Carolyn, who never doubted her choices and had happily ignored social life to study her tail off until she achieved her greatest desire to become a veterinarian.

Kat wouldn't have traded socializing for anything. With boatloads of friends and sorority sisters, college became first and foremost, a whirlwind of fun. One year she even got voted KU's homecoming queen, not because she was pretty—Kat knew better—but because she enjoyed people and loved to make them laugh. If those around her smiled, she did too. This made life extraordinarily pleasant, except for one insignificant detail. Earning a degree.

She'd switched majors more than half a dozen times and still wasn't satisfied, scoring mediocre Cs in classes that bored her silly. If professional student had been an academic choice, she'd have gladly majored in it—as long as part of the bargain meant she didn't have to sit through any more lectures.

But look at her now. How cool she'd finally found her passion. A chance to be something, to be *somebody* besides a silly, feisty girl, who had no goals or direction. You'd think her mother would be delighted. Kat snorted. Nope. For quite some time now, she held a sneaking suspicion her parents viewed Carolyn and Kat like the yin and yang of their offspring: one centered and one blurry around the edges.

She wasn't unfocused anymore. Kat shook off the past and proceeded to do what made the most sense. Head to her room for a nap so she could stay up late packing while Jenna cheered her progress via speakerphone. She grabbed Charlie and climbed the stairs to her bed.

First thing the next morning, Kat awoke to sunshine on her face and a bossy cat tapping her cheek. Charlie meowed, eager to rouse her. She groaned and rolled over. He climbed on her back and kneaded with pinpoint claws. "Ouch, ouch, *ouch*, Charlie!" There wasn't any point in shooing him away. He'd fuss nonstop until he got what he wanted. That's what happened when a person treated a cat to a bit of canned food each morning. He'd grown to expect it, and heaven help her if she wasn't a prompt provider.

"Okay, you win." She picked up the animal and cuddled him. "Today's the start of our big adventure, even if I didn't get much packing done last night." She padded downstairs without bothering to change from her pajamas.

In the kitchen, French doors framed Mother and Daddy outside with their morning coffee. Mother carried on what looked like an animated conversation, while Daddy sipped from his mug. Planning strategy? Kat curled her lip and dished out food for Charlie. "There you go, your majesty."

He gobbled like he'd been starved, a condition his portly figure disputed. Kat ruffled his fur and strolled outside.

"Morning," she said.

"Darling. Did you sleep well? You look pale. Maybe you're coming down with something." Louie sat perched in her mother's lap, the happy recipient of repeated nervous head rubs. The poodle's eyes gleamed like tiny chunks of onyx hidden in a mass of curly hair. He was long past due for a grooming appointment.

Her mother inhaled a deep breath, and Kat could all but read her thoughts. She prepared to defend herself, but surprisingly her father beat her to it.

"She'll be fine, Elise. Don't worry so much." He grinned. "You look great, Kitty-Kat. What time do you plan to leave?"

"As soon as I load the car—Charlie, my guitar, and my other things—then I'll fill up the tank and be on my way."

"Your tank's already full. While you were being lazy this morning, I took it to the shop and had them check everything over to make sure the car's in good shape. You've got a nine-hour drive ahead of you, and the last thing you need is a vehicle problem." He took another sip of his coffee. "You have your AAA card, right?"

"I do. Thanks, Daddy. You think of everything. Ruby's great on the highway. She never lets me down." Kat's Kia hatchback had been a gift from her parents when she graduated high school. The boxy bright red car had quickly become a loyal friend, and Kat adamantly refused her father's offers to trade it in for a newer model.

"That's what I'm here for, right, Elise? It's my job to take care of my girls."

Her mother spared him the hint of a smile, and Kat sniffed. *Aww, Daddy.* She sniffed again. *Could the pollen count be high?*

Mother pushed a plate in Kat's direction. "How about coffee and a bite of breakfast? I have some lovely bagels and cream cheese with fresh strawberries."

"No, thanks. I'm too pumped to be hungry. I'll grab something along the road. If I don't get a move on, I won't be in Nashville until midnight, and I still need to book a hotel."

"I do hope you won't try to make the whole trip in one day. It's too much."

"Mother, you know perfectly well I love to drive, and nine hours is nothing when you're listening to good music."

"Still…"

Kat kissed her mother's cheek. "Stop. I'm only a phone call away, and I'll keep you posted. Daddy, would you give me a hand loading stuff?"

Thank goodness the drive away from home hadn't been as bad as she'd feared. No major drama. Even though his eyes were shinier than usual, Daddy kept a smile fixed firm on his face. Mother gave her a tight hug. "Call us when you stop. No texting while you drive, please."

She must have been coached on limiting her farewell remarks because she bit her lip and didn't say anything more. Standing at her husband's side like a soldier, Mother held up her hand to shade her eyes.

Kat waved and pulled onto the street. Her tiny tug of guilt didn't hang around long. By the time she reached the highway, thoughts of home faded into the background and her excitement fired up. Who knew what awaited her in Nashville? A recording contract? A career doing what she loved? Maybe the same kind of luck her sister had would strike. She might even find a soul mate of her own.

She set her pace to music, adjusting the volume on songs she'd downloaded, driving her car based on tempo. Fast songs pushed her over the speed limit. Ballads slowed her down. When Charlie meowed, she opened the sunroof, put on her shades, and let him smell the outdoors while she tapped beats on the steering wheel and harmonized with melodies. A warm breeze blew her curls willy-nilly around her face and time melted away. Between tunes, an idea for a song about leaving home tickled her brain.

When the need for a bathroom break grew urgent, Kat pulled into a rest stop. First, she texted "Still alive!" to her mother, then put on Charlie's halter and leash. He'd learned to walk with her almost as well as a dog. She had trained him to do so because he loved to be outside and she couldn't trust him not to dash away from her to chase a bird. Now a seasoned traveler, he knew the drill when she put a small litter box on the ground.

It wasn't much longer until the night sky deepened to purple, and traffic grew thick. Kat figured she must have gotten close to the city. A few miles later, her car rounded a curve, and sure enough—she'd reached her destination. Up ahead loomed the glorious skyline. "Oh, man, this is so cool," she whispered.

Lit brighter than the Las Vegas strip, downtown Nashville was a sight to see. She felt like Dorothy catching her first glimpse of the Emerald City. Even though she'd been to Nashville before for a bachelorette party, they'd arrived during the day, not at night. This was a completely new experience.

Her GPS piped up to instruct her what turn to take off the highway and which roads led to the hotel room she'd hastily reserved. A good thing too. Cars bunched together as heavy as she remembered. Trying to find the right street while watching the road at the same time would have been an invitation to Accident City. She stopped at a red light near the gigantic Batman Building and stared up at it, lost in thought. *The top floor must have a great view of the city.* A car behind her honked long and loud. The signal had turned green. "Don't get your drawers in a wad. I'm going," she said out loud to no one and stomped on the gas pedal.

By the time she pulled Ruby into the parking lot of her hotel, just outside the bustle of downtown, an ache pinched her lower back. "I'll only be a minute," she called to her cat and exited the car.

The first thing she saw in the cramped hotel lobby was a notice tacked to the wall. No Pets. *Uh-oh.* Ignoring the sign, she checked herself in. A bored-looking woman behind the counter fake-smiled and entered information into a computer. She handed Kat a card key. Another stroke of luck: her room had an outdoor entrance. What management didn't know wouldn't hurt them.

It took less than twenty minutes to unload her guitar and her bags and then sneak the small cat carrier inside her room. She blew out a breath and looked around. The place wasn't anything fancy, but at least it didn't smell like mildew the way some hotels did. Kat opened Charlie's crate, and he immediately set out to explore each corner. Then he bounced from one piece of furniture to the other, obviously ecstatic to have more space than the inside of Kat's car.

Her tabby had no problem making himself at home. Neither did she. Her room's front window had a dark tint, presumably to keep peeping Toms from seeing anyone in their undies. "It's your lucky day," she told Charlie, and opened the drapes a few inches. He jumped on a chair near the window and stared outside. Kat smiled at him. Then she collapsed on the double bed. *Not as comfy as home, but it'll do.* She picked up the remote to turn on the television and promptly fell sound asleep.

Tap. Tap. Tap. Kat brushed a paw away from her face and opened her eyes. The bedside clock read nine. "Morning already?"

The cat yowled. "All right, all right. I'm up." She rose to feed him so he'd stay quiet, and then peeked out the window. Dark clouds cluttered the sky. Cars zoomed down the road. People paced along the sidewalk, all of them obviously filled with purpose. She needed to do the same. First thing on her agenda? Find a small furnished apartment near Belmont University and Music Row. Colleges always had housing nearby, so it shouldn't be hard. Renewed by a sense of adventure and a full night's rest, she pulled off yesterday's sleep-rumpled clothes, showered, and dressed.

"You behave yourself," she admonished Charlie. "I'm going out to find us a place to live. Keep quiet. No talking."

His expression remained inscrutable as always, and Kat kissed the top of his head. Then she hung a Do Not Disturb sign on the outside doorknob to keep the maid out.

Traffic appeared almost as bad today as it was when she'd arrived, but at least she could see better in the daylight. She eased Ruby into the street, saw a light at the corner turn red, and stomped on the brake pedal. Before she could blink an eye, *Bang!* Someone crashed into the back of her car, pushing the vehicle several feet from where she'd stopped.

Luckily, the seatbelt kept her from hitting the dashboard. Kat took a second to ponder what had happened. Rubbing her neck, she glanced down. No blood. A good sign. She opened her door. A white-haired man who looked no less than ninety years old emerged from a blue car as big as a tank. "I'm sorry, miss. I had to blow my nose and didn't notice you'd stopped until it was too late. Are you okay?"

"I'm all right. My neck hurts a little, but—"

"Oh no! Don't move. I'll call for help."

"Look, I'm just a little sore." She walked to the back of her car and spied a huge dent in Ruby's bumper. The sight turned her stomach, and she swallowed hard.

The old man yammered into his phone and then addressed her again. "Stay calm and don't worry your pretty little head about anything. I told them you've been injured, so they're sending an ambulance along with the police."

"An ambulance? I don't need an ambulance." She pointed at the big scrunch in her car. "What I need is somebody to fix poor Ruby."

A group of onlookers apparently had nothing better to do than stand on the sidewalk and watch. She eyed them. They stared back. "This isn't the way things were supposed to happen," she finally announced. "Not at all." Her lower lip quivered, and before she knew it, in front of all the gawking busybodies, Kat did something she hadn't done in ages.

She burst into tears.

Chapter Three

D r. Dan McDonald leaned over his young patient and completed the fifth in a neat row of stitches to close a nasty wound in the boy's upper arm. Tim's eyes were bigger than truck wheels, but he hadn't cried out or shed tears during the process. In fact, Dan noted, the eight-year-old appeared to be doing a whole lot better than his anxious mother, whose face looked close to the same color as a fresh piece of printer paper.

Dan patted the boy's knee. "You're a brave man. You didn't move a muscle while I put those stitches in. I owe you a lollipop for being such a good sport."

He turned to address Tim's mother, who stood frozen in place. "Mrs. Sheraton. I think maybe you'd better sit down and take a couple of deep breaths before you end up on the floor. If you hit your head, you might need stitches too."

"All right." Her voice was barely audible. When she thudded into a chair, Dan wasn't sure if she'd obeyed his suggestion or if her legs had simply given way.

"You probably shouldn't have watched. It's not an easy thing for a parent to see." He pulled off his gloves. "A nurse will be in shortly to finish up, and she'll give you discharge instructions. Okay, bud, you're done. Try to be a little more careful when you get back on your bike."

Tim grinned. Once the ordeal ended, his spirits had improved considerably. "Hey, Mom, take a picture of my stitches while I'm on the bed."

Kids. Now Tim had a war wound to show off. Something to tell his friends about, Dan mused. Or fodder for his next school essay titled "How I Spent My Summer Vacation." Tim's mother still looked a little green around the gills, so Dan offered a suggestion to his patient. "I'm sure the nurse will be glad to take some pictures for you."

Unlike most nights, this one had been slow for Vanderbilt Health Center. For a change, he might just finish his shift on time. So far, he'd seen someone with a minor concussion, chest pains that turned out to be indigestion, and Tim. Then there were the people who checked in with a virus or sore throat because they didn't have a regular doctor. And, as always, he treated tourists who'd come down with an illness, or too much alcohol, or an injury—often because of too much alcohol—who had nowhere else to go. You simply never knew what was in store when you worked in the emergency room of a hospital serving a populous city full of people who often did things that weren't very smart.

On the other hand, he'd made his own share of unwise choices, so who was he to judge? Dan finished typing notes into Tim Sheraton's file, closed the computer, and yawned. The lull brought a moment to consider the fact he'd soon be able to stretch out and unwind at home. But his shift wasn't over yet. He needed coffee.

The first thing anyone learned in medical school was the value of fortification by means of caffeine. The hospital always kept a full pot available in a tiny staff area, where Dan found a foam cup and filled it to the brim with a dark wicked-looking brew. A young, shapely brunette nurse, one of the hospital's latest recruits, came in for a refill. She glanced at him with naked adoration. What was her name again? Karen? Susan?

She batted her lashes. "Can I get you something for your coffee, Doctor?"

"No, I take it black. Thanks anyway."

He sipped from his cup and moved past her to avoid the potential for more conversation. Karen, or Susan, or whoever, was fresh out of school and had been following him around the ER with puppy-like devotion bordering on stalkerish. He wasn't particularly flattered. Once it became known he was a free man, he'd been hit on by more females than he cared to count. Why was any available doctor who wasn't a Frankenstein clone considered a "catch"? He found it hard to come up with an explanation. Most of his fellow doctors weren't exactly a joy to be around, and he wasn't an exception. Doctors had to juggle far too many life-altering decisions to make a satisfactory spouse or partner. Wasn't he proof of it? In fact, he couldn't pretend to understand why any woman would want to become involved with a physician. Lousy hours and every phone call carried the potential of an emergency dress-and-dash to the hospital. It could tear apart even the most devoted relationship.

"Hey, Dan, I heard something last night you might be interested in." Stuart, one of his nurses, brought a clipboard to the desk and sat. "Rumor has it there's an opening coming up for a new dementia research project at the hospital. That's the area you've talked about before, isn't it?"

"Yes." Dan's brow rose. "How'd you find out about it?"

"On a date. I took out one of the assistants from research. She says they're getting ready to post the opening soon. It sounds like a good opportunity for somebody."

Curiosity over the project set Dan's mind in motion. A research opening didn't come around very often, much less in the field of dementia. Maybe he could make a few discrete phone calls for more information. Dan picked up his desk phone, held it a moment, and put it back. The initial prickle of excitement faded. Research didn't pay nearly as well as the ER. He remembered what a salary cut would mean. "Thanks, Stu, but I'm not in a position to make a change at the moment." It pained him to admit it out loud.

The new brunette nurse scurried toward him, bustling with importance. "Dr. McDonald, we have a patient on the way who's been in a car accident. The ambulance should be here within five minutes."

Instantly alert, he got up from his chair. "Serious?"

"It sounds minor, but you never know."

"Okay, thanks."

"Certainly, Doctor." Her voice fluttered.

Dan held in a sigh and hoped one of the more experienced nurses would set her straight before she said something to embarrass them both. They did, after all, need to work together.

The jangle of the ER phone and a distant shriek from an ambulance were sure signs things were about to heat up. Dan drained what remained in his cup and then tossed it away. He stood at the sink and vigorously scrubbed his hands with antiseptic soap. Though he hated the thought of anyone suffering, he did welcome the challenge of keeping busy. It was a good excuse not to brood over less important things.

As he dried his hands, the shriek of a siren grew louder. Within less than a minute, the automatic doors swooshed open, and a paramedic rolled in the gurney. Dan could hear a woman crying. Her words were garbled, but it sounded like she said, "Why won't you listen to me?" Her voice seemed more upset than pain filled, though it was hard to be sure. The burly paramedic who pushed the gurney caught Dan's gaze and rolled his eyes.

Fantastic. It must be hysteria. Or a psychiatric issue? What a great way to end his shift. He waited long enough to give the nurse time to help the patient change into a gown, take vital signs, and gather information. Then he moved toward Bay 1, counseling himself to remain calm, tolerant, and professional—the best antidotes he knew for dealing with an overwrought patient.

By the time he entered the bay, she wasn't crying anymore. She had her cell phone to her ear, talking a mile a minute to somebody. At first glance, he observed an attractive young woman with reddish-blonde hair all fluffed out around her head. A cervical collar had been fitted to her neck, which emphasized her wild curls and tear-steaked face. Dan tapped her shoulder and pointed at a sign on the wall that clearly said: No Cell Phone Use.

The woman ignored him. He checked the computer screen to find her name and spoke in a no-nonsense tone. "Miss Becker, you need to put your phone down so I can examine you."

She held up her forefinger, indicating he should wait, and kept talking.

"Put your phone down *now*."

When she still didn't comply, the calm and tolerant part of his resolution dissolved. He marched to the bed and snatched the phone from her hand. "Can't you read?" He pointed at the sign again.

"Oh. Sorry, I didn't see it." She sniffled a little, but no more tears appeared. "I was only trying to get my insurance information from my father. One of your people wanted me to give her the card, but I don't have it with me."

"You don't carry your insurance card?"

"What can I say? I left home in a hurry. I do have a Triple A card, if that will get me anywhere." The glint in her eyes told him she was trying to make a joke. If she'd been hysterical when she arrived, at least it had passed, thank God.

Dan looked at the notes left by the nurse. "Tell me what happened."

She directed a look at his name badge. "Well, Dr. McDonald, somebody rear-ended my car and bashed an enormous dent in it. My car is not fine, but I am, which I kept telling everyone. Then an ambulance showed up, and they basically forced me to come here to get checked out. So that's what happened, and here I am."

"I see." Dan removed the cervical collar and started his examination. He asked her questions about her level of pain and watched her face when he gently pressed the area on her neck where she said it hurt most. Better to err on the side of caution. He had a tech take the girl for films and refreshed his cup of coffee. When the tech brought her back, it was just as he figured. No fracture.

"It looks like you have a soft tissue injury of the neck, more commonly known as whiplash. If you feel you need the support, wear the collar for a day or two. I'll prescribe some muscle relaxants, and you can use ibuprofen for pain." He typed into the computer. "Don't be worried if you have a slight headache or feel more sore tomorrow, and call if you have any other problems. Follow up with your regular doctor. The nurse will print out the instructions on your discharge summary."

He noticed how much she'd perked up since her arrival. She'd even kidded around with the tech, who had appeared thoroughly disarmed by her efforts. Yet as soon as Dan finished speaking to her and signed off the computer, the expression on her face went from smiles to what he could only describe as sick, like someone with a stomach gone sour. He watched her for a moment. "Are you okay?"

Her lips thinned, and he grabbed the kidney-shaped pan, thinking she was about to vomit. She gulped a few times and he kept the pan ready. It occurred to him that despite her drooping chin and red, puffy eyes, she was prettier than his initial impression—even with the cervical collar he'd once again buckled in place. She had a combination of innocence and womanhood any men's magazine would kill to feature. The gunny sack hospital gown didn't hide her shape, which would most likely be a popular feature in a centerfold. He shook his head to dismiss the thoroughly unprofessional thought. In his driest and most matter-of-fact demeanor, he pointedly asked her again. "Miss Becker, what's wrong?"

A crooked smile tilted her mouth. "Oh, just about everything," she replied.

Chapter Four

Did hospitals buy uncomfortable beds on purpose to give patients more to feel bad about? Kat shifted her position and returned Dr. McDonald's steady gaze. She'd never met a doctor with hair as long as his. Dark brown strands brushed just past his collar. And those rich chocolate-colored eyes? They practically X-rayed her.

He lobbed another question her way. This time she noted how a very appealing and distinct Southern twang made a melody of his words. "Can you tell me what you mean? Do you feel sick?"

She considered his second question. "Maybe a little."

"Exactly what does 'a little' mean?"

"It means I just got to Nashville." Kat attended to an itch on her neck under the ugly plastic collar. "My car is who knows where. I'm stuck in a hospital bed. I don't have a doctor to follow up with. And I have no idea what I'm going to do next. If that isn't enough to make a person feel sick, I don't know what is."

"There's no reason to be upset. You're released to go home and you have permission to use your phone if you keep it short. Call your father to come and pick you up."

"My father is a nine-hour drive away in Kansas City."

"Well, why don't you call one of your friends?"

"I came to Nashville alone, and I don't have any friends here." She didn't like the way her comment sounded. "Not yet, anyway."

Dr. McDonald's brows pinched together, and he crossed his arms. "Let me get this straight. Are you telling me there's absolutely no one who can pick you up?"

"That's exactly what I'm saying. And I can't drive myself home. I don't have a car because paramedics shoved me into an ambulance. Somebody said my car would be towed, but nobody said where. Any suggestions on what I should do, Doctor?"

He rubbed the side of his head. "I'll be damned if I know."

She thought for a moment and took a deep breath. "Wait. I've got an idea."

Dr. McDonald squinted at her with suspicion. "Just what are you thinking?"

"The nurse who took my blood pressure told me it was almost shift change time. That means you'll be leaving and somebody else will be coming in. How about this? You can take me to my car on your way home."

"What?" His voice notched up in disbelief. "You don't know me and I don't know you. Besides, it's against hospital policy."

"Oh, pooh on hospital policy. Would the hospital rather have me camp out in the parking lot until I can figure out where my car is?"

"Look, Miss Becker—"

"Call me Kat," she said, interrupting him with her most charming smile.

"Miss Becker," he repeated firmly. "I cannot drive a patient anywhere."

"Once I'm discharged, I'm not a patient. And once you're off work, you're a civilian, aren't you? Or does the hospital tell you what to do even when you're not on duty?"

He flinched the slightest bit, and she realized she'd struck a nerve. Silence between them filled with hospital noise—soft-soled shoes squeaking on linoleum and beeping machines. She primly laced her fingers together and waited for him to answer.

"I need to brief the incoming doctor." His voice rumbled like a grizzly's. "I'm not sure how long it will take."

"It has to be faster than nine hours. I can wait outside for you."

He exhaled heavily. "I guess I can take you to your car."

"Thank you." Her neck ached, but her outlook felt tons lighter. "Any ideas on who I should call to find it?"

"Try Mid-Towne Towing. I understand they handle most car accidents in the area." He turned away so she couldn't gauge his expression. "You can get dressed. The nurse will give you your instructions."

As soon as he left, she jumped off the bed. Bending over made her wince, but she had no trouble exchanging the silly-looking gown for her clothes. The nurse handed her several pages of instructions, but Kat declined the offer of a wheelchair ride to the door.

Once outside, she seated herself on a metal bench and filled her lungs with clean, fresh air. Hospitals had a singularly bizarre smell. A mixed-up aroma of antiseptic, sickness, and fear. Kat couldn't imagine spending any more time in one than necessary and wondered if the smell clung to her clothing. The thought of a warm shower sounded like a dream destination.

She searched for Mid-Towne Towing on her phone and placed the call. An attendant offered to check his computer for her information and confirmed they had her car in storage. He even said it was drivable before he added, "You need to bring photo identification, proof of insurance, and proof of ownership. There's also a two-hundred-twenty-five-dollar towing and impound fee."

A car backfired, and birds that had been sitting in a nearby tree took flight. What a crazy-ridiculous list. She was an accident victim, not a potential criminal. "I have my license and credit card for payment. You'll find the other stuff in my glove box. At least I think so."

"You must have the paperwork with you to get your car."

"Well, I do have it…in my glovebox. They made me go to the hospital. I didn't have time to take anything but my purse from the car."

"I'm sorry, but those are the rules," he droned on.

"Oh, for crying out loud." She ended the call. Her first full day in Nashville wasn't going even remotely the way she'd hoped. Maybe Dr. McDonald would have a suggestion. If all else failed, she could call Daddy, who had a lawyer's knack of making things happen.

While she waited, she entertained herself by observing people who either walked toward the hospital or away from it, watching the expressions on their faces. Happy or sad? Scared or confident? All of them material for a song.

After a half hour passed, the exercise grew boring. Kat glanced at the time on her phone. Just when she wondered whether Dr. McDonald had snuck out another door and left her, she caught sight of him. He'd changed from scrubs to jeans, a dark T-shirt, and tennis shoes. His forehead furrowed in thought. It amazed her to notice how much younger he looked outside the hospital setting. Not nearly as exhausted either.

She called out and waved at him. "I found my car. It's right where you thought it would be."

"Good. Mid-Towne's close to the hospital. It won't take long to get there."

Kat wanted to look at his face but found it nearly impossible. He stood at least a head taller than she did, and even wearing a cervical collar, it hurt her neck to tilt her head back. He motioned for her to follow him into the hospital parking lot and gestured toward a late-model silver Impala. "Here it is." Like a gentleman, he opened the door for her and waited while she climbed inside. Then he closed the door and walked around the back of the car to the driver's side.

When he got behind the wheel, a rush of nervous gratitude coursed through her. "I really appreciate you helping me out. I'd love it if I didn't have to call my father again. I told him Ruby had a little fender bender, and I ended up at the hospital as a precaution. Fingers crossed he doesn't say anything to my mother. She wasn't happy about me coming here, and she'd probably flip out."

At her rush of words, he glanced at her. "Wait a minute. Who's Ruby? I thought you didn't have any friends here."

"Oh," she laughed. "Ruby's my car. I got her right after high school. She's cardinal red and the best ride ever. I sure hope they can fix her."

"I don't think I've ever heard of anyone naming a car before."

"A name gives her personality. Don't look so cynical. It's only for fun."

He ran a finger between his neck and his shirt collar like it choked him. "If you say so. Sounds to me like you're worried about upsetting your mother. Are you in the habit of keeping secrets from her?"

"Sometimes. But I only do it for her own good—not to mention mine. It keeps her from getting all worked up. She comes unglued easily."

"And your father doesn't?"

"Daddy's a lawyer. A calm examination of the facts are his bread and butter."

"I guess that makes sense." He pulled the car out of the lot and onto the road, merging into a crowded lane of slow-moving traffic.

She glanced at his profile and did a double take. Was it her imagination, or did he resemble Keanu Reeves? Her heart skipped a beat. Dr. McDonald's hair wasn't quite as long, of course, and he didn't have a beard, but still—so easy on the eyes.

"Miss Becker, I asked if your neck is bothering you much." He enunciated each word loudly and clearly, as if he thought she'd gone deaf.

Apparently, she hadn't been paying attention. "Uh, it's doing okay I guess."

"I know it's none of my business, but why on earth did you decide to leave your family and come to Nashville?"

Her face warmed with enthusiasm at the chance to discuss it. "I'm here to become a singer. And songwriter. Oh, and finish college too."

His grip tightened on the steering wheel. She could tell because his knuckle bones pressed underneath the skin. "Do you have the slightest idea how many people show up in Nashville every year thinking they'll get a recording contract? People with so many stars in their eyes they couldn't recognize the truth if it hit them over the head. Ninety-nine percent of wannabe performers end up leaving within a year or so, once they realize their dream is too far out of reach. If I had a dollar for every person here who had a music career in mind, I could retire." He shook his head. "My advice is to pack up and head right back to Kansas City."

What a downer of a speech. "I'm sure plenty of people come to Nashville with a dream, but tell me how many come here because Trevor T. Ray sent them?"

"What in blue blazes are you talking about?"

"Trevor heard me sing when he was in Kansas City. He videoed me and said I ought to go to Nashville. He even put the video on his Facebook page, and it went viral!"

Dan's shoulders lifted and dropped. "So he gave you fifteen minutes of fame. How are you going to turn a video into a career?"

"I don't know yet, but I will."

Traffic slowed to a crawl and then stopped. A siren shrilled.

"Great." He tapped the wheel impatiently. "Must be an accident ahead."

He may be cute, but he sure is a grouch. She decided to overlook it. After all, he'd been at the hospital dealing with crabby-assed people all day long.

"You seem to know Nashville pretty well, Mac. Are there any furnished apartments near Belmont University?"

"Miss Becker, my name's not Mac. It's Dan."

She grinned at him. "No. You look like a Mac to me. It suits you. And please don't call me Miss Becker. Call me Kat."

"Kat? Your chart said Kathryn."

"Yes, but everybody calls me Kat. You too, I hope."

He sighed again. She'd never heard anyone exhale as much as he did.

"All right…Kat. I do know of an apartment complex near the university. A lot of students live there, and they seem to like it. Lucky for you it's summer break. You'll stand a better chance of finding a vacancy."

"Sounds perfect. Is it far from Music Row?"

"Not at all. Music Row is within walking distance from the complex."

Music Row. The street of dreams. Filled with businesses, recording studios, and licensing firms. She envisioned herself knocking on every single door.

"That's exactly what I'm looking for." A moment later, her mouth dropped open. "You know what? Must be fate. If the accident hadn't happened, I wouldn't have met you. I'd have been hunting all over town and probably never would have found the perfect place to stay. It's kind of amazing, Mac, if you stop to think about it."

"It's amazing all right." Traffic had begun to inch forward, and he hunched over the wheel. "There it is. The towing company is up ahead." A few minutes later, they reached the entrance. He expertly maneuvered the Impala out of traffic and into the lot, then stopped near the front door. "Here you are."

She hesitated. "I know it's a lot to ask, but do you mind coming in with me? There's a little issue with my paperwork being in the car instead of me having it in my hand. Maybe you could vouch for me, if your wife wouldn't mind you being a few minutes late."

"I don't have a wife," he ground out through tight lips as he switched off the ignition.

He turned off the car! She took this as a hopeful sign and headed toward the door. He followed her, though she thought she heard him mumble under his breath. Oh, well. With a shred of luck, the attendant she'd spoken to on the phone would listen to reason.

Kat didn't time the transaction, but it took what seemed like forever to wrangle her car back. Thank goodness Mac had been there to show his identification and confirm her explanation. She paid her bill, got her keys, and with Ruby officially in her possession again, walked outside with Mac beside her.

"What a relief. Poor Ruby's dent will need fixing, but things are already looking up. Thank you so much for your help." She beamed at him and thought she detected a slight thaw in his demeanor.

"I'm…happy I could lend a hand. Good luck to you, Kat. Take care of yourself and follow your discharge instructions."

He sounded so coolly professional, she saluted him and said, "Yes, sir," but his lips remained in a straight line. "Thanks, again, Mac. Cranky or not, you're the most helpful doctor I've ever met."

He waved at her, looking slightly befuddled as he got into his car. She stood near Mid-Towne Towing's wide double doors and watched until he drove away. How could such a cute guy be such a total bear and even saltier than her mother? And why did it seem like he couldn't wait to get away? Most people enjoyed being around her. The speed with which he gunned the car felt downright insulting, like he feared she'd contaminate him. Not once in her entire life had she met a person she couldn't charm if she wanted to. Could he possibly be the first one to flat out dislike her for no reason at all? She shook her head and dismissed the idea, but to salve her self-respect, she'd figure out a way to prove it—assuming she ever saw him again.

Moving a sulky mountain of a man wasn't hard if you worked the angles bit by bit. Kat wasn't in the habit of shying away from a difficult situation. Or a difficult person.

Yes, indeed, Dr. Dan McDonald. Challenge accepted!

Chapter Five

Dan pulled his car away from the towing company. He caught a glimpse of Kat in his rearview mirror as she watched him leave, and wondered if the day's events would serve to wake her up. Based on the firm set of her jaw, he doubted it.

Traffic hadn't tapered off, so he moved his car into a crowded lane, knowing he'd only creep along until he left downtown. An added bonus to the strange way his day ended. Almost every muscle in his body felt tied up in knots. How could he have been idiot enough to let an empty-headed slip of a girl insert herself into his personal life? He should have told her to call a cab or an Uber. Why hadn't it occurred to him? With her lawyer father and reckless demeanor, he instinctively knew she came from money. She could certainly afford the fare.

Kat Becker. If he'd ever met someone who needed to grow up, it was her. A spoiled little rich girl used to getting her own way. No wonder she'd barged into Nashville thinking she'd set the world on fire. Twenty-four years old in only a few days—he saw it on her chart—and she behaved more like someone half her age. She reminded him of a cheerleader from high school who talked too much and too fast while saying absolutely nothing of substance. Lord help anyone who got pulled into Kat's orbit.

His hair turned damp with Tennessee summertime, so he cranked the air conditioner to full blast. A hell of a finish to a long shift in the emergency room—not the most stress-free place in the world. The ER often felt like hanging from a ledge by the tips of his fingers. There were nights when crisis after crisis landed in his lap, often all at once. Staff had to be on their toes every second, prepared for anything from influenza to a multiple-car pileup. Not to mention all the bureaucratic red tape the hospital expected him to contend with. Or the needier patients who required more counseling than they did medical assistance.

An image of Kat drifted to his mind again. Surprisingly, his original exasperation had dwindled. To be honest, something about her appealed to him, although defining what it was seemed impossible. Her arrival in Nashville had turned into more of a hideous nightmare than a grand entrance, but other than crying over the damage to…Ruby…she'd turned everything that had happened to her from a fiasco into a silver-plated door of opportunity. Kat spent more time trying to be funny than most people—maybe a nervous habit?—but her smile looked real as rain, softening the angles of her face into an unsettling winsomeness. His original position against her thawed further until the reason she left Kansas City reined in his charitable line of thought.

She was just another fool lured by dreams of stardom.

Nashville. He'd lived here all his life and loved the area, but if he didn't have family in town, he'd seriously consider a move to Alaska, where people were smarter about their choices. No dreamy-eyed potential singers showed up in the forty-ninth state, only seals and polar bears who minded their own business and stayed at home where they belonged.

Dan rounded a curve in the street and touched a remote to open his garage door. He pulled in and spied his beloved Indian Roadmaster parked nearby. It reflected light in an eye-blinding gleam of bronze and chrome beauty. He'd purchased the motorcycle as a gift to himself after he'd finished his residency and landed the ER job. The bike had been a major splurge, and guilt still sometimes jarred him. Yet nothing could take away the utter exhilaration whenever he took time to climb on and ride.

His stomach gurgled, reminding him he had a carryout box of yesterday's beef and broccoli in the refrigerator. But first things first. A shower. Then he could eat and venture back out to wash the car and pick up shirts from the laundromat, the mundane things he scrambled to do in his off time. Dan tossed his phone and keys on the kitchen counter and thumbed through a few days' worth of mail sitting on the table. Most of it went straight into the trash. He rolled his neck from side to side and yawned. A research job. He mulled over the news Stuart had shared but quickly dismissed it again. No reason to consider the impossible.

Maybe he ought to take the Roadmaster to run his errands. He could shower later. Dan rarely rode anymore, but he'd long ago learned the value of wind therapy. It worked wonders in turning a rotten day into a fine one. Or when the necessity arose to abolish wishful thinking.

His cell vibrated and buzzed. Dan spotted a name on the caller ID, but he didn't pick up. Better to let the call go to voice mail, assuming she'd bother to leave a message. Ava's typical approach leaned more toward the expectation he ought to immediately return any call she made to him. Once the buzzing stopped, he picked up his keys, but then his phone pulsated again. *Bloody hell. What now?* Dan grabbed his cell and saw his younger brother's name on the caller ID. He put the phone to his ear. "Hello?"

"Hey, Dan, is your shift over?"

"It is, thank God. I'm home now."

"Another bad day, huh?"

"More annoying than bad, I guess. What's up?"

"I wanted to talk some more about what we discussed last week. This may tick you off, but I'm sure you're making a big mistake."

"Really? This is what you felt compelled to call me and say?"

"I can't help telling the truth. You need to quit the emergency room and move on to something else. Don't argue yet. Just listen to me. Everybody sees how much the pressure gets to you, especially me. Sometimes I can barely stand to be around you."

"Then don't be," Dan said curtly. "Anyway, you know why I can't leave."

"Cash doesn't make the world go around, so it isn't smart to base your decisions on money. Who cares if you earn less than you're making now? Isn't it better to be happy? We both know you're not delighted about shift work in the ER."

His brother's tone reeked of thinly disguised good intentions, which irritated Dan even more. "Excuse me, but I'm in a better position to know what I should do than you are. Why don't you concentrate on finishing school and get your own career squared away before you tell me how to handle mine." He didn't bother to mask his annoyance.

"Hey, don't turn the microscope around to examine me. I'm going after what I want. You ought to do the same thing, big bro, and your attitude is exactly proving my point. As usual, you're in a mood, and guess what? You just got off work. Point goes to me, and here's a news flash. I'm not letting this subject go, so get ready to talk about it another day."

The screen went dark.

Dan slammed his phone down. When had his brother turned into such a buttinsky? If only it were so simple. The notion of a research job in dementia, the disease that killed their mother—would be a dream come true. He'd held Mom's hand and promised, right before the end. If he couldn't save her, he could at least help others with the same grim diagnosis. She'd been too out of it to know what he'd said, even though he meant every word. But he'd sold out. Instead of following through, he took a job in the ER, reasoning she'd never know the difference. The money was decent and the openings frequent because the field had one of the highest burnout rates in medicine.

What else *could* he do? He wasn't some sort of fool who'd jump into a half-baked idea without weighing the odds in order to make the right decision. Unlike his brother's nutty choices. Dan loved him, but at times could cheerfully throttle him. Or Kat Becker. Come to think about it, his brother and she were like the poster children for people who could use a kick in the pants to become more practical and prudent.

Dan couldn't imagine taking a chance that might cause his family to suffer financially. He owed his father too much to ever disappoint him. It would be preferable to weather a thousand worse problems than working in an emergency room before he'd ever let his loved ones down. Not to mention the other obligations he'd assumed. The ones he'd been handed whether he wanted them or not.

Dan grabbed his keys and headed to the garage. A ride on his bike would help him settle back into the certainties of the real world.

Wishes, pipe dreams, and deathbed promises were off the table.

Chapter Six

Kat snapped up the only vacancy immediately, sight unseen. She'd contacted the agency handling rentals at the apartment complex suggested by Mac—her imagination preferred the nickname—and grabbed it before anyone else could. The location, off Wedgewood Street and near both Belmont University and Music Row, would be perfect. Even if the apartment wasn't as pristine as the enthusiastic real estate agent said, Kat would make it work. She signed the lease, took the key, and to celebrate her acquisition, treated herself to a decadent mocha latte. Who said adulting was difficult?

Within a day she packed up the hotel room, then traipsed back and forth, filling Ruby with her luggage, a guitar case, and a box of sound equipment. She sneaked her cat's supplies to the car before loading the animal into his crate. "We're on the road again," she said to Charlie, who peeked at her from his temporary prison. She couldn't wait to see her new digs in a place they could spread out and call home. Charlie serenaded her during the short drive to a three-story apartment complex. She braked in front of the weathered, peach-colored brick building to examine it. The place looked sort of 1970ish, with mature trees shading the grounds. A breeze ruffled their deep-green leaves.

"Well, it doesn't look awful," she said to Charlie as she turned Ruby off. "You're coming with me, and we'll have our first look together. It's too hot to leave you in the car." Thrilled to find a place in the exact area she wanted, Kat had barely skimmed the contract and hadn't bothered to ask any questions. Therefore, it made sense to be cautious until she knew whether the building was pet friendly. She looked both ways before picking up Charlie's crate. This wasn't easy. She'd put her cervical collar back on since her neck ached from lugging things to the car. *Not a soul in sight.* Kat scurried to the main entrance. Stairs were used less, so she opted for them over the elevator and climbed to the third floor. She peeked out the door to an empty hallway and blew out a breath of relief. Apartment 3D. She stuck her key in the lock and opened the door.

Her nose wrinkled right away. *Ugh! Musty.* She kicked the air conditioner on, hoping it would help and looked around. The place was super tiny, and the complex exterior certainly matched the interior. She noted a round wood table and two chairs pushed against the wall in a corner eating nook. A sofa the color of burnt orange filled the living room, and the kitchen had Formica countertops. The place reminded her of a step back in time. Thankfully, the carpet looked new, though she smirked when it occurred to her the furnishings would make Elvis feel right at home.

A full-size bed with a bare mattress and one side table provided a place to sleep. One bathroom with chrome fixtures completed the necessities. The tub appeared to have been covered with a quick-fix vinyl liner. She hoped nothing too horrible had been hidden underneath.

All righty then. She'd brought a few things but obviously hadn't considered a furnished room would be so Spartan. A trip to the store for sheets, towels, a lamp, and a few kitchen necessities would be at the top of her list. She inspected the mattress and didn't see any stains, but still figured buying a cover would be a smart investment.

"Guess I'll need to write all this down, buddy," she said to Charlie. "I'll let you out to explore while I bring in the rest of our stuff."

With his crate door opened, Charlie stepped out to sniff his new kingdom. Kat left him to his own devices and went back to her car. Another glimpse at the big dent in back reminded her for the millionth time she'd need to get it fixed soon. At least the hatchback still worked, although it and her bumper were crooked. What a pain in the neck— literally. Each throb reminded her it would take longer to haul everything in. *Most important items first.* Kat grabbed her guitar case and the tote with her music.

"Looks like you're moving in. I live here too. Would you like a hand?"

The voice of a tenor with a Southern twang came from behind her, and she turned toward it. A tall dark-haired man, a little on the thin side and wearing a generous smile, watched her. He looked close to her own age. The thought crossed her mind that her mother would freak over a random stranger offering help, but with a pinch in her neck, she didn't hesitate. "That would be great, thanks. My name's Kat Becker. And who are you?"

He lifted her suitcase and her laptop from the back of the car. "Shawn Wright." He gestured toward the items in her hand. "I assume you play guitar?"

"I sure do." She started off along the sidewalk toward the apartment building, swinging the case as she walked. It reminded her of a scene from *The Sound of Music.* If she remembered correctly, the song featured lyrics about confidence. Shawn interrupted the tune her mind had turned on.

"Let me guess. Are you a student? Most of these apartments are rented by students."

"Not yet, but I'm filling out an application for Belmont as soon as I get unpacked. I promised my parents I'd finish my degree here."

"No kidding?" His voice lifted. "Belmont's where I go. I can answer any questions you have."

"Wow. Perfect serendipity. Don't you just love it?"

Shawn laughed easily. A nice laugh. "Of course. And as long as we're deep in the sea of serendipity, what's with the neck brace? It doesn't look very comfortable."

"Didn't you see the back of my car? Somebody plowed into me. Thanks to one little old man who needed to blow his nose, Ruby got smashed and I have my very first case of whiplash." She contemplated the situation for a moment. "I wasn't even in town for twenty-four hours before it happened. Luckily, the old guy's been sweet about it. His insurance will fix my car and pay for the medical stuff."

"Looks like you arrived with a bang." Shawn chuckled. "I'm a lifelong Nashvillian, but I don't hear a trace of Tennessee in your voice. Where are you from?"

Elevator doors slid open, and the pair exited. "I grew up in Kansas City." She stopped to fumble with her key.

"Wait a minute," he said. "This apartment is yours? I'm right across the hall."

"No kidding? Well, come on in and check out my blast from the past." She opened the door with a flourish. "Do all the apartments look like this?"

"Mostly. I've lived here for a couple of years. Some of the rooms have been updated. Others are scheduled. This one just went vacant a few days ago."

"They say everything old is new again. If we wait long enough, this junk may come back in style. Until it does, I'll hang some cute art prints and think of it as trendy."

Shawn snorted. "A stretch, but go ahead and keep your glass half full, girl."

Charlie meandered from the bedroom into the living area with an inquisitive meow.

"You have a cat?" Shawn's voice rose with delight. He put down her bag and laptop to hold out his hand. "Here, kitty, kitty."

Her cat, who didn't know a stranger, followed the call. Shawn bent to stroke the animal with a gentle hand. A robust airplane-engine purr followed.

"Meet Charlie Daniels. I've had him since I was fourteen. He's such a good boy."

"Love the name, but I didn't think management allowed pets. Did the policy change?"

"Um, I didn't read the contract to find out. You won't tell on me, will you?"

"Hells no. It's ridiculous they don't let people have pets. Be careful though. The manager can be a witch, and she patrols this place like the Gestapo. Good news is the residents are cool." Charlie put his purr on hold to groom the tip of his front foot, and Shawn's mouth tilted up. "So Kat has a cat. Too awesome."

She liked Shawn already. "Okay, I think one more trip and I can start unpacking."

"I have a suggestion. Since you're the walking wounded, do you want to stay here while I bring in the rest of your stuff and lock the car? I know we just met, but I swear I'm not a desperado or serial killer. Do you trust me with your key? I understand if you don't."

His statement completely disarmed her. She held the keys between her forefinger and thumb. "Here you go. And thanks."

Shawn left, and Kat sniffed again. The air conditioner had kicked on, but now it smelled worse than before. She jostled through her bag to find a pen and scrap of paper. Might as well start a list of what she needed to make the place less like a cheap dive than it looked. She wrote "air freshener" at the top and filled a quarter of the sheet before a knock stopped her.

"Just me," Shawn called.

She opened the door for him. He plopped her bags and Charlie's stuff on the floor. "Thanks a billion, Shawn. Hey,

I'd love to know more about Belmont. Can you come in and chill for a while?"

"Sure. Here, I grabbed a water for you from my place as a moving-in present." He pulled a bottled water from his back pocket.

"How'd you know? A cold drink is exactly what I need." She placed the bottle against her forehead for a moment, then twisted off the cap and took a deep swallow. "Now that I think of it, I don't even know if the kitchen has cups. Or plates. Or forks either."

"The apartment comes with a few bargain-basement dishes and utensils. If you want anything nice, you'll have to get it for yourself."

Kat jotted a few more items on her paper. "Man, if this keeps up, I'll be shopping forever. Let's have a seat on my lovely orange sofa, and you can tell me all about Belmont."

She sank onto the sofa. Down. Way down. A spring poked her backside, so she shifted. "Dang. This thing has seen better days. I feel like I'm on the floor."

Shawn sat beside her. "It's a pip all right. You better buy some big pillows to boost yourself up."

"Who knew? I might as well have rented a moving van and brought furniture from home. Live and learn." She made a face and leaned back. "Now, what's the story on Belmont? I hear it has a good music program."

Shawn's eyes flared wide. "Hey, I'm in the music program! Songwriting and production. You?"

"Writing songs and performing is my thing. Are you saying they have specific classes in those areas?"

"They sure do. Is your computer charged?" When Kat nodded, he grabbed the laptop and carried it to her. "Fire 'er up. I'll show you all kinds of amazing stuff."

Shawn pulled up Belmont's website. Kat nearly jumped out of her skin with delight when she saw what he pointed out. *A bachelor's degree in composition? In performance? Commercial music? Wow!*

"I hated most of the classes I had to take at Kansas University. This is over-the-top fabulous. I can't imagine skipping these." She realized how her words sounded and her cheeks warmed. "I didn't skip a lot, but most of the courses I had to take were a complete snoozefest."

Shawn grinned. "Tell me something I don't know. If you're into the music scene, Belmont is the place for you. Will you be transferring credits?"

"Yes, and I only need a few more semesters, unless…"

"Unless what?"

"Changing majors again might add more time, but you know what? I don't care. Who'd ever have thought I'd be excited to sign up for school?"

"If you plan to start in the fall, you'd best get on it." His face sobered. "The School of Music is a popular one. It's tough to get in. A good application and an audition tape are required."

"I'm only planning to go part time. I hope it'll make it easier to be accepted. Most of my focus will be on getting a foot in the door somewhere on Music Row. If somebody offers me a contract, I might not even need to go to school. Ha!"

"I've lived in Nashville all my life, and a contract hasn't happened yet for me."

"I know it's hard, but I might have a teeny tiny edge. Trevor T. Ray sent me."

Shawn's forehead wrinkled. "What do you mean?"

"He's the one who told me I should come to Nashville. He even videoed me performing and posted it on his page."

"Wait a minute." Shawn scrutinized her face. "Did his post go viral?"

She produced her best Kat-that-ate-the-canary smile.

"No way. The singer on the video was *you*?"

"Yep," she said, practically bursting with pride.

"I don't know if it'll help, but it sure can't hurt your chances."

"I thought so too." She dug out the card she'd found in her guitar case. "Trevor told me to contact some guy named Pete Casson. The name sounds familiar, but I haven't had time to look him up. Do you know who he is?"

Shawn whistled. "He's a big-time producer. For Trevor, among other names. Have you called him?"

"I've left a few messages. No call back yet. I guess he's busy."

"Seems like I read something about him being in LA for a while. At least you have a name and a number. It's more than most of us hopefuls have."

She studied her computer screen. "Do you mind giving me a hand on the application? I'd like to get this moving so I can let my mother know I'm keeping my promise. She's a worrier."

"Sure thing. Click over to the application. I'll get you started, but you'll still need to send a video."

She looked at a thousand blank spaces, sighed, and began to type. During more than an hour of work, she asked Shawn's advice and pondered how to phrase her answers. Once the blanks were finally filled, things got easy. The instructions allowed her to forward a video and her transcript later, so she submitted the application with a single touch. An item off her list and one that would most certainly please her parents.

"Done." Kat blew out a puff of air and closed the computer. "Are you alone in Nashville like I am, or do you have family here?"

"My family lives here. Good people but not thrilled with my desire to major in music. They think it's frivolous and impractical."

"I hear you. My parents wanted me to stay in KC and become a teacher. Totally not my thing."

"It makes it all a little harder, doesn't it?" Shawn's voice held an undercurrent of hurt.

"True." An empathetic pang forged an instant connection for her with Shawn. They had met a little over an hour ago, but already she felt as comfortable with him as she did with Jenna. Like they'd been friends for years. "I'll call my mother later. She'll be thrilled to know the application is in progress—and without a single reminder. Now all I need to do is come up with a part-time job."

"I've got a paid internship with Spot-On. It's a small recording company. They don't need anyone right now though." Shawn thought for a moment. "Wait a minute.

My dad has a restaurant, Pop's Place. He's always looking for a new server. I'll call him. He's got live music every weekend and sometimes during the week. If he likes you, I bet he'll give you a chance to perform on one of his slow nights."

Kat squealed with delight. "Are you kidding me? That would be perfect. If I can work evenings, it gives me all day to knock on doors." Her stomach rumbled. "Speaking of restaurants, I haven't eaten in forever. What if I order us a pizza? Unless you have other plans." She didn't want him to think she'd commandeered his life.

"Pizza sounds good to me. Cleary's has a great pie, and they deliver."

"Thin crust supreme with extra mozzarella?"

"Of course. What monster would order any other kind?"

She giggled and picked up her cell. "Really, Shawn, you're a lifesaver. Seriously though, I don't want you to force yourself to stick around because you feel sorry for me. If you have a date or plans or whatever, don't worry. I'm fine."

"No plans, and no date." He stood and cradled Charlie, his expression veiled. "You don't know me well, and I appreciate it that you trust me. It's flattering. But just for the record, you don't need to worry about me putting the moves on you. Not to say you aren't cute. It's only I'm not into…" He flushed and didn't finish his sentence.

The hint of unease in his manner made her eyes burn. It was as though he wasn't sure how she'd accept what he so clearly implied. Maybe he'd grown used to being kicked to the curb. The thought slammed her brows together. She had more than one gay friend in KC, and the way some people treated them made her furious enough to spit nails. Why did others feel entitled to be so freaking mean? She grabbed his arms and pulled him into a tight hug.

"You're my first official friend in Nashville. Who cares about anything else?"

The corners of Shawn's lips turned up. "I think this is the start of a friendship that will go down in history. I may not be Trevor T. Ray, but I'm sure we can still help each other out."

"You bet we can." She turned on her phone. "Spell 'Cleary's' for me. I'm half starved. Let's get them moving on this pizza."

Chapter Seven

Pop's Place had a settled, old-school look with white-washed brick and a wide wraparound porch. Only a few blocks off Broadway, the eatery fit perfectly into a setting where several other shops and small restaurants stood. There were half a dozen tables placed outside, presumably for diners who preferred the great outdoors. Kat noted the sidewalk wasn't bursting with the same crush of tourists that packed downtown, but it did have a cozy ambience. Stepping inside, she admired walls lined with brick and slotted boards, which gave a country-style rustic atmosphere. Booths and tables in a spacious area reminded her of Krazy's back in Kansas City, which put her right at ease. Only the stage surprised her. Rather than a platform standing against brick, Pop's stage backed to a wall of windows. She grinned. Passersby could check out a performer before they came inside.

Shawn swore he'd perfectly paved the way for her. "I sang your praises to high heaven. You're a shoo-in. Pop'll love you."

She hoped he wasn't kidding. Earning a few bucks would keep her from dipping too heavily into the cash Daddy had deposited to supplement her savings. Though she knew he'd give her more if she asked, a plan of self-sufficiency sounded much more mature than one of pathetic beggary. Kat had removed the cervical collar before she left her apartment, even though her neck still ached a bit from move-in day. Participating in a job interview while looking like she'd absconded from a hospital wouldn't be the best first impression.

A man behind the bar matched Shawn's description of Pop: receding gray hair, a slight paunch, white shirt with the sleeves rolled up, and a navy-blue tie. She bit back a smile and approached him.

"Hi, I'm Kat Becker. Are you Pop?"

The man wiped his fingers on a towel before shaking her hand. "I am. Shawnie told me you live in the same building he does. He went on and on about you. Makes me think you've got my boy charmed. I keep hoping he'll find a good woman one of these days to settle him down. Somebody like you."

Uh-oh. "He's my neighbor and we've become good *friends*," she said, emphasizing the word "friends" just in case. Pop's overly animated tone indicated he either didn't have a clue or chose to ignore the truth. Could this be the reason for Shawn's distress?

"Good, good. I'm glad to see he has a new gal-pal." He scratched his ear. "Some nights the restaurant gets pretty busy. Do you have any experience?"

"I had a part-time serving job for a while in high school if that counts." She decided not to bring up the fact she'd been fired when she sat at a table too long talking to Jenna, who'd come in to sob over a breakup with her boyfriend. Leaving the job had worked out for the best, since her mother nearly flipped out over the notion of her youngest daughter waiting tables.

"Great. Then you know how the basic routine works. Write down the orders, turn 'em in, and bring the people what they want. We have a cashier, so you don't need to worry about working the register. As far as I'm concerned, you're hired. My manager will train you on how to handle things." Pop looked around the room and then called out to a neatly dressed, auburn-haired man. "Jett, come here and meet our new waitress."

Jett joined them and he slowly appraised her from the top of her head to the tip of her toes. *Geez, buddy. Take a picture why don't you?* Once his eyes stopped bugging out, his mouth took over and widened into the biggest, phoniest smile she'd ever seen.

"You must be Kat Becker," he said, extending his hand. "I was told you'd be here for an interview. I run Pop's Place. He must have been impressed to hire you so fast. Can I schedule you for Thursday? It'll be easier to go over the ropes with you on a night that's not so busy."

She pulled away the hand he still held. "Works for me."

"Good. I'll see you at five o'clock. Black slacks and white blouse. We want our staff to be recognizable."

"Okay. I'll be here. All decked out in black and white."

He gave her another look that narrowed her eyes before he turned away. Pop seemed sweet as can be, but Jett? What a stuffed shirt. *Meh.* She'd dealt with his type before, and she could again.

She chatted amiably a few more minutes with Pop, until a man walked in and took a seat at the bar. He raised his forefinger to interrupt the conversation. "Do you have any craft beers on tap?"

"See you Thursday," Pop said to her, and left to attend to his customer.

Kat's drive home brought an odd mix of feelings. On one hand, her plans were coming together. Apartment secured. School application in progress. Part-time job. Most of the boxes had been checked, except for the big one. She still hadn't gotten a call back from Pete Casson. Kat knew he was an important guy, and important guys were busy, but why hadn't he answered her messages? A possibility chilled her. Maybe he'd looked at Trevor T. Ray's video and hated it. The way she looked? The way she sang? Her gigantic hair? It wasn't her fault the humidity had been 85 percent that day. Had she known Trevor would show up and video her, she'd have visited her stylist.

Crap. So much for sudden stardom. What had made her think Trevor's producer would hang out a welcome sign for her?

By the time she got back to the apartment building, the weight of the world dragged her down. She got out of Ruby and mourned again over the dent. An insurance agent had sent her an email telling her where she could take the car to be fixed, but she hadn't made an appointment yet. *Double crap.* Another item leaped to the top of her list.

She trudged to her apartment door just as Shawn was coming out of his.

"Hey, girl," he said. "What's wrong? You got the job, didn't you?"

"I got it. Come in if you have a minute."

He followed her into the apartment, and Charlie came from the bedroom to greet them. Shawn picked up the cat and took a seat. "So spill the goods. What gives?"

"Second-guessing myself. I haven't heard a word from Pete Casson. Do you think he watched the video and is staying as far away from me as possible? Maybe even changing his phone number?"

"I told you the scuttlebutt. He's out of town. You have to be patient. Drop the idea of overnight success. There's. No. Such. Thing. It only happens in fairy tales."

"I guess. It's just so frustrating."

"Get used to it." He chuckled. "Hey, here's something to cheer you up. I've got a place for you to do your audition tape. You know, the one you need to send for school. One of my friends has a studio in his basement. He says we can use it."

A grin lifted her mouth—and her spirits. Shawn held up a hand, and she high-fived him, to Charlie's annoyance. "Thanks, buddy. You always come through."

Shawn bowed at the praise. "One of my instructors gave me some very good advice. I'm going to pass it on to you. Every path has roadblocks. Climbing over them is what makes you stronger. It'll make your songwriting better too because you've got a hard-luck tale to tell."

"I'm not used to roadblocks." She smiled ruefully. "Most things come easy for me, except classes of course. They were too much of a drag, and Cs were always good enough to get by."

"My point is, don't let the roadblocks trip you up. Keep plugging away. If you do, I predict success. Hopefully, for both of us."

Kat's phone vibrated and she picked it up. "Hi, Daddy." She scrunched her face at Shawn.

"Hello, Kitty-Kat. How's your neck feeling?"

"Much better, thanks. How's Mother?"

"Don't worry about her. She's just fine. Have you gotten your car fixed yet?"

"I've been busy, but I'll schedule it as soon as I have a chance."

"I suggest not waiting too long. Get it done." He paused. "I've got some news you need to know about." Father-voice gone. Now he was using his lawyer-voice, which nearly always meant trouble.

"What is it?"

"The video. We've had a horde of media people calling and even showing up on the doorstep. They want to arrange an interview with you."

"Why?"

"So many people shared it, you've become a minor celebrity, sweetie. I don't intend to disclose anything unless you want me to. It might not be a good idea to have a bunch of vultures swarming after you to get a story. Too many times they don't get things right."

Kat put the phone to her chest to muffle the side conversation. "Shawn, my father says some media people want to interview me about the video. What should I do?"

"Let them! It'll be great publicity. Get it set up before things cool off. Fame comes and goes in a New York minute. Cash in now."

She put the cell back to her ear. "It's okay, Daddy. Go ahead and give them my number."

He sputtered and coughed. "Are you sure?"

"Absolutely," she assured him.

"Very well." She heard the soft murmur of her mother's voice in the background. "Oh, and your mother says to be careful what you share."

Kat ended the call. Shawn whooped and said, "Maybe this will get Pete Casson's attention."

"Do you really think so? I am totally pumped!"

"This could definitely be a career launcher for you." Shawn put Charlie on the floor. "Much as I'd love to stick around and celebrate, I've got to go to work. I'll let you know as soon as I have a definite date and time to record your audition."

"Perfect. See ya."

When the door closed, Kat launched into a foot-stomping happy dance. Maybe everything would work out a thousand times easier than anyone else thought possible. Wouldn't it be a hoot? To think how bummed she'd been only a few minutes ago. She closed her eyes to imagine the triumphant scene and danced a little more, until her heel accidentally came down on the tip of Charlie's tail. The cat yowled, and she jerked her head downward to make sure he was all right. A sharp twinge in her neck indicated this move hadn't been a good idea. First, she verified her cat was more aggravated than hurt. Then she sat on the sofa, rubbing the sore place above her spine. Time to strap on the goofy collar again. Resentful thoughts about her injury led her to another pain in the neck—Dr. Dan McDonald.

There'd been so much going on, she hadn't had time to wonder when or if she'd ever run into him again. It still bugged her Mac had seemed to dislike her so much. Especially since she couldn't figure out why, other than his weird grudge against the music scene. Like anyone could be annoyed by music.

A broader notion dawned. People-pleasing had never been a problem for her in the past. Had she lost her mojo? If she no longer had enough charisma to captivate one crabby but normal, average person, how could she possibly charm a superstar like Pete Casson? Kat massaged Charlie's stepped-upon tail with one hand and her neck with the other as she concentrated on how to refine her people skills.

By the time Charlie forgave her enough to crank up the volume on his purr, she had an idea.

Chapter Eight

Dan took a moment to fill a cup with coffee. It would have to do as a substitute for dinner. His day had been rougher than usual. He'd seen to a man with chest pains who he admitted for further evaluation, three people hacking with flu symptoms, a woman with a gall bladder attack, and a multiple-car accident that brought in six patients, but—thank goodness—resulted in only one truly serious injury. He'd even treated a fisherman who'd accidently hooked his own ear while fly-fishing. The hook had prevented too much bleeding until Dan removed it, at which time the previously stoic patient had passed out cold.

Dan tossed his empty cup into the trash and collapsed on a chair in the staff room. If he could get a five-minute respite, he might just make it through to the end of his shift. A glance at the wall clock showed one hour to go.

The brunette nurse—he'd discovered her name was Kimmie—breezed in with a cup of coffee in her hand. "Oh, here you are, Doctor. There's a phone call for you at the desk. A woman. She didn't give me her name." Kimmie's tone held a trace of reproach.

Surely it couldn't be Ava. He'd avoided calling her back, even after she left a voicemail. He considered telling Kimmie to take a message, but the nurse had already left the staff area. There was nothing to do but pick up the call. Otherwise he wouldn't put it past Ava to arrive at the hospital in person to get his attention. He stood and stretched. A dull ache throbbed behind his eyes.

Stu sat at the main ER desk, tapping notes into the computer. He dipped his head toward one of the phones. "Your call's there," he said.

Dan picked up the receiver. "This is Dr. McDonald."

"Hi, Mac. I took a chance you might be working today."

He didn't even need to ask her name. What in the world could Kat Becker want? On the bright side, at least it wasn't Ava. "What can I do for you?"

"I have a gigantic favor to ask."

Another one? He didn't reply. A gigantic favor did not sound auspicious.

"Are you there?" She raised the volume of her voice.

"I'm here. What is it you need this time?"

"Now don't get all grouchy, before you hear what I have to say. I found a part-time job at a restaurant in town, and I thought it would be a good idea to get a customer's point of view before I started working. This probably sounds kind of weird, but I don't want to sit there alone, and the first person I thought about was you."

"Me? Why?"

"Because at the moment, I only know one other human being in Nashville and he's not available. Anyway, since you helped me get my car back, I feel like I owe you a dinner."

"You don't owe me anything," he replied too quickly.

"Sure I do. Besides, I'll have you know I'm not horrible company, and from what I've seen, you could use some entertainment in your life. What about tomorrow? It'll be fun, and I can tell you about some cool things you might find interesting." She paused for a moment. "Please?"

"I don't think this is a good idea." His fingers tapped the desktop, although he had to admit her offer intrigued him.

"Really? I think it's a fabulous one. Besides, it's my birthday and I'd rather not celebrate alone."

He glanced over at Stu, who stared unabashedly back at him. Eavesdropping with no shame at all. Dan turned his head away and lowered his voice to gather more information. "Where and when?"

"Any time after five. The restaurant's called Pop's Place. I understand the food is great. Have you heard of it?"

Dan's brows twitched up toward his hairline. "Yes, I've heard of it. Okay. I'll meet you there at six-thirty."

"Thank you so much! Truly, I am fun to be with. At least that's what my friends tell me. I promise you won't regret it."

"I'll see you then," he said stiffly and hung up the phone. He already regretted it. Ever cognizant of Stu, Dan shuffled through some papers on the desk.

"Sounds like a strange phone call. What's up?" Stu asked.

"Nothing. Just doing a favor for someone I know."

"A female, according to Kimmie, which by the way certainly jaded *her* disposition." Stu swiveled his chair to the side, and it squeaked in protest. "Look at your face. A sour puss if I ever saw one. You must not like this 'friend' much."

"You don't have to like someone to do them a favor."

"Nobly spoken." The phone buzzed, and Stu reached to pick it up. "But the idea of Dr. McDonald doing a favor for someone he doesn't like is new."

Dan grabbed a file and moved away from the desk before he said something in violation of the hospital's lengthy code of conduct policies. Kat Becker had crossed his mind more than once since the day they met. She was a cute girl, sure, but far too excitable and flighty for his taste. Everything she said to him lacked common sense except for one—her request *had* sounded weird. Yet strange as it seemed, his curiosity had been piqued more than his annoyance. Of all the places in Nashville where she could have found a job, she'd gotten hired at Pop's Place.

The fates certainly had a peculiar sense of humor.

Kat avoided her normal tendency to be late and took a table at Pop's. She studied the menu while she waited, wondering whether it would be wise to memorize the selections. The offerings appeared normal but with a silly twist on the names. Good Golly Dolly Burgers. Music City Caesar Salad. Tubb of Sweet Potato Fries. It made her smile. Pop must have a great sense of humor. Or could this be Jett's work? Somehow, she doubted the restaurant manager had anything to do with it. He didn't seem like the jolly type.

The back of her neck prickled. She sensed someone behind her and turned her head. Speak of the devil.

"Well hello, Kat. I didn't expect to see you before Thursday," Jett said.

"I thought I'd get a feel for the place before I actually start working."

"What a great idea." He grinned at her. Or was it a leer? "I'll even give you your employee discount. What would you like to try?"

"I'm waiting for someone. For now, just water, please."

Jett leaned against the table and hauled her into a one-armed hug. "What about a beer, hon? We've got a great light craft you might enjoy."

She shook his arm away, ready to snap a sarcastic response, but stopped herself. Jett would soon be her manager. He might also have a lot of input on whether she'd be allowed to sing at Pop's. Clearly though, she needed to put him in his place. Right now.

"I won't be ordering anything until my boyfriend gets here."

"Boyfriend? Pop told me you were new in town. Did you bring someone with you to Nashville?"

The intrusive question ruffled her good nature. Jett wasn't only a jerk, he was nosy and obnoxious to boot. "No, I met him in here. The minute we saw each other, we knew it was fate." She wondered if the comment called for a swoony blush.

Jett cocked an eyebrow at her and backed off. "Is that so? I didn't figure you for a fast mover. I'll tell the waitress to bring your water."

Good. The less she saw of him, the better. However, she certainly would like to see Mac. It was six forty-five. Where could he be?

She went back to studying the menu, repeating the words out loud until Mac finally joined her, his hair ruffled in a charmingly disheveled way. "Sorry I'm late."

"I was starting to wonder whether you were going to stand me up. I'm glad you didn't." She looked at him and showed off her best smile.

"There were a few things I had to take care of before I could get here. I didn't mean to make you wait." He slid into the booth and probed his shirt pocket to pull out a tiny envelope. "This is for you. Happy birthday."

She had to restrain herself from squealing out loud. "You got me a gift?"

"No big deal. I figure everybody deserves a present on their birthday."

She dimpled and opened the card. "A Starbucks gift card. Thanks, Mac. I've been craving an iced cinnamon latte all day. How did you know?"

"It's nothing." His voice went cool and brusque. "How does your neck feel?"

"Much better, thanks. It only twinges occasionally."

"Have you followed up with a doctor? I can refer you to someone if you'd like."

"I'm not worried about it. Hey, no more doctor-patient talk tonight. Let's pretend we're friends." She tucked the gift card into her bag. "Did you have to work today?"

"Nope. My day off. I needed it too. Yesterday beat the hell out of me."

"I'll bet. I can't imagine being in the emergency room is much fun."

"It can be trying at times, but a given when in ER medicine."

She set her menu on the table. "How'd you ever pick such an area? Sounds like a stressful place to work."

"I got a great offer, but you're right. There is a lot of pressure in ER and therefore a lot of turnover, hence a good place to quickly find a position. Vanderbilt's ER is where I did my residency, and they hired me right away."

"My sister's a veterinarian, and when she talks about her job, she practically lights up. You don't seem nearly as enthusiastic."

"It's a job."

"Shouldn't you do something you see as more than just a job? Something more satisfying."

He snorted. "You mean like breaking into the music business?"

"Well, yes. A career you can be passionate about. And by the way, my fifteen minutes of fame is about to get a lot bigger. One of the local affiliate television stations called, and they're interviewing me the day after tomorrow on a national broadcast. This could lead to…to who knows what?"

"You do understand a viral video isn't a guarantee of stardom, don't you?"

Joy-killer. "Isn't inspiring people part of the Hippocratic Oath? If it is, you need to brush up on your skills."

"It is not part of the oath, but that's beside the point. You seem to think success is going to drop right into your lap. Reality is a lot different from fantasy. Perhaps you better lower your expectations."

"Why would I do such a thing? I intend to pursue what I love. Otherwise, what's the point? Who wants to be in a job where you end up spending most of your time counting the hours until you're off work and then counting the years to retirement?"

He looked around, hopefully for a waitress and not an escape route. This certainly wasn't any way to soften his attitude toward her. *You can do better than this.*

Kat put her hand on his arm. "Look, I don't mean to upset you. I guess I'm just pumped that after years of meandering through school, I finally found something to excite me. Everybody deserves to be happy with their life, don't they? I'm afraid you aren't."

He looked down at her hand but didn't pull away. It thrilled her to see one side of his mouth lift the tiniest bit. "You sound like an amateur philosopher with a tendency to overshare. I appreciate what you're trying to say, but let's drop the subject and order dinner. Do you know you want?"

Subject shifted. All right then, Mac. "I'm going to try the Music City Caesar Salad. Here, you haven't even looked at the menu yet."

"That's not necessary. I've been here before."

Jett appeared out of nowhere with a glass of water in each hand, his eyes nearly bulging from their sockets. "Hello, Dan." He plopped the glasses onto the table so hard, water sloshed over the side. His head swiveled toward Kat, disbelief radiating from his face. "Dan McDonald is your boyfriend?"

She gulped, aware of a sudden blast of fire in her cheeks. *Uh-oh. Jett knows Mac? No good can come of this.*

Dan's expression reflected a moment of shock before he shot a swift glance from Jett to Kat and smoothly dodged the question. "I think we're ready to order. Kat will have the Music City Salad. Bring me a Broadway Burger—medium rare. A couple of beers too. The usual. Sound okay, Kat?"

Speechless, she nodded.

"Sure, Dan. I'll take care of it right away." Jett retreated with an expression so quizzical, Kat wished she could pull out her cell and snap a photo, although putting it on Instagram might not be wise.

Dan's forehead creased. "You told Jett I'm your…boyfriend? Is this why you asked me to meet you here tonight?"

"Well." She picked up her glass and took a swallow to give herself time to think. "Not exactly. Jett is a little too touchy-feely for me, if you know what I'm saying. He got grabby, so I blurted out the first thing that came into my head to keep things from getting personal. He's the manager, and I don't want to start out on the wrong foot with him. I'm sorry if I overstepped."

Dan crossed his arms. "As a matter of fact, I do know Jett, and unfortunately your assessment is right. I've heard a few complaints about him from staff, but Pop had a talk with him and told him to cut it out. He likes Jett and feels he does a good job, so I haven't taken it any further."

"Why would you get involved in anything Pop or Jett do? What's in it for you?"

A slow grin tweaked his mouth. "As it turns out, Ryan McDonald—also known to one and all as Pop—is my father."

The wheels in her brain spun into overdrive. "Are you kidding?"

"I am not. Pop's had this restaurant for quite a while, and he's getting on in years. He needs someone like Jett who knows the business in and out to help him. God knows I don't have the time to do it."

"This is totally unbelievable." Her eyes widened. "But in a way, kind of cool. I met you because of a crazy random accident, and now I'm working for your dad. Pure and simple kismet—meant to be."

"Kismet has nothing to do with anything. It's only a fluke. I'm a doctor and you got hurt. You needed a job and Pop needed a waitress. End of story."

"How many flukes does it take to turn you into a believer? Hold on a minute." Kat chewed over what she'd learned. "I just realized something. My friend suggested I apply for a job here. He said Pop was *his* father. But his last name isn't McDonald. It's Wright…Shawn Wright."

"Now I see how you ended up here. Shawn's my younger brother. He uses the name Wright as his…What do you call it? Stage name. I assume you met him at the apartment complex. He's a student at Belmont. I sent you to the place where he lives because I know he likes the location."

"Shawn lives right across the hall from me." She palm-slapped the table several times like a judge demanding order in court. "Seriously, do not try to tell me this is a bunch of arbitrary unrelated events and not our cosmic fate."

Dan rubbed the back of his neck. "I'll admit it feels like more than a coincidence. But I don't believe in the idea of anything happening because it was meant to be."

"You don't? Maybe you ought to think again, Mac."

Chapter Nine

On her first evening of work at Pop's, Kat clomped up the steps in her new high-heeled boots, arriving ten minutes ahead of her start time. She felt ready for the challenge until she saw the judgmental look on Jett's face.

"You were supposed to be here thirty minutes before your shift begins to fill out all your paperwork."

"I was? You didn't say anything about that."

"I'm quite sure I did." His superior tone annoyed her to high heaven.

And I'm quite sure you didn't. "I must not have heard you." She feigned a smile. "Maybe you should speak a little louder next time."

"Let's get something straight. You're not going to receive any special treatment just because you're dating the boss's son."

"No worries. I wouldn't expect any special treatment no matter what the situation is. I'm sorry I didn't get here at the time you wanted."

Pop joined them. "Don't worry about it, Kat. We can get everything taken care of before you leave." He chuckled. "It's interesting you know both my boys. Here I thought Shawnie might be sweet on you, and now I find out it's Danny. Whichever way you look at it, this is great news. There's nothing more I want before I die than to see each of my sons with a wonderful woman…just like the one I had."

His gaze went to a framed photo hanging on the wall behind the bar. It was a younger version of Pop next to a fetching brunette. The couple's eyes crinkled with laughter, like they'd shared a private joke. The snapshot had been taken quite some time ago, but Kat still recognized Pop's warm smile. The sentiment he expressed had been sweet, but his meaning made her shift uncomfortably. Jett must have blabbed what she said, and now Pop practically had Mac and Kat on their honeymoon. "You look pretty healthy to me. There's plenty of time to see your boys settled and happy."

She didn't dare correct his assumption, so diversion would do for the moment. Mac had been a champ at her birthday dinner, playing along with the unspoken plea in her eyes. He even requested a slice of cake for her. But how long would he keep up such a charade? Maybe she could call and beg for his cooperation, at least for as long as it took them to find a reason to break up. Of course, breaking up could leave her to the mercy of Jett the Wolf. But a break-up might be better than the alternative. If Pop found out she lied, he might fire her. As far as Pop's hopes for Shawn, *that* was none of her business, though she made a mental note to ask Shawn about it.

Pop beamed at her—future-father-in-law affection written all over his face. "Luckily, it's slow on Thursdays.

Meryl, the other waitress scheduled to work with you, called in sick so you'll be learning on the fly." He walked away with a self-satisfied smile, leaving Kat in Jett's much-more-hostile custody.

"I'll show you around and then go through our routine." His tone was a tad less contentious, which suited her. Even better, he kept his hands to himself. Dating the boss's son might not bring many benefits, but it certainly helped keep Jett in line.

She followed him into a small but neat kitchen, and he introduced her to the head cook, a man named Rory, dark-skinned and big as a linebacker, who looked up long enough to wave and shoot a gap-toothed smile her way before turning his attention to burgers sizzling on a grill.

Jett took her from the kitchen to where she'd pick up food to the restroom area. He explained each day brought a special deal. Thursday's menu featured Hot Hit Chicken. Jett showed her where to find flatware wrapped in napkins and water glasses, then handed her an order pad. "If you have free time, take a good look at the menu. Sometimes customers ask for a recommendation. You'll take the order, deliver it to the kitchen, fill the drink orders, and then bring the customers their food."

As she hovered on the edge of boredom, he announced she should make the guests feel welcome—she'd ace that!—and finally left her on her own. The process sounded simple as could be.

Until a party of twelve arrived.

By the time Kat had scrambled around to drag tables together and added enough chairs so everyone could be seated, moisture gathered at her hairline. She'd clipped her curls away from her face but felt confident any loose strands had exploded. Jett leaned on the counter with a smug expression and didn't offer to help. Nice guy.

Still, her smile didn't falter. She seated the eight women and four men, handing menus to each person. "I'll get you water while you decide what you want," she chirped helpfully. "Special of the day is Hot Hit Chicken." *Ha! I remembered.*

Kat went to the bar, counted out twelve glasses, and placed them on a tray. Then she scooped ice into each glass before pouring the water. Satisfied, she put down the pitcher and prepared to pick up the tray. It wouldn't budge.

"Do you want to drop the whole thing? Don't try to deliver more than a few drinks at a time. Shards of glass would *not* make a good customer experience." Jett glowered at her. "And never touch glasses near the rim."

Drop the tray? Why did he mention such a thing? The ominous thought echoed through her mind as she removed all but three glasses. This time she could lift the tray without a problem. If Jett the Wolf was nice, he'd give her a hand, but he sniffed and scribbled something on a pad of paper.

It took Kat four trips to successfully deliver the water, and she managed it without a single misstep. By the time the final glass had been put in place, the group was ready to order. She opened her pad and started with a pleasant-looking, gray-haired, grandmotherly woman.

"Bring me the Broadway Burger, honey, and make it halfway between medium and well done. I don't care for any lettuce, but if the tomatoes are fresh, I'll take a slice on the side with some mayonnaise. Oh, and give me extra onion, please. Onion doesn't really agree with me, but I like it. Let's see. Along with the burger, I'll have chips and some iced tea. Oh, and we'll need separate checks." She finished her dissertation pleasantly.

Kat hadn't written so much since her last college term paper. All in all, it took twenty minutes for her to gather the group's orders. Only a few were as picky about what they wanted as Grandma had been.

She took the food lists to the kitchen and gave Pop the drink orders. "We usually don't have much traffic on Thursdays," he remarked. "Guess you got lucky."

"Lucky? If you say so."

"Hopefully they'll leave you a nice tip." Pop's gaze brushed Jett. "Why don't you give her a hand?"

"I'll assist when the food's ready." He disappeared into the kitchen.

"Well, okeydokey," she said, filling the first few drink orders, this time with four glasses on the tray. Her arm muscles burned while she carried them to the table. With a workout like this, there wasn't any need to spend money on a gym. Was it wrong to feel so inordinately pleased? "Your food will be coming soon," she announced gaily.

"I hope so." One of the men looked peevish. "I'd like to get home and watch that talent show before it's over. Forgot to set my DVR."

"We'll do our best," Kat replied.

Even after they got their food, the group kept her busy. She raced around the table refilling glasses, delivering another burger to Grandma—who'd complained hers was too well done—and fetched a replacement salad for a customer who'd forgotten to mention she wanted dressing on the side. Sheesh! It had been baptism by fire, yet she seemed to be surviving the test. When the group finally finished and got ready to leave, they complimented her work and awarded her a twenty-percent tip to show their approval.

Gratified, she glanced at the clock. Closing time wasn't far off, and she could already envision soaking in a warm bubble bath. Kat filled a tray with glassware. One minute she was on a swift step toward the kitchen. The next minute, her feet slipped out from under her. She and the tray hit the floor with a loud clatter. Surrounded by three broken glasses and puddles of liquid everywhere, she sat up and brushed herself off.

Pop helped her stand. "You okay?"

"I'm fine."

Jett crossed his arms and narrowed his eyes. He pointed at a closed door. "The mop and bucket are in there."

She gazed at the wreckage. She'd never had to take care of such a mess before, thanks to Mrs. Caldwell. Her mother's longtime housekeeper did the heavy cleaning at home. Kat did her best. She mopped, then squeezed water—and glass shards—into a bucket while Jett shot daggers at her.

Pop sent a sympathetic glance her way. "Don't worry about it, hon," he said. "This is your first night. You did great."

Maybe not great, but she'd learned the two most significant lessons for anyone who planned to be a waitress.

First, patience. Second, cute boots were not a substitute for comfortable rubber-soled, non-slip, sensible shoes.

As she helped Jett with the closing routine, he didn't comment on her accident. If nothing else, she hoped her klutziness had dampened any attraction he might have felt for her. This would come as encouraging news to Mac, who most assuredly would love to end their pretend relationship—the sooner the better.

Kat had almost finished filling out her employee paperwork when Pop muttered, "Oh, no. This is the last thing I needed." He banged down the phone installed behind the bar.

Jett hurried to the counter. "What's wrong?"

"Music for tomorrow is canceled. All three of the band members came down with food poisoning. Friday's our busiest night, and people expect live music. What the h-e-double hockey sticks am I supposed to do now?"

"I can call around and see if anyone is available," Jett offered.

"You know anyone worth spit is already booked."

"For God's sake, Pop, this is Nashville. There are musicians everywhere. I'm sure I can find somebody to do it."

Heart pounding, Kat waggled her fingers at the two men. "I'm available."

Both turned toward her and said at the same time, "You?"

When she took a second to consider it, the incredulous look on their faces felt rather rude. "Yes, me. It's exactly why I came to Nashville, for a chance to sing. I've got experience. Not a lot, but enough. I play guitar and I can perform the sets I've done before in Kansas City."

Jett's taunting look was nearly as dismissive as his words. "We hired you to be a waitress, not a performer. I'll find a real musician."

His remark stung. "You go right ahead and spend your time making calls, although I have no idea who you expect to hire with less than twenty-four hours' notice." She lifted her chin. "I'll wait."

She turned to go help Rory in the kitchen. It sounded like Jett and Pop were arguing. *Good.*

She loaded dishes into the washer, then grabbed a pan and started scrubbing. It motivated her to pretend the pan was Jett's smirking face.

"I thought you wuz in a hurry to leave," Rory said to her.

"I am, but the band for tomorrow canceled, and I volunteered to step in." She pushed the scouring pad harder across the pan's surface. "Jett apparently thinks anyone would be better than me."

"That's Jett, all right. He can be an ornery one, and he makes it tough on anybody who crosses him. You don't want to be on his bad side."

"Too late," Kat replied. "I already am."

By the time she and Rory had the kitchen cleaned and sanitized, Pop rushed in and took Kat's arm. "Jett's called all over town with no luck. I told him we might as well try you. What have we got to lose?"

Kat ignored the less-than-resounding endorsement of her abilities and focused on the positive. She'd just secured her first gig in Nashville. Adrenalin pumped her into action, and she impulsively threw her arms around Pop to hug him.

"Thank you so much! I won't let you down, I promise."

"I'm going to call Danny tonight. He's got himself all twisted up about people who work in music, and he usually won't set foot in the restaurant on band nights. But don't you worry. I'll tell him he better be here. It'd be a dirty shame if he hid out at home instead of watching his sweetheart sing, wouldn't it?"

Double crap!

Chapter Ten

Bam! Bam! Kat opened one eye as somebody banged on the door. She squinted at the bedside clock. Four thirty? She'd been up late scheduling posts for her father's law firm and wondered what sort of weirdo would plan a visit at this hour of the morning. "Go away," she muttered. The pounding didn't stop. She rubbed her eyes and sat up. Cobwebs in her mind lifted, and at once realization hit.

She scrambled out of bed and dashed to open the door. Shawn stood on the other side tapping his watch. "I figured you'd forget to set your alarm. Get with it, girl. We need to be at the studio by six o'clock."

"Six o'clock didn't sound as early yesterday as it does today. Come in."

Shawn entered and pushed her from a slow stumble to a trot. "Don't blow it. People would kill for this kind of exposure."

"Maybe you should become a professional Ted-Talker instead of a producer."

"Never mind. You've got thirty minutes to get ready." He pointed Kat toward her bedroom and gave her another little shove. "Move it."

Kat groaned and stumbled to the bathroom. With each step, she woke up a little more, even though it was stupid o'clock. Her interview on the video had been set with a local affiliate of some television station—NBC or CBS, she couldn't remember which—for a morning show segment. Thank goodness. Evening news programs tended to focus on grim depressing stories while everybody on morning shows smiled a lot and didn't dig deep into the gloomy news of the day.

In what had to be record time, she showered—rejected the idea of washing her hair—gave her face a light touch of makeup, and donned a pair of jeans and a tank top. Shawn paced the floor in her living room, his hands laced behind his back.

"Come on, let's go," he said. "Have you given any thought to what you're going to say?"

"Not really. The person I talked to told me they'd ask all the questions. It sounds simple, only a sixty-second spot." She pulled on her boots.

"A sixty-second spot on a nationally televised program is priceless, so think before you talk."

"If I waste time thinking, I won't have a chance to answer."

Shawn shook his head and sprinted for the door. She dashed after him. He'd offered to drive her in his rickety old Chevy, possibly because he didn't trust her to get to the station on time. She couldn't imagine why he'd think such a thing.

They jumped into Shawn's car and sped off. At such an unholy hour traffic was light, a good thing since he ignored the speed limit to screech around corners, getting them to the studio parking lot with minutes to spare. A guard checked their IDs, and a woman ushered them into the greenroom—a room that was, in fact, green. Glazed doughnuts and coffee sat on a table under the monitor mounted high on the wall streaming the station's live broadcast. Kat kept an eye on the screen as she reached for a doughnut.

Shawn grabbed her hand. "No way."

"But I'm starving."

"Did you bring a toothbrush?"

"Why would I?"

"Do you want millions of people to see you with doughnut pieces stuck between your teeth? No eating anything. Television close-ups are murder. They show stuff even a magnifying mirror misses."

Kat cast a longing eye toward the sweet treats and shoved her hands into her pockets. She went to sit by Shawn on the green sofa where she couldn't smell the sugary delights.

A few minutes later, a harried-looking blonde wearing headphones came into the room. "Kat Becker?"

Kat jumped up. "Yes, that's me."

"We'll be ready for you after the next commercial break. Callie Covington will handle your interview. I recommend you either look at Callie or at the camera and answer her questions in your own words."

"I wouldn't think of using anybody else's words." Kat grinned, but the blonde didn't respond.

The woman pointed at Shawn. "Would you like your boyfriend to come on camera with you? It adds interest to have more than one person."

"We're friends, but I'm not her boyfriend," Shawn said smoothly. "If Kat wants me to be there, I will."

"Why not?" Kat said. "The more the merrier."

"Okay. I'll come get you in about five minutes." The blonde put her hand to one of the earphones like she was listening to someone and scurried away.

Kat turned toward Shawn. "You know what? There sure are a lot of people in Nashville who don't want to be known as my boyfriend."

"I'm sure that comment would make sense to someone, but I don't get it. What are you talking about?"

"I'm talking about your brother."

"Dan? What's he got to do with this?"

She proceeded to explain how they met and the tiny white lie she had told Jett, who'd blabbed the information to Pop.

By the time she finished the somewhat convoluted story, Shawn stared at her in open-mouthed disbelief. The blonde reappeared. "Show time," she said brightly. "Come with me."

The woman led them to a set where three separate cameras were aimed at a sofa and chair. A pretty redhead with helmet hair and a huge smile greeted them. She had pink-tinted papers in her hand. "Hi, I'm Callie." She spoke as if her name ought to mean something. Since Kat rarely got up early enough to watch the morning news, it didn't. Callie tottered to her chair on five-inch spike heels, sat, and crossed her legs daintily. Kat and Shawn sat beside each other on the sofa.

Someone shouted, "Ready! Three, two, one." He pointed at Callie.

She over-smiled at the middle camera. "I'm sure many of you have seen the viral video posted by music legend Trevor T. Ray. Today we have with us Kat Becker, the singer from Trevor's video. She and her boyfriend, Shawn Wright, are here with us exclusively." She swiveled her head toward the sofa. "Hello, Kat and Shawn."

"Hello," Kat said.

Shawn sat still as a stone. He looked like he was suffering from a bad hangover.

"Your video has been viewed by over a million people. I loved your performance. Let's take a look at it." A monitor showed a snippet from the video. The picture appeared a little grainy but who cared? Callie flipped through her notes until the camera returned to her. "You must be thrilled. Tell me, Kat. How did you connect with Trevor?"

"Well…" A single strand of hair on Kat's forehead distracted her. She pushed it away. "I was singing at a little place in Kansas City when who should walk in but Trevor T. Ray. I didn't know he videoed me until my friend called the next day."

"Wow. Trevor must have been impressed."

"I guess so. He told me I should come to Nashville, so here I am."

"How amazing. Have you been offered a contract yet?" The woman chuckled.

"No, but I'm hoping something will happen soon."

Callie turned toward Shawn. "You must be so proud of her. What a lucky break your girlfriend got."

Shawn's eyes went glassy. "Um. Uh-huh."

Callie waited a moment. When she could see he had nothing further to say, her gaze returned to the camera. "Thank you so much for your time and good luck! Okay, Nashville. Send Kat some love."

The interview ended. Callie shook Kat's hand then Shawn's before she raced away to her next segment. Shawn stood rooted in place like he'd turned to stone.

"Come on," Kat said, taking his arm. "Let's go."

He allowed her to lead him from the studio and down the corridor to the exit. "This is a hot mess," he finally said.

"Why does it feel like you're mad at me?"

"Here's the deal. First you blow me out of the water by telling me everybody at Pop's thinks my brother is your boyfriend. A man who, by the way, never ceases to let me know how much he despises anything related to the music business. Then it's announced on national television that *I'm* your boyfriend. Am I the only one of us who thinks all of this is a disaster?"

"Hey, I wasn't the one who spread it around he was my boyfriend. The only one I said it to was Jett, so he'd keep his hands to himself."

"At least that part makes sense. Okay, I get it. But still…this is a train wreck."

"I know," Kat agreed mournfully. "But what can I do? I don't want to get fired. Not when I'm scheduled to sing at Pop's Place tonight."

"Wait. What? You're singing at Pop's tonight? When were you planning to tell me this?"

"Sorry. I'm still trying to totally wake up. Pop had a last-minute cancellation. Guess he was desperate enough to give me a chance."

"Oh, boy. This is a very good thing. It means Pop definitely likes you."

"I think he does, but mostly because, you know, he thinks I'm your brother's girlfriend."

"Maybe. Pop sees things his own way. He's had issues with Dan, but more of them with me. It can be hard to read him. He takes the ostrich approach to any topic he doesn't like. If he saw the interview, I hope it doesn't give him any wrong ideas. You know…like about me and you."

"He already got the idea…for about a second. I set him straight. Anyhow, he's convinced the action is between your brother and me." When Shawn bit his lip, she added, "Pop's a good man. Give him time. Everything will work out…eventually." She hoped she was right.

"Things were easier before Mom got sick. She ran interference for us. Now it's three guys butting heads, each one of us intent on getting our own way."

"Family life can be stressful—don't I know it—but love is still there to link everyone together—whether they like it or not."

"A nice sentiment, but we'll see how reality turns out. Tell you what, I'll come over later and help you get set up for tonight."

"You'll come with, won't you?"

"Wouldn't miss it for the world." He scratched his chin. "Too bad you didn't think to plug the gig during your interview."

"Lordy, I hardly had time to say anything worth hearing." Promotion obviously wasn't her forte. "Do you want to stop and get some coffee?"

"As long as we're quick about it. I've got interference to run. I told my friend—the one with a recording studio in his house—to watch you on the show today. Now I need to find a way to tactfully explain to him you are *not* my girlfriend."

"Oh, no. I'm sorry. I don't know why Callie said such a thing."

"Not your fault. Just another potential nail in my coffin."

A thought occurred to her. "Speaking of nails in a coffin, Pop plans to strong-arm Dan—you know, my other boyfriend—into watching me sing tonight."

"He'll be de-lighted." Shawn gave Kat a hard stare and snapped his fingers in front of her face. "What's the strange sparkle I see in your eyes? Wait a minute. Are you into my brother?"

Her cheeks grew hot. "That's ridiculous. He doesn't even like me."

"Not what I asked."

"He's not my type."

"Still not what I asked."

"He and I are only talking, so chill."

"Not gonna answer, huh? I'm not sure how this situation could get any crazier—or more interesting."

Moving Shawn away from the subject sounded like a good idea. She blurted, "Last one to the car buys lattes," then took off running. Despite the head start, Shawn beat her. He was as fleet of foot as anyone she knew. He had told her his speed was a by-product of a childhood spent running from bullies. Her eyes welled up to think how he'd been treated, but she had no doubt Shawn would someday have the last laugh. As a successful music producer.

Puffing, Shawn opened the car door for her. "You've got equipment to haul tonight. How about I drive? Then I'll be there to help with setup and takedown."

"Would you? I'd love it."

"Done. Do you have your sets figured out?"

"Mostly."

"What will you wear?"

"I don't know. Maybe a sundress?"

"Kat, this is Nashville. Dress the part. Boots and jeans plus a little sparkle. That'll do the trick."

"Okay." She laughed. "Any other advice, coach?"

"I'm glad you asked. Keep your head up when you sing. If you let your chin droop, it looks sloppy. Feel the song and make each person in the place think you're singing it just for them."

She digested his soliloquy. "What about the songs I've written? Do you think I can sneak one or two of them in?"

He shook his head. "Nope. They don't know you and they'll want familiarity, something to hang on to. There's time enough to play with original stuff later."

"Okay." She leaned over and kissed his cheek. "I don't know what I'd do without you, Shawn. Thanks."

He blushed and steered his car toward the street. "Two music wannabes against the rest of the world. What else *can* we do but stick together?"

Chapter Eleven

The stoplight turned green, and Dan twisted the handlebar grip on his Roadmaster. The bike zipped forward at a faster pace, moving through traffic like water around rocks. Evening air cooled his face and calmed his soul. He needed it. The upcoming charade called for the hum of tires on pavement. He throttled up again. How could his situation be anymore ironic? Dan McDonald, a normally level-headed and sensible man, had been sucked into an utterly ridiculous position. It felt like something straight out of a romantic comedy chick flick.

Pop had called him, insisting he come see his girlfriend perform. Dan had offered a dozen excuses. His father argued against each one. It took practically biting off the tip of his tongue to keep from revealing Kat's silly story. What on earth had stopped him? With a frown, Dan maneuvered the bike into a faster lane. Kat's off-the-top-of-her-head schemes had dragged him into a complete farce, yet he'd kept his mouth shut, not telling his father a thing. Maybe it was her relentless enthusiasm. Or her exuberant approach to whatever life threw her way. His mouth curled at the corner. Possibly even how she said exactly what she thought without a shrewd filter. At least not that he'd noticed so far. Kat certainly wasn't like any other woman he'd met.

There was also the issue of Jett. Dan had heard enough rumors—of how tough Jett made it on female staff—to believe every word Kat said about him. Jett had gotten away with his conduct for a while now, but it was only a matter of time until someone sued for harassment. He had to confront Pop on the subject, and if the inappropriate behavior continued, Dan resolved to take matters into his own hands. In a way, Kat's scheme was Jett's fault. This made it Dan's business to share his opinion, whether Pop liked hearing it or not.

Dan slowed his bike to pull into the lot at Pop's. He claimed one of the few remaining parking spaces, turned off the engine, and locked his helmet in a storage compartment behind the seat. Running a hand through his hair, he glanced toward the wall of windows framing the featured performer. A petite blonde with abundant curls cascading down her back stood on stage next to a tall wooden chair. Kat. A quick pull of empathy made him hope she knew what she was doing. Pop certainly hadn't spared the speakers. Music throbbed so loud he could feel the vibrations. He inhaled a bracing breath and headed for the door. By now, Pop must have figured his first-born wasn't going to show up at all, since it was close to an hour later than the time Kat had been scheduled to go on.

Inside, he found nearly every table filled. Dan stood next to the door. His eyes drew straight to the stage where Kat now sat perched on the stool, her wild hair fringing around her face. She was in the middle of a slow song, and couples filled the dance floor. He ignored them to study the singer. Soft pink stage lights showcased her dreamy expression as Kat twanged a tear-jerking melody. She shifted from one chord to another and sang in a low husky voice. Sometimes she finger-picked the notes, other times she strummed.

To his untrained ear, she sounded good. Better than good. No wonder Trevor T. Ray had taken notice. Dan tried to make out the lyrics of the song. Something about a lost love—he'd bet on it. From what he'd heard, slow songs almost always featured a sad tale of how the singer got dumped. Not his idea of a delightful event, but it sure looked like Kat had each dancer on the floor in the mood for romance. She finished the song, looked out at the audience, and smiled. Dan felt something move in his chest.

"Danny-boy!" Pop patted him on the back. "I was getting worried. What do you think about your girl? Isn't she something special?"

"Um." Dan swallowed. *Tell him the truth. And while you're at it, tell him to get rid of Jett.* "Yes. She sure is…special."

"I've got a seat reserved for you right up front. Shawn's already there. You boys can have a few beers together."

"Okay. But, Pop, I need to talk to you later."

"Sure, sure. I gotta get back to the bar now." He gave a nervous chuckle and then hurried away.

Through the sound of appreciative applause, Dan wound his way around tables as quickly as he could to take a seat next to his brother. Shawn pointed his bottle at Dan in greeting.

Kat locked eyes with Dan. She looked surprised but pleased and waved at him before speaking into the mike. "I feel the need for some boot-stomping music. How 'bout it, folks?"

Applause filled the room again, and Kat launched into a wild rendition of "Redneck Woman," which had every female in the place on the dance floor gyrating to the beat and shouting a chorus of "hell yeah" every time Kat prompted them. Dan crossed his arms and listened. If this wasn't Kat Becker's theme song, he didn't know what was.

Shawn's eyes gleamed. "She's got them eating out of her hand!" He hollered the comment. If he hadn't, Dan never would have heard him.

"Where's the rest of the band?" He shouted back. "I can hear them, but I don't see anybody else."

"She has a synthesizer. It's operated with your foot and gives all the accompaniment needed. A solo artist would be sunk without it. You have to have percussion for a beat, especially with fast songs." He looked impressed Dan knew enough to ask.

A waiter dropped off two chilled mugs filled with beer for Dan and Shawn. When Dan reached for his wallet, the man muttered, "Pop says it's on the house."

Dan gave the server a tip and sipped from his mug as Kat worked the crowd. The interaction seemed so fluid, so effortless, he nudged his brother. "She acts like she's had a lot of experience."

"She does have some experience. But you can tell she's a natural. Knows exactly what to do to connect with the crowd. That's beyond gold—it's platinum."

"I guess so. The audience sure seems to be having a good time."

The boot-stomping song ended, and Kat started another slow one. The women who'd been on the floor hollering had calmed down and pulled their significant others out to dance. Most partners were so twined together it was hard to tell where one began and the other ended.

Shawn dipped his head toward Dan. "Good to see you here, big bro, even if I had a bet with Pop you'd be a no-show."

"Thanks for the vote of confidence." He wanted to add he always tried his best not to disappoint his father but figured the comment might provoke an argument.

"You're welcome." Shawn took a drink. "Yep, you don't want to be known as the kind of guy who'd fail to support his girlfriend."

"Cut it out," Dan growled and banged his mug on the table. "This whole thing is out of control. Kat seems like a whirlwind blowing nice neat stacks of papers into an absurd shamble and then swearing it's an improvement. If she wants a stage name, I've got a good one for her: Calamity Kat."

Shawn stopped mid-drink to sputter and cough.

Kat put her guitar onto a stand and spoke into the microphone. "I'd like to take a short break now. I'll be back, so don't you go anywhere."

She waved and then headed straight to the table. Her mouth widened into a contagious grin, like a kid's on Christmas morning. Despite himself, it prompted Dan to smile in return. He noticed Jett approaching them—not bothering to hide his interest in what was going on. In a lightning jolt of irritation, Dan rose and pulled Kat against him. "You did great," he said and pressed his mouth against hers. *Under the circumstances, wouldn't this be what a boyfriend would do?* Her lips, stiff at first, softened as Dan held the kiss, and her arms went around his neck.

Jett said, "Excuse me," and coughed loudly. Dan found himself pulling reluctantly away.

Kat seemed dazed and a little confused. Dan wondered if his own face reflected something similar.

"Dan," Jett said. "Nice of you to come hear our new girl sing." He turned toward Kat and put his hand on her back. "You sound good."

She jerked away from him, almost imperceptibly. Dan shot a narrow-eyed frown Jett's way and then slipped his arm around Kat in a possessive signal. Jett was wise enough to back off.

Kat glanced between the two of them and lifted her chin. "Thank you, Jett," she said, and picked up Dan's mug. She raised it to her mouth and took a deep pull.

Jett's face reddened as he moved away from the table, disappearing into the thick crowd.

Shawn's brows shot up. "That. Was. Epic."

"Pop needs to do something about him." Dan's neck itched like he'd brushed against poison ivy. "No wonder he has a hard time keeping help."

Kat returned Dan's mug to the table. "Rory warned me he's a problem. Thanks to you, Mac, I think he'll steer clear from now on." Pink bloomed high on her cheeks.

"Hey, did you just call him Mac?" Shawn cocked his head to the side.

"I did," she said brightly. "He looks like a Mac to me."

Dan shrugged. "I'm getting used to it."

"I like this new casual mindset," Shawn teased.

"Gentlemen, you'll have to continue your discussion without me. I need to run to the ladies' room and then work on keeping this party going." She touched her fingers against Dan's cheek for a moment and mouthed the words *thank you.*

As soon as Kat left, Shawn tugged Dan's sleeve. "You plan to stand there all night like a zombie?"

His equilibrium returned, Dan folded into a chair.

"She's a hoot, isn't she?"

"You can say that again." His brother cackled, which irritated the hell out of Dan. "What's so funny?'

"Just thinking about Ava and Kat. You've got two women in your life, and they're about as different as people can be."

The remark echoed Dan's earlier thoughts, which irked him even more. "Correction. I don't have any women in my life. Exactly what are you driving at?"

"Oh, nothing. Even though it means I lost a bet with Pop, I'm glad you're here. It's nice of you to help Kat keep Jett in line."

"We need to talk to Pop about him. He seems to be getting bolder."

"Shh," Shawn interrupted. "She's getting ready to sing."

Dan let it go and leaned back to listen. After eight more songs, some fast, some slow, he had to admit he enjoyed hearing her. When she ended the last song of the final set, Kat acknowledged the applause and whistles with a bow and a wave. Then she put her guitar in its stand and stepped back to the table, glowing like a firefly.

Shawn gathered her into a bear hug. "It went great. Pop'll have you sing again for sure. Not to mention, you never know who might have been here tonight, just like the Trevor T. Ray thing. You could have left an impression on somebody big."

"I hope so." Laughing, Kat turned toward Dan. She put a light hand on his arm. "I know the music scene isn't something you're crazy about, so I love it that you came. And thanks again for running interference with Jett. He's a pest."

"Jett needs to be put on notice or fired." Dan's voice went gruff. "I don't care which, as long as we can stop lying to everyone."

"Speaking as a bystander, I kind of like the arrangement." Shawn smiled irreverently. "It's like watching an amateur juggle fire and waiting to see what happens next."

"Mac's right. I feel bad about this whole thing. Pop's such a sweet man. I don't like deceiving him." She glanced fondly toward where Pop worked behind the counter.

Dan's gaze followed hers. Pop looked more tired than usual. The man worked too damn hard. Another thing they needed to discuss.

"Forget about it for now. Tell me something," Shawn said. "How did it feel to get up in front of everyone?"

"Wonderful. I love looking out at the crowd. Their reaction helps me see whether or not I've bridged the gap with them. Tonight, I'd say yes."

"This place was crawling with people. Are you saying you can read everyone who comes to watch you?" Dan knew his voice registered incredulity.

"With the lights shining in my face, I can't see much beyond the first row, but those I see, I can assess and remember. Don't you do the same thing with your patients?"

"In an emergency room, people come and go all the time. I can't remember them."

Kat tilted her head. "If you can't take a minute to know the folks you see, what's the point of working with them?"

The guileless statement took him aback. He coughed and decided to change the subject. "We certainly won't resolve such questions tonight. Look, I've been thinking. It might seem odd if you and your boyfriend went their separate ways tonight. In the interest of improving Jett's behavior and keeping Pop from snapping my head off over my lousy manners, maybe I should take you home. Or do you have your car?"

"Shawn brought me, but I have a lot of equipment to haul."

"No problem." Shawn inserted himself in the conversation. "I'll take your things home." His words tumbled out so fast, his voice broke. Kat gave him a curious look.

Dan rolled his eyes. "You're about as subtle as a sardine sandwich."

"That's because subtlety doesn't work with you," Shawn said, slinging a fast retort.

"Mind your own business." Dan turned to smile at Kat. "Would you like me to give you a ride home?"

Her lips curved up. "Absolutely."

The three of them made short work of hauling her equipment to Shawn's car and loading everything in the trunk. When they were nearly finished, Jett traipsed outside with Kat's book of sheet music. "Pop will have a check for you next week," he announced.

Dan snatched the book from Jett with a stern glower. He handed it to Shawn and took Kat's hand. "Later, guys," he said to the other men.

"Wait a sec." Kat pulled away to hug Shawn. "Thank you. You are the best. We'll talk tomorrow."

Shawn hissed into her ear, loud enough for Dan to catch what he said. "I like what's happening. Don't blow it."

She stuck her tongue out at Shawn, gave Jett a cool nod, and grabbed Dan's hand. "Let's go, Mac. Wherever you lead, I'll follow."

Her response pleased him, and he squeezed her fingers lightly as they walked through the lot to his Roadmaster.

She took one look, and her eyes went big as saucers. "You have a motorcycle?"

"I do. Is that a deal breaker?"

"No way. I love bikes. This one's a beauty."

She ran her hand lovingly across the leather seat, forcing Dan to censor his thoughts. "Here. Let me get the helmets."

"You carry a spare?"

"I've seen enough accidents to favor safety over sorrow."

She took the helmet he handed her and shoved it onto her head. He clamped his lips together to keep from commenting on her appearance. Loads of thick curls hung below the helmet like a skirt. Dan turned to swing his leg over the bike saddle. "Hop on," he said.

Kat climbed behind him and nestled her body against his. He noted the neat fit of her form as he revved the engine. She wrapped her arms around his waist, and the bike roared onto the road.

Stars sparkled overhead, a crescent moon gleamed, and he felt like he owned the night—until Kat's body trembled. He wondered for a moment if the rapid acceleration had scared the living bejeebers out of her. But before he could slow down, he realized the truth. Maybe the night belonged to both of them.

Kat wasn't afraid. She was laughing.

Chapter Twelve

s Mac guided the bike from the street to the highway, wind rushed past them in the most intoxicating way. Kat wished he'd go faster and almost suggested it, until she concluded exceeding the speed limit at night on a motorcycle probably wasn't the best idea. Instead, she settled on savoring the experience. When had she last been on a bike? High school? Her senior year sweetheart's scooter couldn't even reach fifty miles an hour. Nothing at all like Mac's beautiful machine. This ride could be described in no other way than sensational. His body blocked the swiftest streams of air, which made snuggling against his broad back not only beneficial, but also a teensy bit…sexy. As an added perk, not once did she get face-smacked by a bug. Win-win.

The bike slowed and they leaned into a turn. Mac drove into what looked like a park. Near the entrance a lake sparkled with moonlight. Trees outlined the setting, and a couple of benches sat near the water's edge. She thought he might stop there, but Mac pushed on around a few more curves into a nearly empty parking lot. When he stopped, she raised her head and saw a colossal building lit all around by accent lights. There were oodles of columns, more than the most pretentious mansion she'd ever seen. It looked old—but also, not old. She stared harder.

Mac pulled off his helmet and pointed toward the structure. "What do you think?"

She yanked her own helmet off and fluffed her hair, squinting to get a better view. "How totally fabulous! Is it a museum?"

"You don't recognize the Parthenon?" His tone teased.

"The Parthenon? Isn't that in…" She searched her memory. "Greece?"

"Yes, but this is an exact replica, found only in Nashville."

"Can I go up and take a look?"

"I don't know why not. But you can't go in. It's only open during the day."

Kat put down her helmet and jumped off the bike. She bounded up the steps and wandered around the side of the building. More columns. She hunted for a window to peek through but found nothing. When she had gone all the way around the perimeter, she found Mac at the top of the stairs gazing upward. She looked up too and discovered tableaus of men, horses, and chariots carved at the Parthenon's top. "This is so cool," she finally said. "I can't wait to come back when it's open."

He gave her a rueful grin. "Believe it or not, I've never been inside."

"What? You've lived in Nashville all your life and have never gone into this beauty? You need to get out more, Mac."

He laughed. "I guess this makes me the perfect cliché. Life-long residents rarely check out the sights tourists flock from all over to see."

She examined a few more places along the exterior, still hunting for a spot to peek inside. After she was satisfied there wasn't a crack to be found, she raised her fisted hands in celebration. "What a night this has been. Thanks for bringing me here. You know what? I ought to be tired, but I'm not. Let's go do something. How about bowling?"

The expression on his face made her snicker.

"I don't know," he said. "I've got an early shift tomorrow."

"It's not quite midnight, yet. Live a little, Mac."

He followed her down the steps. "I've never bowled before."

"What? That seals it." She tugged his arm. "You're going to experience bowling before one more day goes by, and I won't take no for an answer."

He looked at her like she'd transformed into an alarming mythical creature, something straight out of Greek mythology—perhaps Medusa? She remembered the name because the poor woman had snakes for hair, which Kat could fully empathize with. "Come on. I'll look up the nearest alley on my phone."

As she trotted to the bike, Kat saw a flower and plucked it. "A good luck daisy. My favorite." She tucked the bloom into a buttonhole on her shirt. "Let's go."

Twenty minutes later, they arrived at Rock 'n' Roll Bowl. It had been their only choice since it stayed open all night.

Mac followed Kat—who'd lost her daisy on the ride—into a building lit with neon and smelling to high heaven of fried food and…dirty feet. At the counter, they rented some dilapidated-looking footwear. Mac held his up by two fingers like they could bite him. "Why can't we wear our own shoes? These could be infested with…let's not go there."

"You can't wear street shoes when you bowl. It would scratch up the alley. Put them on, Mac. Consider it part of the experience." She hopped down a few steps to where the alleys lined up and pulled off her cowboy boots.

He joined her and wrinkled his nose as he took off one pristine tennis shoe, blew out a breath, and put on a rental shoe. "I cannot believe I'm doing this. It looks like a foot fungus waiting to happen."

"Don't be a poop. You have socks on. You'll be fine."

"Socks I'll be sure to throw away." He stood. "Now what?"

She pointed at a nearby rack filled with bowling balls. "We each get a ball." She picked up one and then another, testing them for how they fit her hand. Finally, she settled on a bright orange one. "I look for the lightest weight I can find."

Mac cradled the green ball he'd selected up against himself, behaving like the new kid at school. "This will do, I guess."

Kat seated herself before a control panel and pressed a few buttons. With her tongue between her teeth in concentration, she typed in "Kat" and "Mac." Someone in the lane next to them threw like a rocket and scored an explosion of a strike.

"See? That's what you want to do. Knock all the pins down."

"I know," he said irritably. "Ladies first."

Kat picked up her ball and stepped to the alley. She stared down the lane to gauge the distance, then walked forward and released the ball with authority. *Dang.* It went halfway down the alley before curving into the gutter. "Oops," she said.

Her second try went a little better. She knocked down three pins and danced back toward her seat. "Woo-hoo! Okay, Mac, it's your turn."

Mac held up the ball as she had done. He walked forward and tossed. The ball bounced once on the wood before careening into the gutter. His face went blood red. "I told you I don't know what I'm doing."

She smothered a smile. "Hey, I've bowled before and I'm only three pins ahead of you. Go ahead and roll again. You get two chances to hit them."

His second throw went the same as the first, and he gave her a frustrated glance. "Are we finished yet?"

"Ha! Nine more frames to go. Don't worry, you'll improve."

He didn't. But neither did she, so she figured they were even. The game continued, and all at once the unthinkable happened. At some point, between bowling and eating fried chicken tenders and fried green beans—she's insisted they have *something* healthy—Mac had actually laughed. He sipped a beer and appeared to be having a good time instead of looking like he'd rather be in the fires of hell than at Rock 'n' Roll Bowl.

After the tenth frame ended, she said, "Look at your final score. You broke thirty-five. Awesome!" She didn't even rub in the fact she'd smoked him by rolling her career-best score of sixty-seven.

Mac's hand went to his midsection. "I ate too much. My stomach feels like a brick is sitting in it. I'm pretty sure I can hear my arteries hardening." He slipped off the rental shoes.

"Let's go to the bar for a few minutes. Some water will settle your belly."

The suggestion had been a shot in the dark because she wasn't ready for the evening to end. When he abruptly agreed, warmth surged through her. They grabbed a table tucked in the corner, where the sound of balls crashing into pins wasn't quite so loud. Kat sipped a Diet Coke and Mac a water.

"I get better with practice," she announced. "When do you want to take on another challenge?"

"I think it'll be a while before I'm ready for this again."

"Chicken," she taunted. "I promise not to beat you so bad next time."

"Is that so? Based on what I saw those other bowlers doing, I'm not at all worried about your aptitude."

She grinned at him. "You know what, Mac? Don't get mad, but I really like seeing this side of you. Here and at

Pop's." She remembered the spine-tingling kiss but stopped short of mentioning it. "A motorcycle ride. A visit to the Parthenon. This red-hot bowling game." She jiggled his arm. "You're much less tight."

He lifted his water glass and hid his smile with a sip. "I admit it's been—okay. I can't believe I'm saying so, but I had a good time."

"Whoa! Did you just admit to having fun…with me?"

"What do you mean by that?" He looked genuinely puzzled.

"From the first minute I met you, I could tell you didn't like me much, so I've been putting in extra effort to change your mind. Your remark tells me it's working."

"What made you think I didn't like you?"

"Oh, I can tell. At the hospital you were kind of a bear."

"The hospital is business. I can't joke around when I'm working."

"Why not? Aren't doctors allowed to laugh?"

He was silent so long, she wondered whether she'd been too presumptuous. Or was there such a thing?

"Let me put it this way. There's usually not much reason to laugh in the ER. It isn't exactly a comedy forum."

"Sounds like all the more evidence it's time for a change. You spend a gazillion hours at work. Do you really want to be out of sorts and miserable the whole time you're on a job? Let's visualize the options. If you had to quit ER medicine tomorrow, what is it you'd really like to do?"

He turned his glass around creating a damp sphere on the table. "I don't have to think about it. My mother died two years ago from a rare type of dementia. It's a God-awful disease and one that unfortunately can be genetic."

Her mouth wobbled. It hurt to hear how flat he kept his voice, as though censoring his feelings. "Shawn told me she passed away, but he didn't mention what happened." She sucked in her lower lip and waited for him to go on.

"During her illness, one thought got stuck in my head. I'm a doctor. Why can't I help my own mother? All I could do was sit by her bedside and watch as her mind slid away. She became more and more confused, until the day she didn't recognize my face at all. Do you know how that feels?"

Kat shook her head, too moved to answer.

"It's replayed in my nightmares ever since. Toward the end, only one thing kept me going. I told myself if I couldn't save her from this horrible disease, maybe I could save somebody else's mother. In medical school, I took as many classes as I could manage in clinical investigations. I've done a lot of study on my own too. There has to be a way to prevent or treat the demon that took Mom, a demon that might eventually strike down Shawn or me."

"Oh, Mac." She placed her hand over his. "I am so sorry. But isn't research a good field for doctors? It seems like every charity organization I know is always raising funds to find a cure for something."

His chuckle was bitter. "Positions aren't as plentiful as you'd think. There's a lot more to research projects than raising money." His gaze dropped to the table. "In other news, here's a crazy coincidence. I just heard about a new study opening at the hospital. And it's in dementia."

"There you go." She squeezed his hand. "Don't you see? Kismet's struck again. You need to apply, right away."

"I'm afraid not. I've got a lot on my plate with Pop and with Shawn and with…other things. I can't afford to take the pay cut. Maybe someday, but not now."

"Why?"

He glanced at his phone and got up—his expression hard. "Look, it's late. I'm tired and I've talked too much. I need to go home."

She rose reluctantly. "Are you sure you don't want to stick around a little longer? It's not that late. I bet it would make you feel better if we figured this out."

"Don't you think we'd be better off finding a way to end a fabricated relationship than analyze my career?"

"Come on now, Mac. Why don't you sit back down? You're all tense again."

"Like I said, I've got an early shift tomorrow, and it's going to be a long day. Time for us to hit the road."

He'd shut her out again. The playful Mac she'd glimpsed had faded. Gloom now dampened an almost perfect evening. Neither of them said much on the walk to the Roadmaster and nothing at all until they reached her building. She offered him a cup of coffee, hoping she could coax him into laughing again, but he shook his head. He looked as cranky as the first time she'd met him. If anyone could use some down time, it was Dr. Dan McDonald.

Kat said good night and swayed her hips—seductively, she hoped—as she strolled to the door of the building, willing him to change his mind. But when she glanced back, he still sat astride his bike, watching her with his arms folded. She lifted her hand to wave, and he acknowledged the gesture with a nod. When she shut the door, she heard his bike rumble to life with a roar. She listened until the sound faded away.

Sorry, not sorry, Mac. He might be ready to break up their fake relationship, but all of a sudden, realization smacked her between the eyes.

She kind of wasn't.

Chapter Thirteen

A ride on the Roadmaster usually cleared his head, but every mile of the trip home from Kat's apartment, he'd had to rein in the impulse to turn around and go back to knock on her door. The way she'd looked up at him from under those long lashes and the sinuous grace with which she moved had almost broken his resolve. What might happen if he saw her again? A sense of uneasiness prickled along his spine. The entire evening had made one fact quite clear. He felt a frightening pull of desire for Kat Becker, a woman who had a knack for gifting him with major headaches.

His first impression of her had been wrong. She'd struck him as more of a teenaged-brain girl—headstrong and silly—than a full-grown woman. Now he knew better. She was naïve in some ways but an ancient soul in others. Worldly yet vulnerable. All in all, a dangerous combination. Look at what she had him doing. Things he'd never have considered possible, including conduct leaning toward reckless. He shook his head in disbelief as he added up the damning evidence. Who'd have thought he'd agree to give a peculiar patient a lift? Lie to his father? Become a pretend boyfriend to someone who was practically a stranger? And now…bowling?

He reached his condo, tapped the remote, and pulled into the garage. As was his custom, he wiped down the motorcycle, cleaning away all road dust and pollen until he could see his reflection in the shiny copper paint. Things lasted when you took time to care for them. He'd learned the lesson years ago. A final pat on the bike seat and he tossed the soiled cloth into a hamper.

The condo felt far too quiet, so he turned on the television. Once he kicked off his shoes, he looked at his socks and made a face. Dan removed them and headed for the trash can. All told, it had been quite an evening. Despite his reluctance to sit through Kat's event, halfway through he had realized how much he'd enjoyed watching her perform. Thank God she had some degree of talent, for whatever that was worth in the big scheme of things. It wouldn't have been easy to add another layer of deceit to his list by telling her she sounded great if she hadn't.

Lies and secrets. They soon became a sticky web. This evening he'd come close to spilling what he knew to Pop, but the old man seemed happier than he had in a while. Even if he'd wanted to, Dan couldn't make himself do it. Knowing his son had lied to him would knock the wind out of Pop, a sin Dan couldn't face. His father wasn't the tough guy he'd been before Mom got sick. He could just about imagine his father's reaction to the deception. Pop would try to hide a hurt look and then he'd assume they'd been playing him for a fool and get mad. Kat was right. He'd probably end up firing her or disowning his son. Maybe both.

Dan filled a glass with water and took a long drink. There wasn't much point in hashing out the truth yet. It would emerge in time. Pop had already dropped hints enough to prove he'd get suspicious about any relationship that carried on endlessly without turning into an engagement. For now, he might as well let things rest. Anyway, the other events of the evening merited much deeper exploration.

A tour through Nashville wasn't something he'd planned, yet giving Kat a simple ride home had grown into a desire to show her the city he loved. Who knew why he'd chosen the Parthenon as a destination? A replica of the Greek monument to the goddess Athena seemed a fitting destination after her small triumph at Pop's. Almost like an omen, even though they couldn't go inside to see it. He caught himself. *Omen?* It sounded like something she would say.

His mouth quirked. The game of bowling had also been unexpected. And not quite the misadventure he'd feared it would be. He couldn't remember the last time he'd laughed like he had. A real honest-to-goodness belly laugh. When had he fallen out of the habit? Probably somewhere between medical school, Ava, his mother's illness, and icy-silent stares between Shawn and Pop. He'd forgotten about the release found in a healthy dose of humor. It seemed to him, Kat had—inadvertently or not—found a way to restore a sense of light-heartedness to his life.

Hold on a minute. Don't forget what she's here for. He shoved aside any softening of his position. The evening had lightened his mood for a while, but dealing with Kat called for caution. If he wasn't careful, he might be hoodwinked again. His heart wasn't daring enough to go through an experience like the one Ava had handed him.

His phone pinged with a text. Shawn's name appeared above the message.

Gave Kat your number. Here's hers.

Wonderful. The two of them must be having a ridiculously late night—or should he say early morning?—tête-à-tête. A second text pinged with a phone number. Presumably Kat's. *Push much, Shawn?* Mood gone from semi-sweet to rancid, Dan selected Shawn's number from his contacts. A verbal warning for his brother to knock off the matchmaking would be much more satisfying than a text. Unsurprisingly, Shawn didn't pick up. True to form. Any time Shawn didn't want to deal with a potential problem, he avoided it. Escape, a characteristic he and Pop shared. Dan didn't leave a message and dropped his cell on the counter. It would be better to catch up with his brother later and have it out with him in person. Even though he didn't mind having Kat's number—or her having his—he didn't need Shawn's heavy-handed interference.

Dan caught a whiff of fried food lingering on his clothes. A long hot shower sounded like exactly what he needed—and right now. But before he made it from the living room, his phone rang. Too coincidental. It had to be either Kat or Shawn. Maybe both on speakerphone. They had probably cooked up some new and devious form of torture designed to drive him nuts. Dan seethed at the scenario he'd created, in the mood to put a stop to any further nonsense. He grabbed his cell from the counter without looking at the screen, and put it to his ear, prepared to unload on whichever one had called him. It was high time he reclaimed his life and enforced the healthy balance of lines which shouldn't be crossed.

"Okay, what are you up to now," he all but snarled into the phone.

"Don't you say hello anymore? Or are you just trying to charm me, lover?"

His stomach turned at the all-too-familiar voice. "Ava. Why are you calling at this hour and what do you want?"

"Don't you dare be short with me." Her tart words were quickly covered with sugar. "I'm calling with the best news ever. My counselor says I'll be discharged in a few days."

He waited long enough to keep his voice calm. "You're finished with treatment?"

"Yes. It's been a long road, but I worked hard. I can now recite the twelve steps of sobriety, and I'm ready to make amends. I want to rejoin the world, a changed woman—filled with wisdom, serenity, and…acceptance." Her tone struck him as a touch sarcastic.

"You need to take this seriously. I hope the program has helped you."

"It'd be an expensive mistake if it hasn't. You should know better than anyone," she said. "And while we're on the subject, I have to ask another favor. Until I can find a job, I need cash. My counselor wants me to arrange a place to stay before I can be discharged and start outpatient. He says it's supposed to demonstrate my coping skills."

Irritation bubbled up like lava. "Just a minute. Why do you keep coming to me every time you have a problem? We're divorced. You're no longer my responsibility."

"Oh, Dan, how can you say such a thing? You know you still care about me. And we have ties no one else can break. Remember?" Her voice quivered with emotion.

Not going there again. "Ava, stop. That's enough. I don't want to hear this story again." He longed to end the call but forced himself to pause a moment and get his temper under control before he said something he might regret. "We'll leave it at this. Let me know when they plan to release you and I'll see what I can do to help you get an apartment or a room somewhere. I prefer it be anyplace but Nashville." He stroked his forehead. "Your mom's still in Iowa, isn't she? What about doing your outpatient treatment there?"

"Are you kidding? I hate Iowa. I've always hated Iowa. And I haven't talked to Mom in months, so why involve her? Besides, I don't want to leave Nashville."

Ignoring her plea, he kept his voice firm and steady. "Aftercare can be arranged in other places."

"I don't want to switch counselors. I like the one I have. If you don't want to spend any more money, here's an idea. Why not let me stay at your place while I finish the program and find a job? Afterward, I'll think about moving farther away if that's what you really want. Who knows? You might discover you like having the new Ava around."

*Not bloody likely. I ought to just…*A twinge of guilt pricked his conscience. Maybe even Ava didn't deserve to be kicked to the curb on the cusp of finishing the program she so desperately needed. "All right. I'll find a place for you to stay, but I guarantee it will *not* be with me."

"Come on, Dan. It must be lonely for you by yourself with no one to talk to about your rotten day. I'm a much better listener than I used to be."

"Ava." He didn't say more, warning himself not to rise to the bait she had blatantly dangled.

She gave a low, raspy laugh. "You're still single, aren't you? It means a lot to know you haven't replaced me." Ava sounded like she was joking and then her tone sharpened. "Or have you?"

"I'd suggest you drop the question. My personal life is not your business."

"Interesting. Question neither confirmed or denied. Why do you seem so determined to hold me at arm's length? Remember, I've known you a long time. Something tells me more is going on than meets the eye. Maybe Ava should do a little detective work."

"If you want my help, then I suggest you stay out of my affairs. As I already told you, find out the date of your discharge, and I'll see what I can work out for you."

"Nice. I love it when you use your macho voice on me. Thank you so much, lover. Ta-ta."

The phone went dark, but not half as dark as his mood. Ava was exactly the new wrinkle he didn't need. His ex-wife would be back in circulation. On the loose without the benefit of twenty-four-hour supervision.

The idea made him seriously rethink a move to the distant shores of Alaska.

Chapter Fourteen

Space in the recording studio equaled the area of Kat's walk-in closet back in Kansas City. But these walls weren't a calming shade of pale teal. Each had been carefully lined with what looked like egg cartons made of a gray foamlike material. The hardwood flooring reminded her of a dance platform and completed the room's ability to provide decent acoustics. A small table held a control board, computer screen, and camera. Light equipment blazed in a way that screamed "put on your sunglasses." So did the temperature. Kat sat on a stool behind a microphone. She balanced her guitar in her lap with one hand and mopped her face with the other. Her throat felt dry as a desert. Too late, she realized a cup of water nearby would have been a sensible idea.

Dylan Younger and Shawn sat with their heads bent together, mumbling in an animated way. She couldn't make out a single word they said, but clearly, they were enjoying the conversation. Despite the heat, Shawn's cheerful demeanor made her smile. She'd been tickled to finally meet Dylan. He'd explained to her how he built the studio in his basement and rented it out to other artists. A man of medium height with sandy-colored hair pulled back into a tail, he treated Kat like a friend—supportive and full of good advice. She couldn't help liking him, and she could tell Shawn was equally captivated. She guessed any obstacle between the men had been smoothed over. Dylan didn't appear the least put off that Callie referred to Shawn as her boyfriend in front of an audience of millions on national television.

Too bad she had to focus on not making a fool of herself. She would have enjoyed teasing her pal. *Time enough for that pleasure later.*

"Okay, Kat," Dylan said. "Let's get some sound levels first. Sing a few bars for me."

She strummed a chord and launched into the first verse of "You're the One" and sang until Dylan held up his hand.

"Sounds great," he said. "I think we're ready to go."

Shawn patted her arm. "You look like you're waiting for a root canal. Relax. Pretend you're at Pop's doing your thing."

"You hit the problem right on the nose. My thing is singing, not recording music videos. Besides, it's hot in here." She pushed damp strands of hair aside.

"If you want to make it in the music biz, you better get used to recording, kiddo."

He was right of course.

Dylan, God bless him, handed her a glass of water. "When I give you the signal, you can start," he said.

She took a quick sip and waited. When Dylan pointed at her, she strummed an introduction and started to sing. The first notes weren't her best. Her voice sounded rusty. She wasn't surprised when Dylan cut her off and patiently explained they'd start over. It took several tries before she finished both songs to Dylan's satisfaction. When he played them back, the sound shocked her.

Even Shawn, pickiest of the picky, approved. "It's a perfect audition tape. Most applicants send a cell phone video. The admissions committee will *love* this."

"Do you really think so?"

"Would I lie to you? Getting into Belmont is another notch in your belt and a great way to meet people who can arrange internships, which can put your foot in a lot of doors."

"Good. Getting an audition isn't as easy as I thought it was going to be." The initial furor over her viral video and television interview had not only died, it had gone stiff with rigor mortis. Instead of the publicity leading to an imme-diate—she'd hoped—recording contract, the entire episode fizzled after the next "big thing" took over the internet. Mac's assessment of her fifteen minutes of fame had sadly come true.

"I've told you a hundred times. The days of instant discovery are over and done. You have to work at getting noticed, and that's just what we're going to do."

"You're right. I'll try to be more patient. One thing's for sure though. When I do get where I want to be, I'm hiring you to work with me."

"And if I make it first," he said and grinned, "I'll hire *you*!"

"Deal," she responded with a thumbs-up.

"Either of y'all can hire me," Dylan said. "Okay. It's a wrap on these tapes. Good job, Kat. You have a smooth-as-butter sound, and I foresee a great career for you."

"Thanks. You've been wonderful. I'd like to pay you something if it's okay."

"Nope. You don't owe me anything but a future job. Shawn's my friend, and I'm glad to do a favor for him."

Shawn's face colored, and he busied himself with bringing Kat her guitar case. She packed up her instrument and her music, thanked Dylan once more, and went to the car ahead of Shawn. She might as well be nice and let them have a conversation without listening ears, even though she'd have loved to be a fly on the wall. Sometimes manners overruled the possibility of gathering ammunition for the ribbing she'd give him later. What were friends for, anyway?

Kat loaded her gear into Ruby and gave the car a fond glance. Newly repaired and repainted, her vehicle looked better than it had in years. She slid behind the wheel, switched on the ignition, and turned up the radio. By the time Shawn joined her, she was snapping her fingers and belting out "Jolene" along with Dolly Parton.

She turned down the music. "What took you so long? I was almost ready to leave without you."

"We had a few other projects to discuss." Shawn climbed into the passenger seat and buckled his safety belt.

"I'll just bet you did." She pursed her lips together and waggled her brows up and down.

"Hold on. We've got other things to figure out before you start razzing me."

She steered Ruby toward the street. "Such as?"

"Dylan will work his magic on the tape and then we need to get it to Belmont." He pointed at the car clock. "Time's ticking away. Soon decisions will be made on who gets into the program. Even part-time students are scrutinized pretty close."

The desire to have fun hazing Shawn disappeared. "Do you really think I might not get in?"

"I think they'll take you. We just need to get all your ducks in a row."

She leaned her head back. "This is stressful. When I applied to KU, it didn't faze me a bit. I couldn't have cared less if they accepted me or not. But now it feels like my whole future music career depends on getting into Belmont." She shook her head. "It's kind of weird how much this means to me."

"Now is not the time to worry. We'll deliver the tape tomorrow, and all will be well."

"Sounds like a plan, unless I get lucky. What if some big shot comes in and hears me sing at Pop's? Wouldn't it be a hoot if I didn't need school to get a contract?"

"I like your enthusiasm, but it's time to get real. Things are a lot more competitive these days."

"I thrive on a positive vibe, and you're starting to sound like your brother."

She braked at a red light, and Shawn said, "Please, I'm not quite as ornery as him yet. Speaking of Dan, I haven't had time to ask. What went on between you and him after you left Pop's the other night? He nearly snapped my head off when I asked about it."

"Nothing. We just had fun riding around on his bike. Oh, and we went bowling too."

Shawn's head whipped in her direction. "My brother went bowling…voluntarily?"

A horn sounded, and Kat spied the green light. "Keep your shirt on," she muttered as she propelled Ruby forward. "Of course he bowled voluntarily. How could I have forced him? Plus, for your information, he had a good time."

"Are you sure you're not exaggerating?"

"Me exaggerate? Why would you say such a thing?" She recalled the evening she'd spent with Mac. "Seriously, he can be so much fun when he relaxes, but he's such a beast the rest of the time. I know he hates his job. I don't know why he won't leave it. He claims he's stuck. I must be missing something here. Why is he so uptight?"

Shawn sighed. "It's a lot of things, but mostly his ex-wife, I guess."

Kat nearly ran Ruby off the road, and Shawn yelped, "Watch out!"

When she caught her breath, she said, "He has an ex-wife?"

"Yep. She did him dirty, big-time. There were fireworks between them from the beginning. Then, while he was working his ass off during his internship, she struck up a love affair with some guy who said he could make her a singing star."

"That must be the reason Mac hates the music business!"

"You got it. She ran off with her new boyfriend. When the love affair fizzled out, she tried to come back, but he wouldn't have anything to do with her."

"Who could blame him? What a nerve she had." Kat seethed at the betrayal, feeling protective as a lioness. She remembered how hard Carolyn's path to become a veterinarian had been—and she'd had her family's support. Mac did what he needed so he could become a doctor, but instead of helping, his wife had deserted him. Ugh. She didn't know his ex-wife from a stranger on the street, but she already disliked her intensely.

"Ava's a piece of work for sure. And in more ways than one."

"What do you mean?"

"She knows how to string him along. She always has. There were problems with her binge drinking too. I'm not sure even I know the extent of it, but I know he referred her to a treatment program. Somehow, she's learned to make him dance to her tune, even when he no longer has to. All I can say is Dan needs to get her out of his system."

"Come on, you can't leave me hanging like this. Tell me more."

"Sorry, but I don't know much more. Anyway, what's it to you?" He fixed her with a tight look. "Seems like you're awfully interested in what goes on with my brother." Shawn waggled his brows the same way she'd done to him.

"I like Mac. He deserves better than to be mistreated by some dingbat woman."

Shawn laughed and then sobered. "You hit on a helluva good description of Ava. She doesn't seem to operate on a full set of cylinders and hides her true colors like a rattlesnake in sheep's clothes."

"Don't you mean a wolf in sheep's clothes?"

He thought a moment. "No. I mean a rattlesnake. Wolves don't have poison in their fangs."

They rode in silence until a thought occurred to her. "You know what? It felt like Dan turned into someone else when we were out on the bike. He seemed—I don't know—free."

"He got that bike right after the divorce. Said he wanted to take a leave of absence for a cross-country trip. He thought it might help clear out all the muck Ava left in his head. But he didn't go. My brother's huge caretaker complex took over. He spent a lot of time with Mom when she got sick. Then he did his best to look after Pop and me."

"I can understand you and Pop feeling terrible after you lost your mom, but Dan had to be hurting just as much. Why did he feel the need to take on everyone's problems?"

Shawn kept his gaze fixed on the road. "Pop had a really rough time. He and Mom had always been inseparable. After she died, Dan and I were both worried sick about him. Then Dan tried to do what Mom did and be the bridge between Pop and me. My dad can't quite accept the fact I am what I am. It's another reason I took a stage name. I don't want to embarrass him."

Her jaw clenched in sympathy. "I don't think he's embarrassed. He just doesn't understand. I'm sorry, Shawn."

"It is what it is. Not much I can do to change anything."

She reached over and squeezed his fingers. "This has to be hard, but maybe if your family sat down and talked about it instead of tiptoeing around the issue, things would improve between you and Pop. And then you could tell your brother you don't need his protection anymore. You're a strong person, Shawn, and you have a lot of people who care about you. Why not help send Mac away on a bike ride like he deserves?"

"I don't know if he'd do it. I once asked him why he didn't just go ahead and leave, but all I managed to do was piss him off. Sometimes it seems better to leave him alone and hope he'll work things out on his own."

"Hmm," she said thoughtfully, wheels turning. "How long was he married?"

"A year and a half, I think. He said it felt like centuries."

She turned two fingers into scissors and made a cutting motion. "Snip, snip. Time to get her out of his life." She paused and swallowed. "Unless…do you think he still loves Ava?"

Shawn snorted. "I seriously doubt it. Seems more like he wants to throttle her."

"I don't understand why people in your own family are usually the hardest to deal with." Kat groaned. "Sometimes my mother drives me nuts, grilling me about school or whatever she thinks I've done wrong. Daddy's great, but he has his moments too. Then there's my sister. She's always been the perfect one. Man do I get sick of hearing my parents brag about everything she's accomplished. But in spite of it, I still love them all, just the way I'm sure Pop loves you."

"I guess so, although he'd love me much better if I could mold myself into the son he wants—instead of the one he has."

She acknowledged his remark with a crooked smile. "Tell me about it, pal."

Chapter Fifteen

The group at table three—among the friendliest customers Kat had served all day—waved at her as they headed for the register to pay for their lunch. She'd had a great time joking around with the playful retirees, but since her arms were loaded with dishes for table five, all she could do was nod and give them a heartfelt smile as they made their exit. Later, she found they'd given her the biggest tip she'd ever had. Oh, for more customers like those senior sweethearts!

She pocketed the money and carried a stack of dirty dishes into the kitchen. When she came back out, Pop motioned for her to join him and Jett at the bar. Pop leaned toward her, his forearms on the counter. "How would you like to sing again this Friday?"

"Sure!" She wiped her hands on the rag in her pocket. "Did you have another cancellation?"

"Nope. I didn't have anyone scheduled and thought of you."

"Me? Wow. Thanks!" Totally stoked, she could have done a backflip of joy if the tables behind her weren't in the way.

"There's been great feedback from customers, so why not? I'll give you the standard contract and same pay as last time if that sounds okay."

"I'd love to!" She grabbed Pop and hugged him tight. His check for her last performance had been more than she'd expected, a nice addition to the money Daddy recently sent her for work on the law firm's social media.

Jett sent her a speculative glance. "Now that Friday's been settled, I've got a question. Have you ever heard of the Soaring Star Competition?"

She shook her head. "What is it?"

"It's a singing contest. Actually, more like a songwriter showcase. Singers perform a song they've written. It has to be original. The winner gets fifteen grand and a recording contract. You might want to look into it."

As much as she wanted to keep a good distance from Jett, instead of backing away, interest kept her feet firm to the floor. "What else can you tell me about it?"

"Portal Productions runs the contest. If you're interested, I can make some calls and give you pointers. This is a competition that could kick-start your career."

Despite a slight buzz on her scammer radar, Jett had definitely grabbed her attention. "I'd love to know more."

"I think they have a website on the internet," Pop said, intervening. "You can probably find out whatever you need to know there."

Jett's mouth puckered. "They don't put everything on their website. I can get the inside scoop if your boyfriend doesn't mind."

Her face warmed. "Umm, I'm sure he won't care. Thanks for letting me know."

The phone rang, and Pop turned away to answer it. Jett's gaze skewered her. "If Dan McDonald doesn't care, then he's not the guy I know. The last thing he'd do is stand by while his girlfriend pursues a singing career. It all sounds rather strange to me."

"Of course he's supportive! *So* supportive!" Great balls of fire. She sounded like a five-year-old child who had devoured a bag of candy corn followed by a side of Skittles. She cleared the exclamation points from her throat. "I mean, he doesn't stop me from doing things I want to do."

"Rrriiight." Jett dragged out the word and gave her a snarky smile before he walked away.

How odd Jett suddenly wanted to be helpful. She supposed stranger things had happened. Maybe he thought if she did well, it would bring publicity to Pop's. On the other hand, he might only want to needle her—and Mac. Whatever the reason, the idea of a contest appealed to every fiber of her competitive nature. First, she'd check with Shawn to see if the competition was legit. He knew about dang near everything going on in Nashville. She imagined a scene where a judge awards her a fabulous recording contract, until the front door opened and Mac stepped inside. His tousled hair and lean torso—he must spend a lot of time at the gym—made her belly flutter pleasantly.

Ever mindful of Pop's and Jett's watchful eyes, she rushed over to greet him. "Hi, Mac." She stood on tiptoe to plant a kiss on his cheek. "I didn't know you were coming."

He placed his hand at the small of her back and left it there. "Neither did I. There are some issues with the restaurant I need to discuss with Pop." His lips clamped together like he regretted his words.

"Issues? Did something happen?" It sounded like she was prying, but curiosity consumed her.

"Forget it. I said more than I should."

"No problem," she quickly replied. "Have a seat. What can I get for you?"

Before he had a chance to answer, Pop charged to the table, a huge grin on his face. "How you doing, Danny? Did you come in to see your girl?"

"No. I wanted to let you know the accountant called. We need to talk."

Pop's expression plainly said he'd rather be on another planet than where he stood. "Let's take a rain check on that, Danny. I've got a kitchen emergency to handle." He nudged Kat. "Since we don't have a load of customers at the moment, why don't you stay here and talk to your fella?" He turned and galloped away from them like his pants were on fire.

Kat perched on the chair opposite Mac. "Okay, what in the world is going on?"

Mac tapped his fingers on the table. "Nothing."

"Your face wouldn't look the way it does if nothing's wrong."

He released a small breath. "Money issues with the restaurant. Pop keeps trying to dodge any conversation about it, but he's got two mortgages on the place. Debts he shouldn't have to worry about at his age."

"Jeez. I had no idea. What happened?"

"Lousy circumstances all stacked up. When I was in school, he borrowed money to help finance my studies. Then Mom got sick, and he had to take care of her medical bills. You have no idea how much skilled nursing services cost. Now he's overloaded with debt and having trouble with payments."

Her stomach twisted. "Oh, no. How did you find out?"

"The only reason I know is because Pop gave me power of attorney when Mom got sick. The accountant called me when Pop didn't get back to him."

"But it seems like we're busy most of the time. I don't understand."

"Me either. All I know for sure is Pop does anything he can to keep from talking about the issue."

"This is awful. I wish I could do something to help." She thought a moment. "Maybe I shouldn't take money from Pop for performing."

"Don't be silly. Pop would never agree. He's a proud man, even if he is in over his head. I'm sure it galls him to see most of his savings gone. He ought to retire, but he can't. I had no idea how limited his resources were until the accountant set me straight. It's me who needs to step in. If Pop hadn't helped with medical school, he wouldn't be in this mess now."

"I'll bet he's not a bit sorry about helping you. Most parents will make any sacrifice they can for their kids. It's like an investment." As soon as the words left her mouth, she thought of her own parents and realized the truth of it. "Your mother got sick, and he did what he could to help her. No one expected her illness to happen. Life is…unpredictable. Kind of like a good pitcher who now and then throws a crazy curve ball no one can catch. Rotten luck, but what can you do? Shake it off and move on."

"I'll grant you sickness is unexpected. A college education isn't." His gaze turned toward the bar. "I think I need a beer."

"You got it." She jumped from her seat. "I'll be right back." She left him at the table. Since Pop wasn't behind the bar, she steered clear of Jett and filled a chilled mug with brown ale. Mac's favorite brand. She carried the drink to him, hating the double lines creased between his brows.

"Thanks." He took a deep swallow.

"Do you want something to eat?"

"No. I'm good for now. Sorry about dumping this on you. I should have kept my mouth shut. It's not your problem."

"I don't mind. You've listened to me often enough."

Mac laughed. "Still, let's change the subject to a more pleasant one. You know, I hadn't thought about it before, but this is the most subdued you've ever been. You're usually a magpie."

"True enough." Heat traveled from her neck to her cheeks. "My friends accuse me of having diarrhea of the mouth all the time, but it really isn't unthinkable for me to listen."

Mac lifted his beer at her. "Proof positive." He glanced toward the bar where Jett stood watching them. "Any more problems with him?"

"Not really, though he still gives me a creepy feeling. But guess what? He just told me about a singing competition. The winner gets a recording contract. Then he offered to help coach me since he knows people involved with it. Isn't that weird?"

"Keywords: Don't trust him." Mac's voice bristled with a sharp edge. "Talk to Shawn instead. He'll know more about it than Jett ever will."

"I couldn't agree more. Hey, Shawn's coming to my place tonight for dinner." She watched Mac's face, determined to erase the lines she saw on it. "Do you want to come over and have pizza with us?"

He toyed with his mug and took another sip. "Thanks. Maybe I will."

One look at the hint of a grin on his face made her good day complete. "Awesome. We'll eat about seven." The front door rattled open, catching her attention, and a young couple stepped inside. "Customers. Enough of listening. I better get back to work. We'll have lots to talk about to-night. You know, I haven't had a chance lately to pester you about the research opening you mentioned." She was a little afraid her comment might make him back out, but his answer came without any hesitation.

"Sounds good. How about…" Mac's phone shrilled. He stared at it, and the lines on his forehead carved deeper. "I'm sorry, but I've got to take this call. I'll be right back."

"Okay." She watched him walk to the front door and pace outside, the phone to his ear. What lousy timing. Whoever called must not be high on Mac's friend list. His face reminded her of dark clouds covering the sun.

He sure had a lot to worry about with Pop's situation, but it seemed like there was more troubling him. Something or somebody had him by the short hairs—she'd bet every dime of her most recent tip on it. What could be going on?

Chapter Sixteen

As soon as he reached the porch, Dan called on the final tiny shred of patience he had left. "What is it this time, Ava?"

"Trouble, trouble everywhere." She hiccupped. "I need your help."

"Have you been drinking?" The sound of her raspy voice and slurred words were all too familiar. "You just got out of rehab. You're supposed to be working your aftercare program. Have you lost your mind?"

"Now isn't the time to lecture me, lover."

"I've already done everything you asked. You've finished months of inpatient treatment—with bills still rolling in. You have a decent apartment right where you wanted it. Now this. What do you expect from me when you won't help yourself?"

"But this is something I can't get myself out of. You have to help me. I'm locked up in the city jail."

"You're *what?*" People on the sidewalk glanced his way with wide eyes, and Dan lowered his voice. "What did you do?"

"I got pulled over for no good reason, and the cop arrested me. I don't know why. I was driving really careful."

"Ava, you don't even own a vehicle."

"I borrowed one from a friend. He and I were at a nice, quiet little bar. He wasn't ready to go, but I knew I shouldn't have anything more to drink. So when he went to the men's room, I took his keys and left."

"Good God. You stole somebody's car? Did you wreck it? Was anybody hurt?"

"Why do you always jump to the worst possible scenario? I only borrowed his car, and I got pulled over for driving too slow. The cop said he smelled liquor on my breath and made me get out of the car. I only wobbled a little bit when I tried to walk his dumb straight line, and the next thing I knew…handcuffs and a ride in the back of a squad car."

"You're telling me you chose to take someone's car without their permission and drive while under the influence? Exactly what do you think I can do about this situation?"

"Don't be so mean, Dan. I was only a little bit tipsy, and my friend won't care once he gets his car back. This isn't a big deal, but I need somebody to get me out of here. I can't stay locked up in a cage like an animal." She sniffed. "They said I could leave if somebody brings bail money and picks me up."

"Why don't you call your 'friend' from the bar? Or anybody else but me."

A long silence ensued. Then she started to cry. "There isn't anyone else to call. Nobody I can trust. Dan, you can't leave me here. I only slipped because I was thinking about Johnny. I hoped a drink would make me feel better, but it took more than one to numb the pain."

She'd always known how to twist the knife. He did his best to keep his voice even. "This has been going on far too long. I've done everything I can for you, but even footing the bill for your treatment hasn't been enough. This habit of heaping guilt on my head has to stop. It's over between us and time to let the chips fall wherever they land. I refuse to pick up after your messes anymore."

Her sobs came harder, now a true crying jag. "If it weren't for you, Johnny would still be here. You admitted yourself it's your fault he's gone. I can't forget about him. Is it any wonder I'm having such a hard time getting my life together?"

An old jab, but nevertheless a painfully effective one. He pinched the bridge of his nose between his fingers. "Stop it, Ava." He waited long enough to conjure his objectivity and temper his words. "You're in a spot, but remember this is something you did to yourself. I'll come down to bail you out and get you back to your apartment. After you sober up, I'll have other things to discuss. And you'd better let your counselor know what happened before I do."

"But, Dan—"

"I have nothing else to say at the moment, except I'll get there when I can." He clicked off his phone. *Let her sit for a while. Maybe it'll teach her a lesson.* He leaned back against the restaurant's front door and realized how tense his body had become. Of all the conniving women he'd ever met, Ava surely took first place. Even though they'd been divorced for more than a year, she still found ways to tighten her stranglehold on him. Guilt. She used it like a weapon. Maybe it was his own fault for being such a pushover. How much longer could he allow this to continue?

Dan shoved his cell into his pocket, sighed, and went back into the restaurant. Kat had seated the young couple, and they were laughing with her about something. How strange the personality of one woman could be so distinct from another. Ava, always out for herself, was made up of deceit and drama. Kat didn't seem to have a complicated bone in her body, a girl who'd do about anything—or say anything—to protect those she cared about.

While he waited for her to finish, Dan drained the remainder of his drink. *Damn.* Too late, he considered the potential repercussion of him marching into the police station to bail out a DWI offender with the scent of beer on his breath. He'd have to go home and brush his teeth first. Who cared if Ava had a longer wait?

Kat flitted back to his table. He noted how sweetly the corners of her lips lifted when her gaze met his, and he turned the full force of his attention on her.

"You okay?" She spied the empty mug. "Can I get you something else?"

"I'm fine. Nothing more for me, but thanks, anyway."

"Today's your lucky day, Mac. No bill. Your drink is on me because…I like you." She picked up the empty. "Want me to send Pop out to say goodbye?"

"I'm sure he's still busy—or at least that's what he'll say. Tell him I'll be in touch."

"Will do. See you at seven?"

"Uh…" How he hated to say it. "Something came up. I'm sorry, but I won't be able to make it tonight after all." On a good day, Ava could be a handful. God alone knew how long it would take to deal with her latest misfortune.

Kat's smile didn't budge, but the part of it that normally lit her eyes disappeared. "Did you change your mind because of what I said about pestering you? I was only kidding…mostly."

"No." He gave himself a mental kick for disappointing her. "It's an obligation I can't get out of. I'd love to take a rain check though."

"Well, sure, I guess."

"I am sorry." He stood and looked down at her, annoyed with himself for letting Ava commandeer his life—again. "Let Shawn know I'll call him later to fill him in on what's going on with Pop."

"Okay." She wet her lips like she was preparing to say something else, when Dan noticed Jett.

The pompous ass had the nerve to strut in their direction. It would be a relief to blast him now, but in fairness, he ought to discuss the matter with Pop first. Jett's superior attitude prompted an idea. As long as they were still deep in a game of make-believe, why not do what any self-respecting boyfriend would do when saying goodbye to his girl? It only took a moment to decide. He gathered Kat close to him and then dipped his head to press his mouth against hers. Her arms circled around him, and he tightened the embrace. The contact between them sparked such a response in his chest, rather than breaking the kiss, he deepened it, pushing Ava far from his mind.

Jett barked out, "Kat. You have customers."

In no hurry at all, Dan waited a moment more before he gently moved away. Kat's eyes were wide and dark, her pupils dilated. She'd been as wrapped up in the moment as him, he noted with not a little satisfaction. She seemed unbalanced on her feet, so he kept an arm around her in a move that steadied him too. "I'll see you later, babe."

Astonishment streaked across her face, but she didn't hesitate a second. "I can't wait…Sexy Pants." The endearment brought a gleam of mischief to her steadfast—and utterly comical—expression. He nearly laughed out loud, until he saw Jett's glare.

Dan fired a warning glance at him. The second-rate Casanova had motives toward Kat other than as an employer—he'd bet his bottom dollar on it. What a sleaze. Add this to the long list of things to discuss with Pop, assuming Pop would ever let a discussion take place.

Kat's nose wrinkled with barely suppressed amusement. Playing her part to the hilt, she blew Dan a kiss, turned, and sashayed past her manager without a second look. Jett stared after her before he sputtered something and turned toward the kitchen.

Dan waited for his equilibrium to return. Kissing Kat had nearly rocked him back on his heels. He scratched the side of his face in thought and grinned. What a fierce woman. She not only thought fast on her feet but managed to do so with a sly sense of humor and a bewitching smile.

Chapter Seventeen

The front door rattled as Kat maneuvered to unlock it while juggling a bag of Charlie's kibble and a box of litter. She noticed a woman standing in the hall—a new neighbor?—and waved as best she could with her hands full before stepping inside her apartment. Charlie came from the bedroom to greet her, his tail pointed toward the ceiling, meowing for all he was worth. "Hi, buddy. Did you miss me?" The cat brushed against her ankles, and she picked him up for a cuddle. "I had a good day. How about you?"

Charlie's contented purr indicated he had no complaints. She put him down to yoga-stretch an ache from her back. She really ought to invest in a hand cart. A twenty-pound box of cat litter and ten pounds of food got heavy fast when climbing stairs. A rap at the front door stopped her mid-stretch. Kat peered through the peephole and then opened the door wide for Shawn. "Get in here and entertain this animal while I call Cleary's."

He grinned and tucked the cat under one arm, then placed a six-pack of beer into the refrigerator, reserving two bottles for them. Kat ordered their usual—a supreme thin crust—toed off her shoes, and joined Shawn and Charlie on the sofa.

"You'll never guess what." She took the beer Shawn gave her, tucking one leg under herself. "Your brother stopped by the restaurant, and I almost got him to meet us here for pizza tonight."

"Dan? You gotta be kidding me."

"He wanted to talk to Pop about some problems at the restaurant, but as soon as he brought up the subject, Pop made himself scarce fast. I think Mac needed to talk, because he ended up venting to me instead."

"Problems at the restaurant? What kind of problems?"

She took a sip of her beer. "Something about too many mortgages and not enough money. He's going to call you later with the details. Anyway, I invited him to join us for pizza and he said yes. Then his phone rang, and he went outside to talk. I don't know who called him, but when he came back in, his face was red. Like fire-engine red. He apologized and begged off for tonight."

"It could be the hospital," Shawn said. "Sometimes he's on call."

"I don't know, but he sure looked ticked off." She pointed her bottle at him. "And get this. Jett was watching us, so before Mac left, he grabbed me and kissed me. I didn't even have to drop a hint."

"So as much as he's complained, he's still playing the part of a boyfriend. Did he land a chaste little smooch on your mouth before he ran off?"

"Nope," her body tingled at the memory. "It was actually pretty spectacular. Hot, slow, and sexy. He kissed me like he meant it. And you know what? I think he did. My knees nearly melted."

Shawn's eyes flew open even wider. "A public display of affection. Are you sure you're talking about my brother? That doesn't sound remotely like him. After Ava burned him so badly, I didn't figure he'd ever get involved with anyone again. This sounds promising." He gave her a sidelong glance. "Now don't take this the wrong way, but I have to ask. You wouldn't mess with his head, would you? He couldn't take another letdown."

Her gaze dropped to the floor. How exactly *did* she feel about Mac? He was hilarious when he let his guard down. Smart. Hardworking. Loving and loyal to his family. Not to mention incredibly luscious looking.

"Of course not," she said. "I wouldn't mess with Mac. I like him. I like him a lot, although I'm not sure he knows what to make of me."

"I don't want to see him get hurt again. It's okay if you keep him on his toes. Just don't tromp on them."

"I love it when you're poetic." Her gaze rolled toward the ceiling in mock reverence.

"I'm not kidding. He's got so many barriers built around himself, it could take a bulldozer to knock them all down." He winked at her. "Or maybe a Kat Becker."

"What on earth did Ava do to him? I feel like I don't know the whole story. Maybe it would help me understand where he's coming from."

"I told you the major stuff. They got married. While he worked, she found another man who said the things she wanted to hear. She tricked my brother and used him on multiple occasions. Even after they divorced, she hasn't stopped interfering. Ava finds ways to guilt him into doing things for her, though he's never explained to me exactly how. I guess it's his business to share whatever else there is."

A nagging thought occurred to her again. "I can't ignore the possibility Dan and Ava aren't finished with each other. He could still have feelings for her."

"That's hard to believe. The main sentiment he seems to have is closer to…how should I put it?" Shawn thought a moment. "Loathing?"

"Love and hate are both strong emotions. There's a fine line between them."

"That's a stretch. You can tell when there's an attraction between two people. It's almost electric."

She waited, hoping he'd say more, but Shawn closed the subject by staying stubbornly silent. This called for some serious payback. "All righty then. Speaking of electric." Kat tilted her head knowingly. "How are things with Dylan?"

All at once, Shawn's face went the same color Mac's had. "Dylan is a good friend. Okay, a very good friend. He's helped me out big-time. And you too. Without him we wouldn't have gotten a quality video to Belmont on time."

"You don't have to convince me. He's a great guy." She tapped a finger against her cheek. "I'd like to repay him somehow."

"What have you got in mind?"

"I know. Let's invite Dylan over for dinner to thank him." She paused. "No, wait. Let's take him out to dinner. No wait, wait." She clapped her hands once with eager inspiration. "Pop's! We'll take him to Pop's for dinner."

"I'm not sure Pop would appreciate us showing up at his restaurant." Shawn looked down to brush something off his jeans. "He prefers not to have his hopes dashed, so I don't see any reason to shove facts in his face."

A hint of raw emotion in Shawn's voice made her throat tighten. *Dang.* Now she felt bad for teasing him. "In some situations, you have to force people to deal with the truth. Or else you spend your life living a lie."

"Yeah, well, I'm not the only one living a lie at the moment, am I?" He nudged her. "I don't plan to instigate family drama any time soon. Let's forget about all this and focus on anything else."

"Wait a minute!" She palm-smacked her forehead. "I forgot to ask. What do you know about a competition called Soaring Star?"

His face lit up. "Of course. Soaring Star. Why didn't I think about it? The competition would be perfect for you."

"Of all people, Jett filled me in. He says he has connections and wants to coach me."

"I hope the look of disgust I see on your face means you aren't dumb enough to let him get involved. I'll work with you. Dylan will help too. It makes a lot more sense than dealing with a sneaky SOB like Jett."

She laughed. "I agree. Mac said practically the same thing."

"My big brother is giving you advice? Like he's concerned about you or something?" Shawn tented his fingers. "This sounds better all the time."

Kat shoved him playfully, causing Charlie to squall a loud meow. "Oh, cut it out, Shawn. It'd be nice to think he had amorous thoughts floating around in his head attached to my name, but show me the receipt. This girl is pretty sure he thinks I'm as flaky as they come."

"He might think you're flaky, but he's still pretending to be your boyfriend. That's gotta mean something."

She grinned at the superior look he gave her and then took a deep swig of her beer. After all, she'd started this. And if by some master stroke of luck Mac did feel attracted to her, she wouldn't be unhappy at all. No, not one bit.

After the ordeal of picking up Ava, Dan returned home, his feet dragging all the way into the house. Bailing her out had been a nightmare, just as he'd expected. The officer who checked his ID and took payment for her bail money looked almost sympathetic. Apparently, Ava wasn't the ideal inmate. He could only imagine. When she drank, the light polish of veneer she maintained disappeared, exposing the jagged fragments of her personality. From the minute she got into his car, she'd whined about how unfair the arrest had been. He had kept his lips pressed together until they arrived at her apartment where she faked—he felt sure—dizziness, so he'd walk her to the door. Then she twined her arms around him and begged him to stay. He disentangled himself from her, sick from the reek of alcohol and cigarettes. His lack of response to her advances propelled Ava into a spirited rage, and she slammed the door in his face.

He felt as weary as if he'd been in a wrestling match— one he didn't win. Dan melted onto the sofa and picked up his cell. On a whim, he decided to call his brother. Venting to someone who'd sympathize with what he'd been through would help lift the weight tightening his chest. Then, after he unburdened himself, he could tackle explaining to Shawn their father's financial woes. But when the call went straight to voice mail, he knew better than to leave a message. "I've been too busy to check voice mail," Shawn always said.

Today was a great night for his brother to be unavailable. Surely, he wasn't still at Kat's. It was past ten. Dinner would have ended long ago. He had no desire to bother Pop with Ava's latest escapade, but if he didn't blow off steam to somebody, he'd explode. He scrolled down his contact list, and Kat's name caught his eye. If he called her, she'd pick up the phone; he knew it. She'd not only listen to what he said, she'd probably also insist they get together and discuss it in person. He'd be quick to agree because—why not? She'd have him laughing before they'd been together thirty minutes. His finger hovered over her number.

Is it smart for me to call her? He'd found himself thinking about Kat more than he should. Spending time with her felt good—so good lessons from the past faded like a bad dream. Yet he'd do well to remember facts. He'd once let a determined woman turn his existence into bedlam. Years later, he was still dealing with the fallout. If he let another strong-minded woman into his life, what if the same thing happened again?

No. He needed to talk to her, but not about this and not tonight. Later, when his feelings weren't so raw. Or his heart so vulnerable. They had to deal with ending the farce she—no, both of them—had started. If they didn't do it soon, he feared Kat might snare his soul completely. Then, when she got her chance at stardom, she'd abandon him to pursue her dream.

Dan exhaled a huge breath he'd apparently been holding and gently placed his cell on the table.

Chapter Eighteen

One of the nice things about having a small place was it didn't take any time to tidy up. One of the bad things about having a small place meant Kat tended to leave cleaning undone until she had a reason to do it. Who enjoyed dragging out disinfectant spray, sponges, and a cheap discount store vacuum cleaner?

But today she had a reason.

Out of the clear blue, Mac had called and reported in his steady, doctor-solemn way he needed to come by and talk. Part of her happy-danced at the idea, while another part of her whispered a more ominous possibility. *He sounds way too serious for this to be good.*

After she hung up from his call, she'd texted Shawn to explain the current state of affairs and asked him to come over for advice and moral support. Rather than returning her text, he telephoned her right back. "No way. If Dan's coming to see you, it's huge. The last thing you want is a third wheel to spoil the fun. This is your chance to do what you do best. Show him how much he likes you."

She snorted. "Um, I think you have that backward."

"I meant it just the way I said it. I'm betting Dan does like you. A lot. He just hasn't figured it out yet."

If only! "I don't know. One minute I think we're on the edge of something major, and the next it's like he can't get away from me fast enough."

"You're reading him all wrong." Shawn's voice turned away from the phone a moment and muffled like he was having a side-conversation with someone else. "Hey, I'm in the middle of a project, so I'll be home the rest of the day. You get your fanny in gear and call me as soon as you can after he leaves."

Kat threw her phone on the unmade bed, and a delectable shiver ran down her back. A strong desire to believe what Shawn said made her feel good enough to turn up her playlist of favorite country tunes, and then two-step around the house while she fumigated her apartment. It would be a shame if Mac felt compelled to turn her in to the county health board.

Charlie watched from his perch on the back of the sofa, lazily flicking his tail.

"You're going to meet somebody new today," she told him. "So you better be on your best behavior."

Unimpressed, he yawned.

Once she had the apartment in order, Kat jumped into the shower and then grabbed her favorite outfit: jeans and a white "Don't Tempt Me with a Good Time" tank top. She put them on and fluffed her curls, then grabbed her guitar. Nerves always drew her to the solace of music. Kat settled on the sofa by Charlie and strummed, singing along with the tunes still blaring from the speaker. She went through several melodies, looked at the clock, and checked her phone.

Nothing.

Did Mac have a sudden emergency? Change his mind? Find something better to do and somebody better to do it with? The last thought brought a twist of unease to her belly. Had he stood her up? That would be a new experience…and not a very nice one. On the other hand, this technically wasn't a date. Therefore, even if he no-showed, she couldn't consider herself stood up, could she? She put her guitar in the case with intentions of calling him to find out what happened. If Mac wasn't coming, maybe she and Shawn could go out and do something later. That would be better than sitting around stewing. She stood and a firm rap sounded on the door.

Kat scurried to open it. "Hi, Mac. I was starting to wonder what happened."

His face flushed. "Sorry I'm late." A moment later he said, "Well, can I come in?"

Heat fired up her own cheeks, too busy staring at him like a love-sick teenager to remember her manners. "Of course."

"Thanks." He stepped across the threshold. If such a thing were possible, she had a notion he looked more uncomfortable than she felt. The thought immediately perked her up.

"Make yourself comfy on the sofa. Would you like a beer? It just so happens I have your favorite brand."

"Uh, sure. I'd like that."

Her cat rose from where he lay and jumped to the floor with a loud meow. "Mac, say hello to Charlie Daniels."

He leaned to pet the tabby's head. "Charlie Daniels?"

"I named him after one of my favorite old-school country singers. Charlie's been my best buddy for years. I got him when I started high school."

The cat sniffed Mac's hand and then took possession of his lap. Mac laughed when the animal began to purr. "How do you do, Charlie?"

The comment seemed genuine. It even lightened Dan's expression, making him look a little less like he was preparing to deliver bad news to a patient.

Dang. What made me think about bad news? Time to deflect and delay. "Guess what? In case you don't know it, I'm playing at Pop's again tonight. If you're free, come on by for a while. Shawn will be there too. When I'm singing, it bolsters my confidence to see you and him at the table right in front."

Dan pursed his mouth together as though holding in a smile. He lost the battle and snickered. "Please. If there's anything you have plenty of, it's confidence."

He looked so much *nicer* when he smiled. "Okay, point taken. But it sure is fun to see you two guys rooting me on."

"You're good, Kat. It isn't hard to cheer for you."

She put her hand on her chest and fluttered her lashes. "Why thank you, kind sir. You even sound like you mean it."

"I do." Right away, what remained of his smile receded.

Uh-oh. Keep talking. "Wait! I forgot to tell you something really important. Shawn's friend, Dylan, recorded my audition tape and we sent it to Belmont. I haven't heard anything yet about my application, but Shawn thinks they'll take me. My mother is semi-thrilled. She still wants me to channel my music into a teaching degree. But somehow, I don't see myself facing a room full of kids day after day."

"Whatever it is you decide to do, I'm sure you'll be successful. Most likely, Belmont will work out. But there is something we need to discuss. It's been put off too long."

"If you're getting ready to ask when we can cruise around on another bike ride, I say let's go for it." Kat wasn't ready for what she feared was coming. Shawn had been wrong. She could read between the lines. Her pretend boyfriend wanted to break up with her for good, when all she wanted to do was drop the "pretend" part of their relationship.

"No, Kat. What I came here to talk about…" he said.

A muffled buzzing noise came from the bedroom. Her phone. Ordinarily, she'd ignore it. Not now though. "Hold that thought. I hear my cell. It might be something important. I'll be right back."

She raced to grab her phone, grateful for the interruption. By the time she got to it, the buzzing had stopped. Her caller ID showed Miss Stenger. The landlady? The meanest—per Shawn—human being on earth? Apparently, the woman had left a message. Who in heck left a voicemail these days? What a dinosaur. Oh well. At least it kept Mac from saying things she didn't want to hear.

Kat started the message and put the phone to her ear.

"Miss Becker, this is Martha Stenger. It's come to my attention you may be in violation of the terms of your rental agreement. The contract clearly states no pets are allowed. If you've broken your contract, it's grounds for eviction. I'll be at your door at five o'clock sharp to address this matter and to inspect the apartment."

Kat dropped her cell and glanced at the bedside clock. *Crap, crap, and triple crap.* It was nearly five o'clock now! She galloped back to the living room where Mac sat with a wish-I-were-anywhere-but-here expression on his face.

When he saw her, his eyes rounded. "What's wrong?"

"My landlady is on her way right now to inspect the apartment. She's going to evict me if she finds Charlie."

"Why would she evict you?"

"Because I'm not supposed to have a pet."

She waited for the words to register, half expecting him to flee the scene of the crime. Instead he said, "Let's take him to Shawn's."

"What?"

"Hurry. If Shawn's not home, I have a key. Let's go."

"Wait." She grabbed a trash bag from under the sink. "Let me get his stuff." Kat threw Charlie's food, bowls, and toys into the bag and handed it to Mac. She tucked a scratching post under her arm and snatched up the litter box. "Okay, I've got everything. Can you carry Charlie?"

Dan scooped up the cat. He opened the door and looked both ways before crossing the hall to Shawn's apartment to pound on the door. Shawn opened it, and his mouth gaped. Dan pushed past him with Kat close on his heels. Dylan was at the table in front of a stack of papers.

"Hey," Shawn said. "What's up?"

"It's Miss Stenger. Someone must have told her I have a cat. She'll be here any minute to inspect my apartment."

"Got it. Leave Charlie here and go deal with her. Good luck."

"Thanks." She whirled around to get back to her own place, and Dan followed. Kat stopped in the living room, her arms hugged around herself. "It's okay. If you'd rather stay out of this, you can leave…or go hang out with Shawn until it's over."

"It might help you to have a witness."

"Oh. I didn't think about that. Thanks." Growing up with a suspicious mother had taught her to handle her own problems. Having help would be a novelty.

They waited without speaking. Kat nibbled at a guitar player's callous on her forefinger, hoping the landlady would change her mind. She already missing Charlie's presence. If it came down to a choice between this apartment and her cat, she'd start packing her bags now, even if it meant sleeping in the parking lot at Belmont. Kat's eyes met Mac's and she calmed a bit, until a sharp bang at the door made her jump. She took a breath and went to open it.

Miss Stenger's normally prim but cordial expression had disappeared behind a mouth pressed into a straight line.

"Hello, Miss Stenger," Kat trilled in her most vivacious tone. "I'd like you to meet my friend, Mac."

Mac gave the old witch a charming smile, but the woman barely glanced at him, anointing Kat with a glare of supreme disapproval.

"I presume you got my message. It's been reported you have a cat."

"I did get your message, but I have no idea what you're talking about." Kat spread her arms wide. "There's no cat here. Except me, of course." She giggled, but Miss Stenger only clamped her lips even tighter together until they practically disappeared. *If looks could kill!* "Please. Feel free to check for yourself. There's no animal in this apartment."

"She's right, there's no cat here." Mac said. "You must be mistaken."

Miss Stenger scowled at him and scanned the room. Then she marched toward Kat's bedroom. From the corner of her eyes, Kat saw Mac surreptitiously kick one of Charlie's toys—a catnip-stuffed mouse she'd apparently missed—under the sofa. She looked at him and smiled gratefully. He disguised a swift grin as Miss Stenger returned.

"All right. I don't see anything, but I'm putting you on notice. There are to be no pets in this building. I'll be keeping a close eye on things, and if I discover you have an animal, you're out. Do you understand me, young lady?"

"No worries. I wouldn't dream of breaking any rules." The remark came out sweet as a slice of angel food cake, just as she'd intended.

With a final narrowing of her eyes, Miss Stenger left. Once her footsteps faded away, Kat turned toward Mac who held his finger to his lips and then spoke in a hushed tone. "You look like you're about to yell. Don't."

How did he know? She'd been ready to whoop with happiness, but Mac was right. Miss Stenger could be lurking nearby, listening for any sign of foul play. Kat satisfied herself by performing an excited but noiseless skitter toward Mac. She threw her arms around him. He appeared to welcome the gesture, and held her in a tight embrace. She sank into the pleasure of pressing her body against his. It felt cozy and lovely and soothing. How could the caress of any other man ever warm her like this? She wouldn't mind a bit if he didn't let her go for at least a week…maybe two.

But after a moment, Dan stepped away. She brushed a piece of lint off her tank top and worked at regaining her composure.

"You okay?" He studied her face.

"Sure. Thank goodness you were here and willing to fib for me. The list of reasons I owe you just got longer."

"Why don't we not keep a list." He gestured toward the door. "How long do you plan to leave Charlie with Shawn?"

"I don't know. I guess I can bring him home after I sing tonight."

"That should work out. Miss Stenger doesn't look like the type to be policing the halls late at night."

"True." She clapped a hand to her cheek. "Oh my gosh! I've got to get ready. My music is all over the place. I'm not sure what to wear, and I have stuff to pack."

He gave her a long and measured look, his expression unreadable. "Right. I better be on my way."

"I'm sorry. I know you had something to say. Maybe we can talk later?"

"Later. Sure. I wouldn't mind seeing Pop tonight. Or Shawn. Maybe we can get together after you finish."

Her throat vibrated with the effort to restrain a squeal. She managed a dignified "That'd be nice, Mac." Then she took his hand with both of hers and squeezed it. "Thanks again for helping me out. You're the best."

His face flushed, and he ducked his head like a schoolboy. It was such a sweet moment, she almost reached out to hug him again, but she wasn't sure how he'd feel about it. Instead, she watched him walk out the door, and tried to figure out exactly what had happened. Mac could easily have waved good-bye and let her ship sink. Instead, he'd stepped right into the middle of a sticky predicament and helped deflect the potential consequences. Maybe because she was his brother's friend? Or could there be some other reason? A glance at the clock kicked her into more concrete action.

As she scrambled to throw her things together, the possibilities of what was on his mind crossed hers. Two options. It could be something good—or something awful. She'd spent a lot of energy tonight skirting around the issue. Maybe she should simply let him say what he had to say. Of course, this tactic would be a lot easier if the nagging voice in her head that kept repeating, *you'll be sorry* would shut up.

Chapter Nineteen

Apparently, he had completely lost his mind. No other explanation made any sense. Dan sat in front of his television and softly cursed himself. Even watching an episode of *American Chopper*, his favorite show, didn't distract him. He'd lied for Kat again. Well, technically he supposed he hadn't spoken a single dishonest word. There really *wasn't* an animal in the apartment— at the time. Still, the reason for the deception had tightened his features and given him a case of cottonmouth while Madame Wicked Witch of the West hurled accusations. He found himself not feeling much pain over misleading her. Seriously, what was the big deal about having a pet as long as the tenant paid her rent and didn't trash the place?

What bothered him more was how natural it had felt jumping in to help Kat. She didn't even have to ask him. What the hell was going on? It seemed like he'd begun to understand the intricacies of her thought process—God help him. Without much trouble, he could decipher her mood by her mannerisms. Like when she chewed her lip pondering a question. The amused side-glance she lobbed in his direction when she teased his brother. How her eyes lit up when he watched her perform. For such a hyperactive woman—the type he usually took pains to avoid—she was ominously easy to be around. As a matter of fact, the more time he spent with her, the more comfortable he felt. She brought him a sense of freedom eerily similar to when he rode his bike.

But he'd do well not to forget they were opposite as the sun and moon. His intention to tell Kat they needed to be sensible and finish the fake-boyfriend masquerade had bounced out of his brain the moment panic filled her eyes after the landlady's call. Defending Kat came naturally, especially when the woman condemned them both with a single caustic glare. Afterward, he didn't have the heart to bring up ending their ill-conceived relationship. Despite her backbone of steel and sass, Kat didn't need to be weighed down with anything else to upset her before a performance. It'd be like disclosing an alarming message to a surgeon just as he picked up the scalpel for a delicate operation. Anyway, what harm could it do if he carried on the lie a little longer?

The argument in favor of his good intentions resolved the problem—for now. He turned off the set and started toward his bedroom to get ready for the evening at Pop's when the doorbell chimed. Half inclined to ignore the intrusion, he stood still a moment, then sighed and turned back to open the door.

Why didn't I look first?

"Hello, lover." Ava stood on the front porch, her brown hair pulled tight and coiled into a heavy bun on top of her head.

Damn. "What do you want?"

"I need to talk to you."

He folded his arms and waited.

"You used to have better manners, Dan. Aren't you going to invite me in?"

"I'm afraid when it comes to dealing with you, manners and I parted company long ago."

The crafty glint in her gaze told him she wasn't going to give up easily. He glanced at the clock. There was a little time before he needed to leave for Pop's. Might as well get this over with. Grudgingly, he stepped aside and motioned for her to enter.

Ava's gaze inventoried the room, and a simpering grin followed. "Black leather sofa. Glass and chrome tables. Blinds at the windows with no curtains. A gigantic television screen. It's obvious no female had a hand in decorating your place."

Her coy undertone overstretched his final nerve. "Will you please tell me why you're here?"

"I just wanted to stop by and let you know the lawyer needs a deposit before he'll take my case. DUIs are a lot more expensive than I thought."

"And this is important for you to tell me…why?"

"You know why. I don't have the money to pay a lawyer. I barely have enough to buy food. I need your help taking care of this so I can focus on my aftercare."

"I've already been more than generous, Ava."

"I know you've spent a lot." She wandered into the kitchen and ran a hand along the counter. "You need somebody to clean this joint up for you. Since no one knows better than me how much time you spend at work, I have a suggestion. There's plenty of room for two people here. If I moved in, it would save a ton of money for both of us and I could help out by taking care of the condo. Plus, if we were together again and I had your full support, I'm sure I'd do much better in treatment."

Of all the absurd things she could have suggested, this one topped everything. "That ship sailed a long time ago. The last thing I want is to have you back in my life."

Right on cue, her eyes filled, and a tear streaked down her face. "Don't be so horrible to me, Dan." She put her hand on his arm. "We've got history, and you know how much I need you."

He shook his head. "I paid for your treatment. I paid for you to have an apartment. Now you want me to pay for your lawyer. Your recovery isn't my responsibility. It's yours."

"What about the reason I got where I'm at in the first place? What about Johnny?"

He steeled himself against the quick stab of pain. "You blame me for everything that happened. Don't you think you had something to do with it? In therapy, you should have dealt with your part in this. If you haven't, maybe it's time you did."

She sniffed a few times, and her tears disappeared as quickly as they'd come. "I have outpatient every day. My counselor's trying to help me get a job, but there's no way

I can do it until full-time outpatient ends. I barely have enough from my treatment stipend to survive. Now are you going to help me or not?"

"Right now, I'm leaning toward not, but I'll think about it." He opened the door, eager to see her go. "It's getting late, and I have plans to hear a friend sing at Pop's tonight."

"What? You're going to watch somebody sing? Have pigs started flying?" She pursed her mouth together. "Come to think of it, I haven't talked to Pop in a long time. What if I come with you?"

"Absolutely not. You're supposed to be in recovery. I don't think visiting a bar is what your counselor would recommend—or your lawyer. Anyway, as I recall, the last time you saw Pop, you threw a shot glass at him."

"He was yelling at me. You know I hate it when people yell at me."

"Pop had a right to be upset, since you were flaunting your new boyfriend…while still married to me."

"I was hurt and lonesome, and you were never there for me."

"If you want to call working my job not being there for you, then no, I wasn't."

"See, even you admit the truth." Her lips twisted up smugly.

"I've had about enough for today, Ava. Goodbye." He swept a hand toward the open door and waited for her to exit.

She walked close enough to brush against him as she strolled past. "Think about it, won't you, lover? Think about us."

Dan slammed the door, afraid of what he might say. How in the name of heaven had he become sucked into the quicksand of Ava? Had she bewitched him at their first meeting? In retrospect, he had no idea what blinded him to how devious she could be. He massaged his forehead. Staying in the peace of his home sounded better than going anywhere else, but he couldn't bear the thought of letting Kat down. It wasn't her fault he'd married and then divorced a woman from hell, the one who should have been out of his life permanently a long time ago.

Somebody needed to kick him square in the pants. He'd let Ava manipulate him for years. For the second time in one day, Dan questioned his own sanity. In a roundabout way, Ava's assessment about him had been correct. Her ongoing demands were no one's fault but his own. As long as he helped her, she'd always be back asking for more.

Chapter Twenty

Dan put the headache of another battle with Ava behind him. He showered and changed, trying to focus on the evening ahead. Never in more need of his own kind of treatment, he ignored the car and chose his bike. The Roadmaster, always dependable, revved into action, carrying him along Nashville streets while a cool evening breeze brushed his face. He passed a slow-moving car and smiled. Anticipation over seeing Kat again helped his troubles recede while the bike carried him closer to Pop's.

He pulled into the lot later than he wanted, and found the place jammed. This meant driving up and down aisles several times before someone left. Dan waited to squeeze his bike into the spot and then took off his helmet. Music pulsated from inside the restaurant. If parking was any indicator, Kat was playing to a full house. He caught a glimpse of her through the window but couldn't make out the number of spectators.

Stepping inside, he found the size of the crowd confirmed his conjecture. Overhead lights had been dimmed, and a soft warm spotlight haloed Kat as she sang a rhythmic tune that had booted feet tapping. He stopped to listen for a few moments, then wove his way through the mob until he reached the empty chair next to Shawn at the table near the front.

"Hey, bro." Shawn mouthed the words and gave Dan a thumbs-up. No wonder he didn't try to talk. Between the music and the sound of the crowd, a person would have to holler to be heard. Within a few moments, a waitress brought Dan a bottle of beer, and he waved his thanks to Pop, who looked a little frazzled at his place behind the bar. Why wasn't Jett helping? On such a busy night, he needed to be out lending a hand, not hiding in the kitchen to boss Rory around.

The moment of irritation passed when Kat began a soft ballad that got what looked like more than half the couples present onto the dance floor—where they clung to each other and swayed to the music. Dan leaned back and watched her perform. What he didn't know about singing would fill the ocean, but he knew what he liked. Kat seemed to have it all. Her voice sounded full and rich and a little torrid with notes she released like butterflies floating in the room. She seemed to hold her entire audience within one small palm. Or was it his imagination? Even so, a strange sense of pride stirred in him. Why, he couldn't figure out, as he certainly had nothing to do with her talent. Shawn winked at Dan and smiled in a see-what-I-mean kind of way. Dan curled the side of his mouth in response and turned his attention back to the show. Kat sounded even better than she had the first time he'd heard her perform.

He took a moment to scan the room, trying to confirm what he thought he was witnessing. Clearly, she'd woven a spell. A sort of magic. Could this be how it worked? The reason a person tackled a path against all odds—for the love of God, becoming a doctor was easier—in the quest to be a performer? For the first time, it occurred to him she just might make a splash in the music world. And then he knew what would happen. She'd leave to chase her ambition. The thought iced the blood in his veins. There must be something he could do to change her mind. He took a sip of his beer. What if he put his cards on the table and confessed to the feelings she'd stirred in him? Would she be willing to let go of this crazy dream and settle into a quieter life?

Manipulation. Would that mean doing to her what Ava's done to me?

Kat finished her song, and when the applause died down, she spoke into the microphone. "Thanks, everyone. There's more to come after I take a short break. My guy is here, and I need to say hello." She looked straight at Dan, who suddenly felt like a deer-in-headlights.

The crowd whooped and laughed in response, Shawn guffawed, and Dan's back prickled with the sense of many eyes on him. Kat put her guitar on the stand and stepped down from the stage.

The spotlight switched off and overhead lights brightened so people could grab another beer or head toward the restrooms. Kat giggled as she reached Dan and put her arms around his waist. "Thanks for coming," she whispered.

It felt right to hold her, so he rested his chin on the top of her head. Her hair smelled of vanilla and something slightly citrus. He ought to let her go, but having her near touched a chord in his heart—hell, she had him thinking in music terms—when she pressed against him sweet as warm honey.

His gaze drew to the bar, where Jett had emerged from the kitchen apparently ready to help Pop. Better late than never. Dan muttered, "It's about time Jett got to work. A busy night like this is too much for Pop to handle alone."

Both Kat and Shawn glanced toward the bar. Before either of them could offer a comment, Dan heard a voice from behind him.

"Well, well. Isn't this cozy?" Ava was dressed to impress in a low-cut, sequined western blouse, high-heeled cowboy boots, and dark blue jeans that looked like they'd been painted on. She clutched a beer bottle in her hand and glared at Dan with eyes hard as hail. "I thought you told me you weren't involved with anyone."

Dan moved away from Kat, unwilling for her to become Ava's target. "I believe I said what I did was no longer any of your business."

"The dragon lady returns." Shawn raised an eyebrow. "What kind of trouble are you plotting tonight?"

"You keep out of this," Ava shot at him and twisted back toward Dan. She pointed at Kat and bellowed. "She's the one you came to see?"

The last thing Dan wanted to do was make an introduction. He had no idea how much Ava already had to drink and calculated the quickest way to remove her from the scene before she got any louder. He didn't count on the fact Kat wasn't one to stay silent in the background while somebody figured out what to say.

"I'm Kat Becker." Normally she'd reach out for a handshake. This time, her hand went to her hip. "And who are you?"

"I'm Ava McDonald. Dan's…wife," she hissed.

"Ex-wife," Dan and Shawn corrected in stereo.

"I see." Kat smiled in the least sincere manner Dan had ever seen her do. "Well, it would be fascinating to stay here and chat with you, Ava, but I need to get back to my set." She rose on tiptoe to kiss Dan's cheek and took her time about strolling away.

Ava pointed at Kat. "So I've finally met your little tart. I knew it. She's the reason you've been so cold to me. Ever since I got out of treatment, I've been doing my best to make amends like my counselor said I should, and it's done me no good at all. Treatment didn't change anything, so why even try?"

She was unsteady on her feet, and her voice had grown so loud, heads turned in their direction. Ava had binged again. He hadn't seen her at Pop's when he walked through the crowd, so she must have been drinking somewhere else before she arrived. No one needed Ava on a rampage. It wouldn't be good for Pop, Shawn, Kat, or the restaurant.

Or for me either.

As proof of his assessment, Jett appeared at the table. "What's going on? Some customers have complained about the racket."

Through clenched teeth, Dan muttered to Shawn, "I've got to get her out of here."

"Still taking care of your ex? Maybe you've got more going on with her than you do with your new girlfriend." Jett jerked his chin in Kat's direction.

For a person who shunned drama, he'd certainly gotten himself into the center of a soap opera. He hated soap operas. Pure frustration—over Ava's behavior and the lie he'd been living—bubbled in his chest, crawled up his throat, and simmered in his mouth until he blurted it out. "I don't have anything going on with my ex. And"—he gestured toward Kat—"she has never been my girlfriend."

Shawn's mouth dropped open, and heat flamed in Dan's face. He'd done it. The words needed to be said, and now he'd said them. A moment of regret needled him, but he put it aside. Maybe this hadn't happened in the best manner, but at least the truth was finally out.

Jett's expression reminded Dan of a shark circling prey. Ava broke into a complacent grin. Dan found his entire esophagus suddenly growing tight, and he swallowed hard.

"You faked a relationship with Kat? I knew something was fishy about this whole thing." Jett's eyebrows butted together. "You need to get Ava out of here before any more customers complain—or she gets Pop worked up."

Shawn recovered himself enough to leap in. "Don't do it, Dan. Call a cab. Don't let her suck you in."

Ava snipped at Shawn. "I told you to stay out of my business."

Dan groaned. Could the evening get any worse? If he sent Ava away alone, it would be a mistake. For spite, she'd do anything. Maybe even get out on the road and kill herself or somebody else. "I don't have a choice. I've got to take her home."

Shawn shook his head. "Everybody has choices. Set some boundaries, bro. You're going to be sorry if you don't."

Dan understood the truth of his brother's words, yet what else could he do? Ava had successfully baited another trap. His conscience wouldn't let him turn her loose on the world, not in her condition. He snatched the bottle away from her, hoping she wouldn't fight him.

Thankfully, she only grabbed his arm. "What would I do without you, lover?"

"Come on," he said, frost dripping from his words. "Let's go."

She'd been curious about the commotion at the table, but as soon as Kat saw Ava take Mac's arm, it made her sick to her stomach. It wasn't until he walked beside his ex and disappeared into the crowd that she stopped wondering what had happened. Ava—Mac's ex-wife. It had been a shock to see her and an eye-opener to experience such blatant hostility. Something about the woman stirred Kat's memory. Middle school? Ava behaved like the pack of mean girls who blustered, bullied, and backstabbed any girl they didn't like. Poor Mac. If this was what he endured from his ex, no wonder he harbored so much resentment. Maybe he'd get rid of her and come back to Pop's later. The weary expression on Shawn's face didn't look promising. Her throat closed up a little, but she lifted her chin and concentrated on her next song, determined not to let anything interfere with what she owed the people who came to see her.

By the time her final song ended, she'd developed a big fat lump in her throat. She wasn't sure how she'd made it through to the end. Kat acknowledged the applause and swallowed at the reminder posed by Mac's empty chair while Shawn pushed his beer around like he'd lost his best friend and avoided meeting her eyes. A few well-wishers had surrounded her, and she spoke to them before returning to the table. "What the heck happened?"

"There are tornadoes, earthquakes, hurricanes, and Ava. Pick your poison. Every single one is a natural disaster. Tonight, she was tanked up and getting rowdy, so Dan thought it best to take her home."

Take her home? "Meaning her place or his?"

"I have no clue. I guess you noticed she's a major challenge when she's in her cups."

Kat's spirit drooped at the thought of Mac and his ex-wife together, no matter whose place they were at. "Oh, I noticed. It's obvious she's been drinking. I thought you told me she went through a rehab program."

"It's my understanding she did. Guess she needs a do-over. But I'm afraid there's more bad news, kiddo."

Jett appeared at the table, and Shawn clamped his mouth shut.

"Good job tonight, hon." Jett squeezed Kat's arm.

She jerked away from him. "Keep your hands to yourself, or I'll tell Mac you've crossed the line. I'll report you for being grabby too."

"Your so-called boyfriend just left to take care of his ex-wife. But he didn't leave until he told us you are *not* his girlfriend. You never were. I knew all along your story was nothing but BS."

Shawn gave Jett a dagger stare. "Knock it off."

Jett didn't smile—he smirked. "I've got cleanup to supervise, so I'll leave you to hash this out yourselves. Remember, Kat, you're on the work schedule. I'll see you then."

Mac had opened the door for Jett to resume his harassment. For once, words failed her.

"That's what I was going to tell you. I don't think Dan meant to blow your cover, but what's done is done. Jett's only trying to bait you. Try not to let him to it." Shawn drained the rest of his drink. "I'd talk to Pop myself, but he listens better to Dan than he does to me. I'll speak up if my brother doesn't, though."

Dang. The breakup of a fake relationship and Mac's quick departure with his ex shouldn't make her feel so—discarded. "Don't worry about it. I can take care of myself." She did her best to conceal the ache in her heart. "If Miss Stenger isn't snooping around when we get back to the apartment, I'd like to bring Charlie home. I need him with me tonight."

"We can do whatever you want. Let's finish tear-down and then we'll go home." He stopped to eyeball her. "Hey, are you okay? You have a weird look on your face."

"Do I?" She attempted a smile and failed miserably.

"Kat Becker, it's time to get real." His sharp stare immobilized her. "You've really fallen for Dan, haven't you?"

"Of course not," she said. "Why would I go and do something as dumb as that?"

Chapter Twenty-One

Music echoed through the apartment. Kat strummed her guitar and sang the tune she planned to enter in the Soaring Star competition. Charlie snoozed on the sofa while Shawn stationed himself in front of her, watching every move with his head cocked to the side. About a minute into the song, he held up his hand to stop her. "I'm not sure about the rhythm. Sing it again, a little slower this time."

Kat obliged, and Shawn let her sing clear through to the end. "Yep, a much better tempo. The music is more solid when you slow it down. Dylan offered his studio again, and I think we're ready to film the entry video."

"You haven't told me yet what you think of my song." The melody had boomeranged back and forth in her head for the past year, but after coming to Nashville, she'd changed the lyrics a lot from the original. Fine-tuning a piece never ended.

"Everything I've studied tells me it has good structure. The music and lyrics fit together well. I like it. After we get

Soaring Star behind us, we'll call the Bluebird Café and get you on the performance roster. It would be great exposure."

"The Bluebird? I thought you had to have name recognition to perform there."

"All you need is to be among the first to call and have original material. An audition isn't required, unless you want to try out for Writers' Night."

"Hmm. Actually, I have a couple of ideas for new music." She gave him an anemic smile. "Getting dumped is great incentive for creating a country song. Do you realize this is the first time a guy ever broke up with me? Even if a fake boyfriend did the dumping, it doesn't feel so hot."

"I take it you still haven't heard from Dan?"

"Nope. I thought he'd at least touch base over the whole debacle at Pop's, but I guess he has other things on his mind." *Like his ex-wife, for example.* "And by the way," she gave Shawn a stern glare. "My rule is still in place. Don't you dare bring up the subject with Mac. I don't want him pushed into calling me because he feels guilty. He gets enough of garbage like that from Ava."

"Don't worry. I'll keep my mouth shut. I won't even mention how you've been acting like you lost your best friend since the big reveal."

"Mac *is* my friend. I *do* miss him."

"Uh-huh." Shawn kept his face averted.

"It's true!"

"Whatever you say, toots. How have things been at Pop's?"

Her neck felt hot, so she held her hair up a minute to cool down. "It's about what I expected. Pop seemed pretty upset with me at first. I got the idea he was real disappointed to find out Mac and I weren't an item. I almost told him about Jett and why the lie got started in the first place, but he had such dark lines under his eyes, I didn't want to bother him. I just left it alone and said the whole blowup was my fault so he wouldn't hold anything against Mac."

"It's good of you to look out for my brother. After everything that happened, most women wouldn't."

"None of this is his doing. I'm the one who got him into it. Besides, the more I know Mac, the better I like him, although how I feel doesn't change anything." She didn't want to admit it, not even to Shawn, but she had a suspicion the word "like" wasn't strong enough to describe the way Mac could turn her body into melted butter. What was the point in verbalizing her feelings? Anyone could see he was still wrapped up with his ex. The two of them looked awfully tight when they left Pop's together, and the entire scenario screamed unfinished business. Until Mac made a clean break with Ava—assuming he even wanted to—she would just have to knock off daydreaming about what might have been.

"Here's some advice if you're willing to take it. Don't give up on my pigheaded brother. Give him another chance. You're good for him. And I think…" Shawn smiled. "He's good for you too."

"We'll never know, will we? I'm not about to become a third wheel in some woman-scorned love triangle. That's not the way I roll."

"I don't know what's up with Dan and Ava, but I guarantee it's not what you think. She's made his life hell, but he's always been a sucker for helping people who need him."

"So I've noticed." *If only he'd get sick of helping a full-of-troubles woman like Ava.* "But never mind me. You've got some explaining to do. I hope your love life is going better than mine." Shawn blushed from ear to ear, which made her giggle despite the funk she'd fallen into.

"I went out on a limb and invited Dylan to Pop's the last time you sang, but he couldn't make it. The crazy way things turned out, it's probably just as well. I'm not exactly looking forward to Dylan meeting Dan or Pop."

She touched his hand. "I'm not in the best position to give advice, but hang in there. It's going to be all right. I know it will."

"Time to lay off consoling each other." He stood and stretched. "Why don't we get back to work? Let me refill your water."

Kat handed Shawn the glass and picked up her guitar. "I'm ready when you are, coach."

On his way to the kitchen, Shawn brushed against a tall pile of envelopes stacked at the edge of the counter. Most of them fluttered to the floor. "That's the biggest batch of unopened mail I've ever seen. Aren't you curious?"

"About what? Besides, I've been busy."

He bent to gather them up. "Good God, girl, here's something from Belmont."

Kat set down her guitar and jumped from her seat. She scurried toward Shawn, knelt, and took the envelope from him. "I'm kind of afraid to look."

"Do it," he said.

She gulped and her fingers shook a bit as she tore open the flap. Her pulse pounded faster than a military snare drum.

Shawn grabbed her arm. "Hurry up. What does it say?"

"It says…congratulations!" She sprang to her feet with a squeal. "I'm accepted into the songwriter's program at Belmont!"

Shawn pulled her into a hug. "Woo-hoo! I knew it. I knew you'd get in. Your audition tape was first-rate, and so are you!"

"You know, this is all so strange. I was just thinking the other day if by some wild stroke of luck I win Soaring Star and get a contract, I might not even need to go to Belmont."

"You just got in and you want to back out already?"

"That's not what I meant. Making the finals, let alone winning the contest, would be a huge long shot, but wouldn't it be cool?"

"Are you saying if you win the competition, you won't finish school?"

"To tell the truth, I don't know why I should. A contract is my goal. It would give me a platform and a chance to show what I can do." She wrinkled her nose. "Mother would kill me, of course, but a degree is her idea, not mine."

"Sounds like you're saying it's the competition or school. Are you going to tell your parents?"

"I won't lie to them, but right now all they need to know is I plan to enter the Soaring Star Competition. There's no need to say anything about whether it would affect school. It's all speculation at this point anyway. One step at a time. I need to prepare for the contest, but I'll go ahead and set up my classes too. Then I'm covered no matter what happens."

"Fair enough, I guess. Okay, let's run through your song once more and then we're going to break for the evening and celebrate Belmont's newest student. By the way, did I tell you how much I like the title of your song?"

"You did. 'Along the Road' describes most everything that's happened to me since I left Kansas City. I've only been here a few weeks, and Nashville feels like home to me already."

Even as she turned a peg to adjust the pitch of her E string, she knew she meant every word she'd said. Nashville did feel like home, and with a few things finally falling into place, she'd welcome any opportunity to give her music dreams a bigger boost.

As for her parents, she'd make the call she owed them tonight. They'd be overjoyed with the good news about school. A mention of the contest would swiftly be glossed over as her mother focused on Belmont and ignored everything else. For a change, it should be a tension-free conversation.

Kat would be elated if it weren't for the small piece of her heart nagging nonstop for her to call Mac. She'd love to hear his voice, but how would he feel about hearing hers? If she told him the latest news, would he be happy for her, blow her off, or hang up so he didn't have to hear another word she had to say? He probably wasn't wasting time brooding over what happened in her life. Not with Ava hogging his attention. *Geez.* She sounded like someone brooding over a fantasy crush gone bad.

Refocus. She didn't have time for romance anyway. She had come to Nashville to establish a career, not get sidetracked by anything—or anyone—else.

Chapter Twenty-Two

Kat mopped her forehead with a paper napkin. Whew! The restaurant had been remarkably busy for a weeknight, but at least her customers had been fun. She'd complimented a young couple, joked with a book club group, and flirted shamelessly with two elderly men who'd appeared to be overjoyed at every minute of her attention. Shawn had suggested she work on building a following, and although daytime diners weren't exactly her target audience, it didn't matter. She extended invitations to one and all, asking them to come hear her when she played at Pop's. Having a good time with others was the best part of waitressing. Pop's Place might not open any important doors for her, but she could still entertain the customers she met—along with herself.

She couldn't call herself a struggling artist either. Between what she made updating the law firm's media accounts, waitressing, and singing, she had no need to ask Daddy for a loan. He'd even texted her to offer help after she'd called home last night. "I'm good!" she'd texted back with no small sense of pride. Now if Daddy had offered to find Pete Casson and get him to call her back…Well, that would be another story. She'd started to wonder if the man truly existed. Her viral video had faded into yesterday's news and, along with it, her high hopes of a handy springboard to a new vocation. But hey, at least the dang thing brought her to Nashville.

What the heck did it really take for true music magic to happen? She stacked dirty dishes and pondered the question. Shawn said hard work and time. Mac's statement had been more blunt. *What was it?* Ninety-nine percent of musicians and singers who came to Nashville left within a year. She found this hard to imagine since it was so easy to fall in love with the town. But truth be told, no major development had happened for her yet, unless you counted her Soaring Star video. An email said she made semi-finalist status, which was cool, although she saw the competition as a crapshoot. Kat reminded herself what Shawn told her—she had as good a chance of winning it as anyone else. *Material. Think of all this as material for a song.*

She picked up another load of dirty plates, and Pop waved her to the bar. "I was afraid I'd have to call in reinforcements. You've done a first-class job keeping up with everything. This has been a bear of a day but good for the cash register."

Appreciation for his kindness brought a smile to her face. Once Pop got past his initial disappointment, she'd been relieved to see him put aside his annoyance at her for the deception. Maybe he understood. Maybe he liked her a little more than he let on.

"It's been a day, for sure." She put the plates down. "And I'm doing what I can to drum up more business. People seem happy to come back."

"We always have a decent crowd when you sing. It's one of the reasons I like keeping you on the list of our regulars. We get plenty of good feedback."

"Thanks, Pop." His praise flooded her with warm affection. "I've been feeling a little down about the state of my career, and you put it all in perspective. Performing makes me happy. Maybe I should just be satisfied with that."

"All anyone can do is keep on trying." Pop swiped a towel across the counter. "Since we have a lull, would you stand in for me a few minutes? I'll be right back."

"Sure thing."

She stepped behind the bar as Pop headed toward the restroom. A couple sat at the only occupied table in the restaurant. Their order had already been turned in and she'd served them drinks, so they'd be fine until Rory had their food ready. Kat leaned against the counter and picked up the towel Pop had used, flicking it against her leg. The towel slipped from her hand, and she bent to pick it up. Somebody patted her behind, and she straightened like a shot.

Jett walked past her. "Nice ass."

"Cut it out, you disgusting creep. I've told you a million times to keep your hands to yourself. I'm about finished dealing with you."

"Oh, get off your high horse. Most women would be flattered at the attention."

"I'll bet Pop will say something different when he hears about you being such a perv."

"Excuse me? Pop won't do anything but tell some convoluted story that makes no sense about the way things were when he was young and how they've changed today. What do you think would be easier for him, saying good-by to you and hiring a new waitress, or replacing a top-notch manager who's been with him for years? He can't afford to fire me."

"Don't be so sure about that." Kat tightened her eyes at him.

"You've already proved you're a liar. If I were you, I wouldn't do anything more to rock the boat."

With that remark, her fingers curled into a fist. She itched to pop him one, but with a truckload of effort, she restrained herself. "You are a total jerk. Take care of the counter until Pop gets back." She threw the towel down and walked away.

Her job had been much easier when she had a boyfriend. Okay, a pretend boyfriend. The last thing she wanted to do was make Pop's job harder. She also didn't want to quit, but what other solution did she have? For a nano-second, Kat considered creating a new boyfriend, but the label "liar" felt a tad uncomfortable. Besides, going from a pretend boyfriend to an imaginary one felt, even to her, a little bit crazy.

Worst of all, Jett had reminded her how much she missed seeing Mac. It had been almost a week. Despite all the silly pushes and pulls between them, she knew they had something, a spark—dim and tenuous for sure, but something she'd love to investigate. Instinct told her he felt it too, but the way things played out, it wasn't likely to go any further. He'd made his ex-wife a priority, which spoke volumes, no matter how noble his intent. If he could put Kat aside so easily while taking care of Ava, what were the odds? He obviously wasn't interested in pursuing a friendship—let alone a potential romance.

And what had started this whole snarl of feelings? One convenient little deception. The kind of foundation destined to crumble.

"Order's up," Rory called to her from the kitchen.

Delighted to think about something else, she picked up two plates, heavy with barbecued pork sandwiches. "Thanks," she said and carried the plates to the couple's table. The man and woman gazed at each other with stars in their eyes. *Sweet.*

"Here you are." She set the plates down.

"Looks good," the man said.

"Oh, it is," Kat assured him. "You'll love it."

The woman studied her. "Don't you sing here sometimes?"

"As a matter of fact, I do."

"I thought so. A week or two ago, we happened to be here when you performed. You were great! Between songs when you shared how you stalked your eighth grade social studies teacher because he was hot, I laughed so hard, I almost peed my pants."

A grin crept across Kat's face. "Thank you. Just another little tidbit from my life story. Hey, I'm performing again next week. If y'all are free…"

"Awesome," the woman replied. "We'll grab a front row table."

One ego boost coming right up. Kat left the table feeling 1,000 percent better. This is what she loved about performing. The chance to absorb positive energy from an audience like a sponge so she could use it any time she felt low. Pop had taken his place behind the bar when the front door opened and a customer entered. She swiveled her head toward the sound.

Mac.

Her heart immediately filled with the warm molasses of desire. At first, Kat wondered whether she ought to disappear into the kitchen and let Pop handle his son—a chicken's escape. Why shouldn't she wait on him? Especially since there wasn't any sign of Ava. Lifting her head a notch, she went to the table where he'd seated himself.

"Hi, Mac. How's it going?"

"Okay." His face turned a slightly deeper shade. "Between work and…other things that came up, I've been busy."

Boy, did that ever sound like a brush-off. "Sure. I get it."

"I owe you an apology. Coming clean with the whole relationship thing was what I'd wanted to talk to you about when your landlady showed up, but I didn't intend to blurt it out the way I did. Ava had me so worked up, the truth just popped out of my mouth of its own accord."

"It's just as well. I understand."

"Have you had any more trouble from Jett?"

She swallowed. "Nothing I can't handle."

"Good. I'm here to talk to Pop. Jett's behavior will be part of the conversation."

"Don't bother Pop on my account. I can take care of myself."

"I'm sure you can, but Jett has no right to harass you or anyone else."

Mac's forehead crinkled in an unnerving way. She looked down to concentrate on cracker crumbs someone had dropped on the floor. "What can I get for you?"

"Just a glass of water, please." He fiddled with a coaster on the table. "Shawn told me Soaring Star is coming up soon. He says you made semifinalist, and he thinks you have a good chance to win. I'll be rooting for you."

The attempt at a topic Mac disliked but was dear to her heart returned her gaze to his. "Thanks. The email was short and sweet. I'm not sure exactly what I'm up against, but I'm trying to get ready. Shawn and Dylan have both been awesome about helping me."

Dan reached out and took her hand. "My brother likes you. Thanks for being such a good friend to him. The last few years, he's had some rough times. There are people who despise him for who he is, and it hurts him. Even Pop has a hard time accepting things the way they are."

Her façade softened. If she and Mac couldn't be anything else, maybe they could be united in helping Shawn. "I think Pop will come around. He's a good man, and he doesn't want to lose his son."

"I hope you're right."

With tension dialed back at least thirty degrees, she decided to plunge in. "I know this is none of my business, but I'm going to ask anyway. What happened with your ex the other night?"

He huffed a sigh. "I guess you noticed she has problems."

"It's hard to miss."

"Ava's had some bad breaks. Sometimes I feel responsible."

Kat's brows arched. "Why?"

"Hello, Danny." Pop appeared at the table. "Welcome back. I'm glad to see you and Kat are still friends."

"We are," Dan said and looked at Kat with an expression so soulful she had to bite back the urge to touch his face.

"That's good. That's good," Pop said. "Your mom always told me, where there's true friendship, sweet things can blossom."

Dan's fingers tapped the table. "Pop, you and I need to talk about cash flow and a few other things we've put off too long."

"But—"

"We've got plenty of time. The evening rush won't start for a while. Jett can handle the place while we meet. Let's go to your office."

Pop hunched over in defeat. He walked with Dan toward the cluttered cubbyhole he used as an office with the air of someone heading to an execution.

Jett reached Kat's side in record time and pointed toward the men. "What's this all about?"

She took a step back. "I don't know. They have business to discuss."

He crossed his arms. "Did you get Dan involved in your petty little complaints against me?"

"I did not." She locked eyes with him and said nothing more.

Jett visibly relaxed. "I'm afraid you and I have gotten off on the wrong foot. How about we grab a bite to eat after your shift so we can get to know each other better? I picked up some information on Soaring Star that might help you."

"No thanks."

"You want to win, don't you? I might be able to pull a few strings with the group in charge of the whole shebang. I know for a fact people with connections are always the ones who come out on top."

She shook her head. "I'll pass. Shawn's been working with me. He knows how Soaring Star works."

"Shawn doesn't have the contacts I do."

"You know what? I don't care. And by the way, my shift is over. Pop's busy at the moment, so I guess you're in charge."

"Don't be so stubborn. I'm only trying to help."

Kat pulled off her apron and tossed it on a table. "See you tomorrow."

And as much as she longed to hang around until Mac finished his meeting with Pop, Kat marched out the front door.

Really, Jett? Enough is enough.

Chapter Twenty-Three

Dan emptied folders from a couple of chairs in Pop's office so they could sit. A look around the Lilliputian space made him grimace. A hoarder's dream. Piles of paper covered every square inch of the desktop. Books, photographs, and memorabilia from years of coaching Little League baseball were shoved haphazardly on a bookcase the size of a postage stamp. Cardboard boxes lined the floor filled with God only knew what. Dan remembered how his mother used to come in once a week to organize and tidy up Pop's office. Now it burst at the seams with debris, and who knew what might be hiding in the mess? There could be a thriving colony of brown recluse spiders in those boxes hosting a dating service to hatch new citizens. Dan shuddered at the thought.

"Have you considered cleaning your office? It looks pretty shabby."

"I don't spend much time sitting around in it, so why worry?"

Dan could bring up several reasons, but today he had bigger fish to fry. "Your accountant called me. He said he's left you several messages about receipts and expenses not adding up, but you never called back."

"I haven't had time, Danny. We're busy around here, you know."

"Exactly. It is busy here, so why is cash flow a problem? Business seems to have picked up a lot. Yet still there are deficits. I don't understand."

"Beats me. You'll need to talk to Jett. I let him handle the books because I can't make heads or tails out of those fancy reports the accountant wants me to use."

"Doesn't Jett show you the expense sheets after he fills them out? Or at least discuss them with you? Do you ever ask him any questions?" Exasperation sharpened Dan's voice.

Pop sat up stiff as a ramrod and fisted his hands. "Daniel, I'll thank you to keep a civil tongue in your head and remember who you're talking to."

"I'm sorry, Pop." Chastened, Dan took a moment to breathe. "Look, it's a big job to run a business. Has the restaurant become too much for you? Do you want to sell?"

"Sell my restaurant? This is all I have left. Even if I wanted to, I couldn't afford to let it go."

"Once we get things straightened out, I'll gladly do whatever I can to help. I still owe you plenty."

Pop's indignant expression softened as he concentrated on thumbing through the papers on his desk. "You don't owe me anything. It was your mother's dream for you to be a doctor. She was so proud of you."

"Medical school costs a lot. Add that expense to the bills after Mom got sick. I know you're in over your head."

"I don't regret it one bit, and I don't want to talk about this anymore. It'll work itself out. We're getting more customers all the time."

"The accountant says there should already be enough money coming in for the business to be profitable, yet…it's not. That's something we need to fix, or you could be facing bankruptcy."

"For your information, Jett and I do talk about the books. Accountants? They only care about crunching numbers and don't consider the way real life works. Every business has ups and downs. This is just a little hiccup, and it'll straighten out soon. I've been running this place for decades and you act like I hide my head in a sack. So far, I haven't seen any reason to ask questions."

Dan could feel his patience slipping away once more. "Isn't what the accountant said reason enough?"

Pop snorted. "I told you how it is. What else do you want me to do? Jett's been a good manager. He took over for me when I needed to be with your mom, so I wouldn't have to worry. He made improvements to the way we operate. I don't want to piss him off and have him walk away."

"Even if he sexually harasses your female employees?" Might as well get it all out in the open.

"What are you talking about?" Pop's face looked like he'd swallowed a truckload of cayenne.

"He makes suggestive remarks to your female employees."

"Who told you that?"

Best not to throw Kat under the bus. She'd been hurt enough already. "Several women have commented on his behavior. Don't you wonder why you have a problem keeping waitresses? We're lucky no one has filed a complaint against him…yet."

"You're making too much of this. Jett's a throwback from years ago. He's like the guys I grew up with. They were always making stupid remarks because they were trying to be funny. It doesn't mean anything."

"I beg to differ. Jett isn't trying to be funny. And he doesn't stop at comments. He has no business touching anyone without their consent."

"Okay. All right." Pop held up his hands in surrender. "I'm too busy to hear any more of this lecture. I'll talk to Jett. About the books and about…this other business."

"If you want me to be there with you, I will."

Pop bristled. "Are you trying to say I can't handle my own employees?"

"No." Dan reminded himself to hold his temper in check. "I just don't want you to ignore the problem."

"I won't, and if we're so free about nosing into other people's business, I have a few things to ask you. Looks to me like Ava's in the picture again. You haven't crawled back into bed with her, have you?" Pop folded his arms and waited. The fuse to his ire had obviously been lit.

"What kind of a question is that? Of course not."

"Then why did you and she leave together? Looks damn suspicious to me."

"She was drunk and needed help. I couldn't in good conscience let her stay here and create a problem or drive off alone and end up killing somebody."

Pop harrumphed. "How long are you going to take responsibility for your ex-wife? It doesn't make sense. You two are divorced, aren't you?"

"All I did was do Nashville a favor by keeping Ava off the road. Then I called her treatment coordinator and reported her relapse. Other than that, nothing else went on between us but several ugly arguments."

"It still looks bad, especially when even a blindfolded man could see there's somebody right in front of your nose you keep shoving away."

"Are you talking about Kat? She's wrapped up in music, just like Ava was. I won't put myself through something like that again."

"How can you compare the two of them? I sure wouldn't mistake Ava and Kat for twins."

"The point is they're both ambitious women. It's hard *not* to compare them." He knew Pop had a point, but he couldn't bring himself to take a chance, no matter what his heart whispered. "Believe it or not, I know what I'm doing. Now, before this conversation deteriorates even more, I've got some news for you, something I hope will make you happy."

Curiosity swiftly replaced resentment and Pop stopped arguing. Distraction worked wonders with patients. With parents too. "What is it?" Pop rumbled, his voice still rough with the embers of anger.

"I've given it my best effort, but the truth is ER medicine just isn't for me. A position in dementia research is available at the hospital, and I applied." He swallowed. "I know the sacrifices you made to send me to medical school, and I know how much it pleased you to talk about your son, the doctor. I hope this doesn't disappoint you."

For the first time since the discussion began, the lines on Pop's face smoothed. "I've never been disappointed in you, Danny. Your mother wouldn't be either. If a change makes you content, then do it." He scratched a day's worth of whiskers on his chin. "You'll still be a doctor, won't you?"

"Absolutely, but it'll mean less money. I won't be able to help as much with the debt you've taken on, at least for a while, but I'll do my best."

"Listen to me, son. The money you make is yours, not mine or anyone else's, including a daffy ex-wife. Do what you want and don't worry so much about other people's opinions."

"What I want is to find a cure."

This time, tears spilled from Pop's eyes. He wiped them away with his sleeve. "Dementia stole your mom's memory and her personality. Then it took her life and sent me straight to hell. I worry every day one of you boys might end up going down the same path. If you can find a cure, nothing in the world would make me happier."

Dan put his arm around Pop. "You okay?"

"I need a nap, but otherwise, I'm all right." Pop pulled away. "I'm getting too old to fret about stupid little things that don't amount to a hill of beans. All that concerns me now is for you and Shawn to be settled and content."

"Don't worry over anything, Pop. Just love us. It's all we both really need."

Pop sniffed. "You ought to know by now family is everything to me." He pulled a handkerchief from his pocket and blew his nose loudly.

Dan hadn't seen his father cry since the funeral. A lump hardened in his throat. "Let me know how it goes with Jett. And slow down a little, old man. Get your checkup scheduled, will you? Some extra B-12 might make you feel a lot better."

"Yeah, yeah. Are we done yet? I need to get back out on the floor."

"We're done. Thanks, Pop."

Pop grabbed Dan's sleeve. "Danny, please do your old man a favor. Will you stop letting Ava's crap keep you from finding somebody to love? Happiness doesn't come around very often, and it sure doesn't last forever. Don't wait too long to find it."

Chapter Twenty-Four

With grocery bags clutched in each hand—she really must put a hand cart on her shopping list—Kat stuck her key in the lock. Shawn trooped from his apartment as her door clicked open.

"Need any help?"

"Thanks, but I've got it." The door swung open. "Can you come in for a minute?"

"Always." He stepped across the hall and followed her inside.

Charlie materialized from the bedroom to meow a delighted greeting. Shawn picked him up. "I miss this guy. He's nice to hang out with. We're buddies—and just in case you don't know, he loves tuna."

Kat put her bags on the counter. "Charlie loves everything edible. And he doesn't mind being spoiled either." She chuckled as the tabby butted his head against Shawn's chest and amped up his purr to high gear. "Are you coming to Pop's tonight?"

"You bet I am. And not only will I be there, but Dylan's coming with me too."

"Well, it's about time. I can't wait to see him again."

"We figured it'd be good for him to watch you during a live performance. He'll be able to spot areas where you need to improve before the competition."

"I hadn't thought about it, but I guess that makes sense."

"His idea. During Soaring Star, you'll be in front of an audience *and* judges. Evaluating how you come across to them is important."

"You're not still worried about introducing Dylan to Pop, are you?" She kept her words light but gentle.

Shawn focused on Charlie. "I've decided I can't bury my relationships forever. If Pop disowns me, he disowns me."

"You sound very Zen. Like a philosopher."

"I'm not a philosopher, but I am trying to stop hiding."

"I think Pop will surprise you." She gave him a hug and went to the kitchen. "I need to put these things away before they start melting. Can you and Dylan meet me at Pop's early and help with set up?"

"Will do," he said and put down Charlie. The cat shook his head vehemently, causing the bell on his collar to jingle. "I'm on my way to Dylan's now. We've got a few errands to run. See you later, kiddo." Shawn closed the door behind him.

"Aww, Charlie. Don't be upset. Your friend had to leave, but I got you some treats." She rattled a small bag.

This news grabbed the feline's attention. Kat tore open the bag, and Charlie sat up like a dog ready to beg. He swallowed the morsel whole and then pawed her hand for more. A firm rap at the door kept her cat from getting another bite. *Shawn must have forgotten to tell me something.* "Coming," she called and pulled the door wide open.

Miss Stenger stood at the threshold, her arms akimbo and her face scrunched together in a portrait of suspicion. Charlie trotted toward her.

Busted!

"Exactly as I thought. The woman who called me was right. You're in violation of your lease. And you straight-faced lied to me about having an animal in this apartment."

Kat gulped, trying to come up with a new and more convincing lie. *Watching Charlie for a friend?* Somehow, she didn't think Miss Stenger would buy it. As the wheels turned in her head, Charlie wandered closer to the landlady. The woman stepped back and glared at him. Then she sneezed.

"Bless you," Kat said. The phrase left her mouth automatically.

Miss Stenger sneezed again. "Get that animal away from me. How deceitful. You not only hid a pet, but you also obviously vacuumed before I got there to inspect. Otherwise, I'd have known a cat was here. I'm allergic to them."

Charlie meowed, and Kat scrambled to scoop him into her arms. "I am so sorry. Listen, Miss Stenger, Charlie really is a good boy and we've been together for years. He hasn't created any problem here at all, and I promise he won't. I'll pay extra rent every month to keep him. Can he stay? Please?"

Another sneeze. Miss Stenger pulled a handkerchief from her pocket and blew her nose. "No tenant is allowed to have a pet."

"Is there someone else I can talk to about this?"

"There's no one else. I'm in charge, and there are no exceptions to the rules."

"What can I say to change your mind?"

"You heard me. Nothing is going to change my mind."

"Why are you being so stubborn about this?" Kat did her best to keep her voice steady and pleasant. "You won't even know he's here."

"I'll know he's here, and if I let you break the rules, everyone else will think they can too."

"But—"

The woman stopped Kat by holding up her hand. "I'm giving you notice. Get rid of him immediately."

"But where? There's no place for Charlie to go."

"I imagine you can take him wherever it is you decide to move."

"Wait. What did you say?"

"You've violated the terms of your lease, so I'm evicting you just as I said I would. You've got thirty days. The cat needs to go immediately."

"How am I supposed to find another place to live in thirty days?" Despite the situation, a thought almost made her break out in a nervous giggle. *Who, what, why, where, when, how.* She'd just asked every question a story…or a song needed to answer. She wanted to turn it into a joke, but Miss Stenger didn't appear to have a sense of humor.

"I'm afraid that's your problem, not mine. Ah-choo!" Sniff. "I plan to file the paperwork today. I'd suggest you start packing your things." Miss Stenger turned and stormed from the apartment amidst a hurricane of sneezes.

"Oh, no. This is not good, Charlie."

He pushed the top of his head against her chin in sympathetic solidarity.

"Now what do we do? We're practically homeless."

She mulled over Miss Stenger's comment. Who could have ratted her out? Kat never had any problem with her neighbors. Wait. Neighbors? A fuzzy image appeared, and she processed the thought until it became crystal clear. The evening she met Ava, she'd noticed something familiar about her. It wasn't middle school nonsense at all. She'd seen Ava in the hall near the apartment, on the day Kat had dragged home supplies for Charlie. At first glance, she'd thought the stranger was a new neighbor. *No. It couldn't be Ava. She has no way of knowing where I live.* But in their weird codependent way, maybe Mac had mentioned Kat's apartment was right across the hall from Shawn's. She felt a sharp little jab to her heart and put Charlie down.

Crap.

She felt like screaming. Or punching a wall. Or bawling. This situation was worse than when Ruby got rear-ended. Kat went to the refrigerator, snagged a chocolate bar she'd been saving for Shawn, and shoved a chunk into her mouth. Charlie stared at her.

"I know, I know. I'm eating my feelings."

Under her cat's judgey scrutiny, she threw the rest of the bar into the trash and hardened her mouth. There wasn't any help for it now. She'd have to figure out something. In the meantime though, she wouldn't let this situation wreck her performance at Pop's. Who knew what might come of it? This could be the big night. She might be one song away from being discovered and then none of this craziness would matter at all. An errant question strayed into her mind.

Would Mac show up tonight? Ha! A snort-laugh followed the thought. He wouldn't be there. He'd likely be far too busy giving Ava more ammunition to use against an upstart singer—one who'd made him feel like a fool.

But he has done things to help me. She disarmed the hopeful speculation right away and reminded herself where Mac centered his attention. Who in their right mind wanted to compete with something like that?

"Okay," she told Charlie. "I feel better now. I'm going to suck it up and get ready for my gig."

A text pinged from Shawn.

On our way. C U soon.

At least he'd be there to support her. And Dylan too. Despite Miss Stenger's callous attitude, Kat decided to ignore the woman's order until later. She'd put everything from her mind except getting to Pop's on time and giving the performance of her life, just in case it mattered to anyone else.

And as far as getting rid of her cat, uh-uh. She'd already been evicted. What else could the landlady do? She certainly wouldn't sneak in to snatch Charlie away—Miss

Stenger would sneeze her head off. Kat and Charlie would leave the apartment the same way they'd arrived.

Together.

Chapter Twenty-Five

At Pop's, cars surged into the lot on the way to filling all the empty spaces. Kat looked for Shawn's car but didn't see it, so she parked Ruby in front of the restaurant entrance and texted him. Moments later, he and Dylan showed up to help her unload.

"Hi, guys," she said. "I really appreciate this."

"It's going to be a full house," Dylan said. "We'll be right up in front taking notes to go over with you later."

"I think it'll be a great night." Shawn hauled a box from the back of her car. "Pop said he had a lot more requests for table reservations than usual."

"Hmm, I hope so."

Shawn, his arms full of speakers, elbowed her. "You seem a little off this evening. Is everything okay?"

"I had another run-in with Miss Stenger today. I'll tell you about it tonight."

"That old crank? Don't let her get you down. She gives everybody a hard time."

"I couldn't agree with you more." Kat decided not to explain how she'd already crossed way past the line of being given a hard time.

Once all her equipment had been set up on stage and her guitar tuned, she realized every table in the restaurant had been filled. Nice. Others stood at the bar and in the back of the room. Pop came over and gave her a thumbs-up of encouragement. "It's shaping up to be a sensational night. Are you ready?"

"I am." She smiled and took her guitar to the stool on stage. The restaurant lights dimmed, and the stage lights flicked on. After taking a moment to center herself, she pushed the day's events away and leaned toward the mic. "Hello everybody. My name's Kat Becker. Let's have us a little fun tonight, shall we?" Applause followed. "Okay, then. This song is the first one I ever performed, so it's kind of sentimental to me. I'm going to try real hard not to cry." Then, knowing she'd led the crowd to expect a ballad, she launched into a lightning-fast number. Squeals sounded and groups of people rushed to the dance floor. During the chorus, Kat stopped playing guitar and clapped until she had everyone clapping along with her.

She interspersed fast songs with slow ones, and the audience showed their appreciation by ensuring the floor stayed tight with people two-stepping or swaying to the music. The evening felt like an utter triumph as she finished her first set of songs and announced a short break.

Shawn's grin said it all. "The sound is fantastic, and the way you engage the audience is perfect. Comfortable and friendly. Exactly what you need to do."

She looked around. "Where's Dylan?"

"Restroom break. He'll be right back."

"Did you introduce him to Pop yet?"

Shawn colored. "I did."

"Well, don't keep me in suspense. How'd it go?"

"It's hard to tell. Pop's voice was softer than usual, but he gets quiet when he's busy, and tonight he's definitely busy."

She fanned herself. "I need to get some water before the next set. I'm a little dry."

"No beer. You don't need to burp into the mic during your next song."

"I know." She couldn't help but laugh at the image as she walked toward the bar. Well-wishers stopped her to chat along the way and a few others waved.

When she'd almost reached the counter, a man's voice called out her name.

She turned, prepared to greet another fan, and then froze. "Mac," she said. "What are you doing here?"

"Pop told me you were singing. I decided to come." He closed the distance between them.

"Oh." Astounded as she was to see him, she still beamed unabashedly. "Why didn't you sit with Shawn?"

"He has his friend with him. I didn't want to barge in on their evening." His expression could melt steel. "Have you got a minute?"

"I sure do," she said.

He led her to a small table and they both took a seat. "You sound great tonight. It's clear you're getting more comfortable with what you do. I can tell by the way you handle people."

"Thanks. I guess I am more relaxed than I was at first. I only hope it pays off."

"If you're sure that's what you want, I hope so too."

She watched his face. "Are you alone?"

"Yes. I was hoping we could talk after you're finished. There are some things I'd like to explain."

Things like you and Ava are back together? "Maybe. It depends on whether Shawn and Dylan want to do a debriefing tonight on my performance or talk about it later. They're going to help me figure out what changes I should make for the competition."

Mac put his hand over hers. "I don't think you should change a single thing."

He pulled her closer, and she held her breath, not sure how she should feel about this. Was he going to kiss her? Should she let him? She leaned closer, waiting to find out the answer to both questions.

"There you are." Ava banged against the table.

Kat pushed away from Mac faster than a repelling magnet.

He glowered in the direction of his ex. "I said Pop's was off-limits for you."

Ava laughed. "When have you ever been the boss of me?"

Not again. Kat stood. "If you'll excuse me, I'll let you two figure this out."

Ava shot a withering look at her. "Stay away from my husband."

"Excuse me?" Both Kat's hands went to her hips.

"I said stay away from Dan. He and I are getting back together."

"Ava, that's not true and you know it." Mac's voice rose.

Kat's face scorched and she could hear her heart pound. "Let me tell you something…Ava. Whatever happens between you and him doesn't concern me, but you need to stay out of my business. I don't even know you, and for some reason your aim is to create problems in my life. Well, congratulations. Thanks to your interference, I've been evicted from my apartment. You've done enough damage, so I'd advise you to steer clear of me."

The shot in the dark paid off. Ava didn't look surprised, nor did she deny the accusation. Kat noticed people turning in their direction to stare, so she stalked away from the table with as much dignity as she could commandeer. "Water, please," she said to the barmaid, a woman who must be a new hire.

While she waited, somebody snaked an arm around her waist. "More trouble with Ava?" Jett asked. "She's a bad trip in action. Looks like Dan wants to keep her around though." His arm tightened.

Oh no you don't. Without another thought, Kat jerked away from him, spun around, and punched Jett square on the nose. He yelped, and both hands flew to his face. Blood seeped from between his fingers and she smiled grimly. She wished she had knocked him into next week.

Moments later, Mac appeared at her side. Without a glance to Jett, he stared at Kat. "Are you all right?"

"Yes." She flexed her fingers, and her hand began to throb. "Okay, maybe my knuckles hurt a little."

"You hit me." Jett's fingers muffled his voice.

"Yes, she did." Mac took a step toward Jett. "And if you don't get the hell out of here, the next punch will come from me."

"Knock his block off, Dan!" Someone hollered over the commotion. The voice sounded a lot like Shawn's.

A drop of blood spotted Jett's white shirt. He twisted around to beat a hasty retreat in the restroom's direction while Kat rubbed her hand.

Mac took her arm and led her through the crowd that had gathered. He called to Pop, "Would you bring me a towel and some ice?"

When they got inside Pop's office, he examined her fingers. Pop hurried in with the compress and Mac pressed it against her hand. "Feel any better?"

She glimpsed Pop's face. "I'm so sorry. This isn't a good excuse, but I've had a really bad day."

"It's all right Kat," he said. "Jett got what he deserved. I guess I should have sent him packing a long time ago. It's just getting harder each year to handle everything."

"I'll help you, Pop. Try not to worry." Mac kept his gaze locked on his father's.

"Thanks, son." Pop pulled a handkerchief from his pocket and mopped his forehead. "I need to get back out there. Will you be able to play, Kat? If not, we can cancel."

"I can do it. Just give me a few minutes."

Pop's face wrinkled with concern as he left them in the office.

"Are you sure about this? It doesn't look like you broke anything, but it wouldn't hurt to get an X-ray."

She clenched and released her fingers a couple of times. "No, I'll be fine."

"I'm sorry, Kat. Ava told me what she did."

"She admitted it?"

"Yes, and I'm afraid it's my fault she knew where to find you. Ava heard me talking to Shawn on the phone and put two and two together. She snooped around near his place looking for something she could use against you. When she saw you bring in supplies for Charlie, she remembered Shawn once told her the complex had a no pet policy. Ava called the landlady, hoping to get you thrown out."

"Why should she give a rip about me? What did I ever do to her?"

"Ava is under the impression…" Mac stopped to clear his throat. "That you and I are an item."

"Oh? What makes her think so?" This new and fascinating territory helped Kat forget the dull ache in her fingers.

"She told me she senses there's something between us."

"What did you say?"

"I didn't answer her. I just gave her cab money and told her she had to leave."

Absolute deflation. He'd chosen to say nothing. An answer of sorts—but not one she much appreciated. "Mac, I like you. I really do. But it's clear there's still something going on between you and Ava."

"All I feel for her is a sense of responsibility. She's hammered it into me for years."

"Why? You're divorced."

"It's a long story. Just know that I—"

The door banged open. Shawn, his face whiter than she'd ever seen it, shouted, "Dan, hurry! Pop passed out."

Kat raced from the office on Mac's heels. Behind the bar, they found Pop sprawled faceup. The ruddy color of his cheeks had paled to gray. He was obviously unconscious. Mac dropped to his knees, felt for a pulse, and began CPR.

Within minutes, sirens approached. Someone must have called 911. She stood with her hands over her mouth, watching as Mac gave firm and steady chest compressions. When the first responders burst through the door, Shawn and Dylan shooed customers out of the way to create a path. Pop's eyelids fluttered open—thank goodness—and Mac helped lift his father onto the gurney. Mac jogged alongside them toward the ambulance, holding his father's hand. He said a few words to one of the attendants as they loaded the gurney and then he climbed into the vehicle. Lights on and sirens screaming, they sped away.

Shawn spoke to Dylan, then bolted out the door. Kat stood rooted in place. Dylan put his hand on her shoulder. "Shawn said to cancel the rest of the show. We'll help staff close up, and then he wants you to meet them at the hospital. Shawn has the car. Do you mind dropping me off at home first?"

"I don't mind." She paused. "Dylan, do you think he'll be okay?"

He patted her hand. "I hope so."

A lump of dread settled like an anchor in her chest as they evacuated the restaurant. Just turning off lights and locking doors would be enough for tonight. Cleanup could wait. Dylan and Kat tossed her equipment in the car and she drove like a maniac to Dylan's townhouse. He didn't speak. A spill of emotion kept her silent too. When Kat braked in front of his building, Dylan squeezed her arm before he got out of the car. Tears prickled at the back of her eyes and she swallowed a sob before flooring it to the hospital, more terrified about Pop's condition than the speed limit. The stars must have been properly aligned. No police car attempted to pull her over.

She passed through the emergency room entrance, dragging her feet with dread as if a ball and chain had been attached to her ankles. A nurse pointed toward the emergency room waiting area where she found Mac and Shawn sitting side by side. Shawn's eyes were shiny, but Mac stared at the wall, his expression blank. She crept toward them, hoping they wouldn't feel she was intruding on their family's crisis. On the other hand, she couldn't bear the idea of going home and flipping out with worry.

Shawn looked up as she walked toward them. "Kat, I'm glad you're here."

"Everything's taken care of at the restaurant, so don't fret about that. Any news on Pop?"

"Nothing yet," Shawn said. "I wish they'd get out here and tell us something."

Mac's bleak silence scared her more than Shawn's obvious distress. "Surely, they'll talk to you. Why don't you go back there and find out what's going on?"

He turned toward her. "In this situation, I'm family, not a doctor. Those are the rules. I imagine someone will be out soon."

She wanted to ask what he thought but feared his response. Nervousness kept her on her feet. "Can I get you both some coffee?"

"Please," Mac said.

It felt good to do something besides pace around the room. She scurried to a coffeepot in the waiting area and filled two Styrofoam cups with black coffee. Cream? Sugar? Sweetener? Who knew? She stuffed her pockets with a little of everything, along with lids and stir sticks, then plodded back to the men without spilling a drop. She'd been gone for several minutes, but they didn't appear to have moved at all.

Kat held out the cups. Neither wanted anything but black coffee, so she arranged the other offerings on a table by the sofa—just in case—and took a seat. Shawn sipped his drink while Mac moved his own cup from one hand to the other as if he didn't know what to do with it. The tiny kernel of guilt she'd been nurturing since Pop's collapse matured into full bloom. This entire incident was her fault. If she hadn't lost her temper and punched Jett, Pop wouldn't have been upset enough to…A tear spilled from the corner of her eye. She turned her head so no one would see it. Even though Jett deserved what he got, she should have been an adult and exercised self-control, rather than behaving like…Kat.

She tried to brush off her regret and fought an urge to apologize. This wasn't the time to turn attention to herself.

All that mattered was Pop. She waited with the men and kept her mouth shut, except for the prayer she mouthed silently. *Let him be okay. Please, please, let him be okay!*

After what felt like at least two centuries, a nurse appeared and called for the McDonald family. Mac and Shawn rose. Shawn grabbed Kat's hand and pulled her to her feet. "Come on," he whispered. "You're like family as far as I'm concerned."

She glanced at Mac, who nodded once. With his approval, she followed them to bay three and brushed past a curtain surrounding the bed. Hope widened her eyes. Pop was fully awake, and he looked one hundred percent better than he had earlier. The heft of a pickup truck ascended off her back.

A doctor at the computer looked up. "Dan, your father had what appears to be a mild heart attack. He's going to need a couple of stents. We'll keep him overnight and do the procedure first thing in the morning. He should be fine, although I told him he needs to slow down and take life a lot easier."

"Thanks, Ted."

Mac obviously knew him. Then she shook her head. *Of course. They worked at the same hospital.*

Pop fretted with the blanket covering him like he couldn't get comfortable. "And who's going to run my restaurant if I have to slow down?"

Guilt pinged Kat again. Pop ill and Jett gone. Who *would* run the business?

"Let's not worry about that right now," Mac said quietly. "First things first. How are you feeling?"

"Better. Better yet when we get this nonsense taken care of. I've been so blasted tired lately. Doc here says it's because my heart's not getting enough blood flow. He says I'll do great once the stents are in."

"I see. Well, I have confidence in Dr. Anthony's assessment."

A nurse bustled in. "We've got a room ready for you, Mr. McDonald."

"Do you want us to stay with you tonight?" Shawn's forehead furrowed in rows of concern.

"Nah. I just want to sleep. Y'all go on home. I'll see you in the morning."

Kat went over and pecked a kiss on Pop's stubbled cheek. "Don't you go scaring us witless like this again, you hear?"

Pop reached for Kat's hand. "Sorry to ruin your big night."

"Cross that off your list right now and buck up, buster. You're in for a ton of attention during the time it takes to get well. Milk this moment while you can." It gratified her to see him laugh.

"Good night, Pop." Mac touched his father's shoulder.

Shawn bent to hug Pop as best he could around lines attached to beeping equipment. "See you tomorrow."

Kat pushed aside the curtain around Pop's bed and walked away in case they needed to say things that weren't meant for her ears. Shawn and Mac's footsteps followed behind. She turned to say, "Everything's locked up, and I drove Dylan home."

"Thanks," Shawn said. "We appreciate your help."

Mac kneaded the back of his neck. "Shawn, I want to stay at your place tonight. You're closer to the hospital than I am."

"Sounds like a plan."

A yawn escaped Kat. "I don't know about you guys, but all of a sudden, I feel like I could sleep for a week."

"My car's still at Pop's. Kat, would you take me over to get it?" Mac's voice went brisk and businesslike.

"I can drive you—" Shawn closed his mouth when Mac shot him a dark look.

Her radar said Mac wanted to talk, and her radar seldom failed her. With a renewed sense of hope and a lighter heart at Pop's prognosis, she couldn't help teasing Mac the same way he had his brother. "I think you're the one who's subtle as a sardine sandwich. Of course I'll take you."

He rewarded her comment with a rare but very sweet Keanu Reeves-style grin.

Chapter Twenty-Six

S tars twinkled in brilliant abundance across a velvet sky. The moon sat low on the horizon, which made it look huge and close enough to touch. Away from the neon of downtown, nighttime appeared sweeter and vastly more mysterious. Mac had suggested Kat drive to Centennial Park rather than to his car. She hadn't argued.

"I'd like to sit outside in the quiet for a while and decompress, unless you're too tired," he'd said.

Tired? Who's tired? "I don't know why, but all at once, I'm wide awake. Let's do it." Exhaustion from the day's events vanished as she carefully pulled Ruby into a spot near the lake and turned off the ignition.

"Come on, Kat. There's a bench." He climbed out of the car.

She followed him and then perched on a seat facing the lake. He leaned back and stretched his legs out, an arm resting casually on the bench behind her shoulders. Other than an occasional distinct roar of an engine or horn honk, the evening was so quiet the buzz, whirr, and click of night bugs surrounded them. Songs of the night.

"I sure am glad to know Pop's going to be okay," she said, finally breaking the silence between them.

"Me too. They'd have said so if there was anything more than the normal risks a person his age has facing surgery. And Dr. Anthony's the best."

"If Pop has to cut down on his workload, what'll happen with the restaurant?"

"I don't know. Frankly, I'm not ready to tackle that problem yet." He turned to face her. "What about you? Have you considered what you're going to do about a place to live?"

His comment whipped up a surge of stomach-churning anxiety. She'd forgotten about her predicament, at least for a few minutes. "I haven't had time to think about it, but I'll be on the prowl in the morning to find out."

"You could always go home to Kansas City."

She frowned at the remark. "What a strange thing to say. I came here for a purpose, and I'm not giving up."

"Settle down, Kat. It was only a thought." He tilted his head back. "Look at the sky. It's brilliant tonight."

She admired the celestial display. It looked like what her father called a harvest moon. Peeking at Mac, she smiled. Commentary on the sky wasn't what she expected from a sobersides type like him. She'd read a full moon could make people do and say crazy things. Could he have fallen victim? She threw out a subtle suggestion to test her theory. "When the moon looks like this—bright enough to cast shadow—it makes me feel like grabbing somebody and dancing."

"The sun is the sun, but the moon cycles and changes. I could stare at it for hours." He took a deep breath, and she waited for him to take her into his arms so she could sing them into a slow and sexy country swing dance. Instead, he coughed. "Well, I guess we ought to go."

Dang. "Wait a minute. I'm sure you didn't want to come here just to gaze at the moon for five minutes. Is there something on your mind?"

"I needed a moment to clear my head. There are a few things I should say, but I doubt this would be the best time to do it. Why don't we head back to your apartment?"

"I thought you wanted to get your car."

"Shawn can take me tomorrow."

Clearly, the anxiety of Pop's situation had shaken Mac more than she'd realized. "Something's bugging you. Why don't you get it off your chest?"

"You sure you want to hear my troubles?" He held out his hand. "If so, let me drive. It's easier to talk when I'm occupied."

"Have at it." She handed him her keys.

They got into her car. Mac adjusted the driver's seat and turned the ignition. He guided Ruby from the lot to the road. "You must think I've lost my mind."

"Not at all. You had a big shock today. It's understandable you're not yourself."

"True, but issues have been fighting it out in my head for a while. It all seemed to start right around the time I met you."

"Oh?" *Now we're getting somewhere.* "Tell me."

"First let's settle something. I know you believe Ava and I are still involved with each other." He turned the steering wheel. "And you're right. We are."

Her stomach dropped to her knees. "You are?"

"But not the way you think. Can I start from the beginning?"

"Please." She swiveled her head to watch him and waited.

"I met Ava when I was in medical school, just getting ready to start my residency. She was softer back then. Affectionate. Pleasant. She helped me when I was operating on only a few hours of sleep at night. Things like picking up at my condo and bringing over a decent meal. I felt grateful. Before I knew it, gratitude turned into habit. I gave her a key and I'd find her waiting for me when I dragged in from work. From time to time we shared a bed. A few months later, she told me she was pregnant."

Kat widened her eyes. "You do know how getting pregnant works, don't you, Doctor?"

"Don't be a smartass. She told me she took birth control pills and said she'd forgotten to refill them."

"Interesting. Do go on."

"Long story short, we visited a justice of the peace. I didn't tell my family why we married. It seemed like the right thing to do."

"Very noble of you. Then what?"

"I was tied up at the hospital all hours of the day and night. Ava got sick of me working so much. She begged for us to go out and party during my off time. She wanted to dance and drink and have fun singing Karaoke whenever she could. All I wanted to do was sleep, so after I went to bed, she started to go out alone."

"She went out to party? Wasn't she pregnant?"

"Yes, but it didn't stop her. Foolhardy as hell, that's Ava. I told her she had to be careful—what she did could harm the baby—but she didn't listen. She miscarried when she was four months along. A little boy. We named him Johnny."

Tears welled in Kat's eyes. "Oh, how awful. I'm sorry."

"Ava blamed me for what happened. She said if I'd been home more, she wouldn't have had to find comfort somewhere else. She said I killed our son." He flinched as he spoke, like each word hammered him.

"It isn't your fault she chose to do the things she did."

"Maybe not. Maybe so. I don't know anymore. Anyway, her drinking became more problematic. We fought all the time over it. Then she met a guy who told her he could help her with a singing career. I said she'd be better off working on her problems…our problems. She made her choice. Ava ran off with the guy who said he'd help her, and I filed for divorce."

"Oh, wow." Her words were inadequate, but what could she say to alleviate the self-reproach Mac heaped on himself?

"I know. It's a nasty story, isn't it?"

"It tells me a lot about the kind of person you are."

"That I'm an unfeeling monster?" He shifted in the seat. "Or so Ava's informed me."

"You're not unfeeling at all. Maybe you feel too much. Besides, if Ava thinks you're a monster, why's she sticking around? And what happened to the man she ran off with?"

"He left her. To Ava, I'm security. If she has a problem, she calls me. If I balk, she brings up Johnny." He kept his tone flat.

"There's a term for what she's doing—emotional blackmail." Kat found it hard to wrap her head around all the things he'd told her. "But if you keep letting her get away with it, she'll think you still care about her. Is that the message you want to send?"

He shut off the car and handed her the key. "Sometimes I haven't a clue what I want."

They both got out and he helped her carry her equipment to the door. His usual swift pace had become a plodding one. She wasn't sure what else she could say to comfort him, until they reached her apartment.

"I'm still not tired, Mac. Are you?"

"Not really," he replied. "Shawn may already be in bed, but I'm too keyed up to sleep."

"Why don't you come in and watch a movie or something? Charlie would love to see you again." She didn't add she hoped Charlie's presence would shake Mac from his current funk. "Doctor's orders."

She led him into her apartment, and they placed her things near the door. Charlie bounded toward them, meowing up a storm. Mac bent to rub the cat's head and then picked him up. A contented purr sounded, and it delighted her to see the magic of an animal crinkle the corners of Mac's eyes. He'd succumbed to one of the most soothing sounds on earth. Pet therapy in action.

Feeling much more cheerful, she turned on the television and flipped through the channels until she found one playing "The School of Rock," a funny movie with plenty of good music. The perfect film to forget your worries for a while and put things into perspective.

Kat handed Mac a beer. Charlie snoozed on his lap, still purring. The cat's engine ran so loudly, she was tempted to notch the television volume higher. She claimed the vacant spot next to them and took a sip of her beer. "You've probably seen this a million times, but it suits my mood."

"Actually, I've never seen this movie."

"What? Well, settle back. You're in for a treat, my friend."

Kat began to repeat her favorite lines along with the actors, then figured she'd better let Mac watch without interrupting. But nothing could stop her from singing along to the songs. He looked at her and laughed. The sound hatched a million fireflies in her stomach.

"Your voice is louder than the guy in the band," he said.

"Oh, sorry about that. I'll tone it down."

"Nothing to apologize for. As a matter of fact, you sing better than he does. It makes me feel...I don't know. Lighter."

She pushed his arm. "Aww. A compliment instead of telling me to shut up. Thanks."

"You're welcome." He paused. "I want to tell you something. Your persistence about that research job wasn't in vain. I submitted an application."

"Seriously? Mac, that's awesome!"

"Nothing definite at all yet, but I talked to Pop and he said it wouldn't bother him if I took the job. We'll see what happens."

"They'll hire you. I know they will."

"I admire your enthusiasm, but there's quite a process to apply, and no guarantees."

"Let's cut a path through the gloom and doom. Think in terms of wonderful things ahead instead of assuming what you want won't work out."

"I've found being prepared for the worst leads to fewer disappointments."

"Oh, Mac." She shook her head at him. "Don't waste your time thinking life will knock you down. Good things do happen from time to time, you know."

He didn't seem convinced, although his eyes had a hungry look, like he wanted to believe her.

Kat took a total of one second to decide. *Why not?* She leaned toward him and pressed a soft kiss against his mouth. "See?" she said.

Only a breath later, Mac's arms went around her. He pulled her body tight against his like she was a lifeline, and her breath escaped in a small gasp. With her head pressed against his chest, she heard the swift rhythm of his heart. Her pulse galloped too. Charlie jumped to the floor and stalked away as Mac held her. It felt tunnel-of-light amazing.

"You're right," he finally said. "Good things do happen."

She lifted her head to look at him. This wasn't her first time in a man's arms, and she recognized a heavy-lidded look when she saw one. Yet a series of summer-sun tingles told her this was something new. Could the intensity be a result of the day's events? Or was it something more?

This time he took the initiative and moved his mouth toward hers. They bumped noses before he tilted his head properly and found her lips. She closed her eyes to enjoy the moment and tasted a kiss so tempting and moist and warm, it made her light-headed. He took his time and then deepened the kiss until his five-o'clock shadow scraped her skin. A swift bolt of energy zapped from her mouth down to her toes in a way unlike anything she'd experienced before. Whatever faults Dr. Daniel McDonald might have, he certainly had no problem whatsoever in the kissing department.

When he pulled back, she noticed how fast his breath came.

Her mouth curved upward, and she traced a finger across his lower lip. "Say it again…good things do happen."

"You're right. Good things *do* happen."

"Now come with me and remember this one factoid: practice makes perfect." She looped her arm around his and tugged him toward the bedroom.

Dan stroked Kat's back. Whether it had been a release from the stress of Pop's illness or some other reason, his libido had never been, well…more cooperative. He glanced at the lovely woman cuddled against him and smiled. With her gusto for life, he wasn't surprised at how eagerly she'd welcomed him into her bed, but who'd have imagined she could also be soft and gentle as an April breeze? The wild tangle of her curls and the tempting way her skin glowed made him wish to high heaven he could stay the night. *Not a good idea.* The last thing he wanted was to have his brother suspect what had happened. He wasn't sure what would sound worse. Spending a steamy night with Kat the evening before his father's surgery, or Shawn's matchmaking inclination. His brother would never let him hear the end of it.

He kissed the top of her head. "I need to go. Shawn will be wondering what happened to me."

She waved a lazy hand. "Just send him a text. He won't mind if you stay."

Dan gave the matter serious consideration. "No," he said at last. "I don't think it would be wise."

"Spoilsport." She sat up and stretched her arms.

The sight made him wonder if leaving her was the most moronic thing he'd ever done. He abruptly rose from the bed before he could change his mind and picked up his pants. He'd enjoyed being with Kat…too much. "Can I ask a question without upsetting you?"

"Sure," she said.

"Exactly how serious are you about becoming a performer? You may not know it, but Nashville is a nice place to live for many more reasons than music."

Her wide eyes met his. "You know very well I came here to pursue a career. Nothing will change that."

He reached out to cup her cheek. "This is a little hard for me to say, but I rather like being with you. Considering what just happened between us, I need to know something. Would falling in love change your plans?"

Her expression went from curious to surveying him like he'd suddenly sprouted a third eye. "Why should falling in love change anything about a person's plans?"

"Don't forget I've been through this before. The career you want has broken a lot of people. I'd hate to see you get hurt, and I'm not sure if I can handle trying to pick up the pieces again."

"No one's asking you to pick up any pieces," she said firmly. "I get the impression you're sure I'm going to fail. What if I make it?"

"What if you do? On the road all the time. In the recording studio. Working to sell records. I'll be honest. Someday soon, I hope to have a wife and children. I want normalcy."

"People in the music business aren't forbidden to have a family, you know."

"And all is cozy until something or somebody better comes along."

"You are a certified pessimist. Have you stopped to consider the possibility if we have something special, we can make it work?"

"Impossible. I care about you, but I can't put myself in a situation where there might be another crash and burn in my life. Never again."

"Music is my dream—my destiny. Just like a research job is yours. Why must you let stuff from the past ruin the chance for a wonderful future?"

What she said reminded him of Pop's lecture. The theory made sense in a purely logical way, but what happened with Ava still haunted him more than he'd like to admit. Would he ever be able to let it go? "I just can't put myself there again. If music is what you truly want, it wouldn't be right for anybody to hold you back—least of all me. Maybe someday one or the other of us will have a change in heart, but for now I think it'll be better if we don't try to move past being friends—if you're still willing to be a friend, that is."

Her shoulders, usually so straight, sagged a little. "Quite a speech, Mac. I guess we can be friends. If that's how you want it."

The evening's emotion muddied his voice. "Much as I hate to say this, it's for the best. I'm sorry about tonight. I think we both got caught up in all of this…stuff with Pop."

She looked away from him. "It's been a hard day for sure, but I get it. I don't need any distractions now anyway. Between school and the competition and finding a new apartment, I'm going to be busy."

Kat studiously avoided his gaze, and he searched for something to brighten his words. A thought popped into his mind and to his horror, flew straight out his mouth. "I have a suggestion. It could take a while to find a place that accepts cats. I've got a spare bedroom at my place. You're welcome to use it until you decide where you want to move. There's no point in trying your hide-the-cat game again."

Her eyes drew back to his, rounded like the full moon they'd earlier admired. "You're inviting me to live with you?"

A full moon. Maybe that's what brought on his unexpected offer. "I guess I am. If Ava hadn't interfered, you wouldn't be in this spot. It's the least I can do." He wiped his damp palms down his pant legs. "Don't worry. The arrangement would be strictly platonic. Two friends sharing a space. You go your way. I go mine."

Kat chewed her lip. "I don't know. Can I think about it?"

He figured she'd have declined such a ridiculous suggestion right away. Maybe he'd even counted on it. But with the offer extended, he could hardly recall his words. In fact, he wasn't lying. He did feel responsible for the problem Ava had created. He did owe Kat something.

But sharing a home with the woman who'd unwittingly chipped an opening into his heart? He swallowed and wished he'd considered the matter longer.

Chapter Twenty-Seven

Nothing moved slower than minutes while sitting in a surgical waiting room. Dan had come to the conclusion while staring at a clock on the wall. Shawn sat beside him scrolling nervously on his cell phone. They weren't the only ones in this place of fearful silence and whispered prayers. An older gentleman was near a window on the other side of the room, his knee bobbing up and down. Across from him, a young couple held hands. Tears streaked down one woman's cheek as another woman patted her shoulder. Worry radiated from each face.

He and Shawn had said their goodbyes to Pop before the nurses wheeled him away. Pop had looked pale, but his spirits were good. He even cracked a few jokes. "Don't worry. Your mother will be keeping an eye on me. If anyone has an 'in' with the Big Guy, it's her."

Shawn interrupted Dan's reflection. "How long do you think surgery will take?"

"Not long. An hour or so, unless there are complications."

"Complications? Like what?" Shawn's voice cracked as it hadn't in years.

"Let's not go there," Dan said gently. "Pop will be fine." He rose and stepped to the window. "Is Kat coming?"

"No. I asked her to, but she said it would be better if she helped at the restaurant instead of sitting here. She told me to keep her posted."

Dan hadn't heard a word from her since he left her apartment last night, not so much as a simple text message about his offer. He wasn't sure what to make of it.

"Did something happen between you and Kat last night? When I called, she hardly said two words. It wasn't like her at all."

"We just…talked. About Pop and Ava and a few other things."

Shawn's mouth opened to respond when Dan's phone vibrated. He glanced at the screen. "It's Pop's accountant."

Dan put the phone to his ear and listened to a string of instructions. He answered with a simple, "Okay," then hung up the phone and sat beside Shawn. "He wants to meet with us. Looks like he's found the source of the problem."

The news diverted them from worry into a discussion. They hypothesized guesses until both half agreed on the idea of an accounting error. Then Dr. Anthony stepped in the waiting room and brought the conversation to an abrupt halt. The doctor, still wearing his surgical scrubs and cap, lifted a hand in greeting. Dan felt weak with relief when he saw his colleague's expression.

"I've got good news," Dr. Anthony said. "Everything went well. We put in two stents. Your dad's in recovery and you can see him shortly."

"Thanks. We appreciate this, Ted." Dan shook his hand.

"My pleasure. We'll keep him overnight to be on the safe side." Dr. Anthony smiled before he left them.

"Whew!" Shawn expelled a breath. "I haven't been this scared since Mom…"

"I know. As soon as they get Pop squared away in a room, they'll tell us."

"Should we fill him in about meeting with the accountant?"

"Absolutely not. Let him focus on getting well first." Too fidgety to sit, Dan rose and shoved his hands in his pockets, pacing from one end of the room to the other.

A gray-haired woman wearing the pink uniform of a volunteer called to him. "Are you Dr. McDonald?"

"Yes," Dan said.

"You've got a message from the emergency department. They tried your cell, but you didn't answer. There's a problem, and you're needed right away."

They know Pop's scheduled for surgery. Why would they page me? "I'm not on call today."

At his abrupt tone, the woman blushed and pursed her lips together. "You were talking to Dr. Anthony when the nurse rang the desk. That's all I know."

"My apologies. I'm a bit rattled. Thanks for telling me." He turned toward Shawn. "This shouldn't take long. It's probably some administrative mix-up. Text me Pop's room number when you get it, and I'll be there soon as I can."

Relieved over the outcome of surgery, Dan paced through the hall to the elevator. As soon as he arrived in the emergency department, the receptionist clicked the door open. "Dr. McDonald, please go to bay one."

It struck him as odd he'd been called to a bay and not to the desk. An adrenalin rush of dread kicked up his heartbeat. He stepped forward and parted the curtain. Ava was in the bed with an oxygen mask on her face and an IV in her arm. Her eyes were closed, and her hair lay in damp strings on the pillow. The scent of vomit filled the room. A nurse he didn't know typed into a computer. "I'm sorry we had to page you, Dr. McDonald, but she had you listed as her emergency contact."

"What happened?" he asked.

"Alcohol overdose. She came in with a BAC of point one seven."

Dan moved to her bedside, and Ava's eyes fluttered open. "Dan?"

He took her hand. "Here I am. What have you done to yourself, Ava?"

She coughed. "I'm so tired." Her eyes closed again.

There wasn't any point in trying to speak to her now. He'd say what he had to say later when she'd sobered up. The slight rise and fall of her chest made him wonder how they'd come to this. He'd once cared for this woman. Hell, he even thought he'd spend the rest of his life with her.

Dan abruptly let go of her hand and looked at the computer screen. "What's the plan?"

"She'll be admitted for observation."

"And then?"

"I imagine a social worker will interview both of you and then make recommendations."

His mouth hardened. "Put this in your notes. Ava needs more help than she'll get from a few days in the hospital. She was just released from a residential treatment program, and she's already been arrested for a DUI. Ava and I are divorced, but her mother lives in Iowa. I can supply a phone number. I suggest the social worker call."

The nurse's eyes went wide. "All right, Dr. McDonald."

"I can give whatever factual information you need but nothing more. Tell Ava I'll touch base with her sometime tomorrow. My father just got out of surgery. I need to be with him."

It felt remarkably good to speak aloud what he'd been thinking, even if it did come off as cold. He swiveled away from the nurse and left the ER when realization hit him. He'd been nothing more than an enabler for Ava. How had he failed to recognize the fact before? Never again. He'd cut the cord that bound him to his ex, no matter what images from their past she invoked to drown him in guilt.

Dan's phone pinged with a text. He glanced at it and left the ER.

By the time he reached room 232, he found Shawn near Pop's bed, chatting about Belmont. The television mounted on the wall showed a baseball game in progress.

"Who's winning?" Dan asked.

Shawn took a sip of bottled water. "The uh…team in blue and white."

"The blasted Cubs," Pop stated. In his off time, Pop enjoyed watching baseball, often lamenting the fact Nashville had never gotten a major league franchise.

"How do you feel, old man?"

"Sore. I have to lie still for a few hours. My back hurts too."

"Don't be a tough guy. Ask for pain meds if you need them."

"Danny." Pop turned his head slightly. "They say I have to take it easy for a week or two. Who's gonna take care of the restaurant?"

"Don't worry about the restaurant. Shawn and I will deal with it. You concentrate on getting well."

Either the comment satisfied Pop, or he was too wiped out to argue. He turned his attention back to the game.

"Sit down," Shawn said. "You make me nervous just standing there."

Dan settled into a chair on the other side of the hospital bed.

"Hey, Pop," Shawn looked up. "I just got a text from Dylan. He and Kat are at the restaurant, and he says not to worry. Everything is running smooth."

"Your friend—Dylan." Pop swallowed. "He's a nice young man."

Shawn broke into a smile. "Yes, he is."

"And Kat. I like that girl a lot."

"So do I," Dan said.

Pop kept his gaze glued to the television screen. "Boys, I love you both and I want you to be happy. Whatever it takes."

Shawn looked as shocked as Dan felt at the comment. Pop had delivered a message, in his gruff, roundabout way. *Whatever it takes.*

It didn't appear a response was expected, and neither of them answered. Within a short while, Dan noticed his father's eyelids drift shut. He smoothed back Pop's thinning hair and glanced at the television screen. The at-bat player hit a home run. As the man rounded the bases, Dan thought about what he needed to do.

The next morning, clouds gathered and a light drizzle cooled the scorching temperature. Shawn and Dylan were scheduled to bring Pop home from the hospital, but Dan had driven in early to meet with the head of staff. By the time he left, he'd been granted four weeks of family leave. That was the easy part. Next, he steeled himself for the tougher assignment. A showdown with Ava.

The bed in her room had been inclined to accommodate a breakfast tray, which sat on the table in front of her. She smiled when he walked into the room. The smile faded when she got a good look at his face.

"Morning, Ava. I'm here to tell you I've given your doctor all the information he needs from me. I didn't hold back on anything. He's going to have the hospital's social worker get in touch with your aftercare counselor. In view of all that's happened, you'll probably go back to inpatient. I suggested they look into a program in Iowa, where you can be near your mom."

She pushed away her tray. "I don't want to go to Iowa. I want to stay here in Nashville with you."

"Staying with me is not an option, so I suggest you cooperate with whatever your doctor recommends. Here are the facts. I will no longer be involved in your problems. I also won't be paying for treatment or an apartment or a lawyer. I've done my penance. You'll have to make your own way now. Only you can fix your problems."

"You can't force me to leave Nashville."

"You're right. I can't. But I won't take any more calls from you. I've blocked your number from my phone. If you're near your mom, you'll have the support you need during treatment. Give her a chance. She's a good woman."

"What about everything we had together? What about our little Johnny?"

He swallowed. "I grieve his loss as much as you. Maybe more. But there's nothing we can do to change anything now. It's time for us to move on."

"This is about Kat, isn't it? I've seen the way your face changes when you look at her. I don't get it. She's a singer, and I know how you feel about singers. I bet you'll be sorry if you get involved."

"To be painfully honest, Ava, whether I'm sorry or not is none of your business. We once were married. We're not anymore. That means we're through. For good."

Ava screwed up her face like she might break into tears. She sniffed a few times instead. "This really isn't fair. That girl's so damn lucky. I wish I was."

He felt a glimmer of admiration for her. For once she hadn't shed any tears or argued or thrown a tantrum. "Ava, when you come to grips with what's happened, you'll make a new life for yourself. I wish you the best."

"Iowa, land of cornfields." She toyed with her spoon. "It's the exact opposite of the lights in Nashville."

"Getting away from here could be the best thing that ever happened to you."

She took a bite of scrambled eggs, and the corner of her mouth turned up in the shadow of a smile.

After he left her room, Dan blew out an enormous breath. Speaking an uncomfortable truth wasn't easy, but it was certainly liberating. Next on his list: the appointment with Pop's accountant. He headed from the hospital to the parking garage with a long-absent spring in his step. His thoughts on all that had happened traffic-jammed his brain as he walked to his car, until an epiphany stopped him dead in his tracks. How much time and effort had he expended in the last few years to help Ava? This morning he'd created a plan to guide his ex-wife toward what she needed, but he hadn't given half the consideration to the woman he'd fallen for.

The woman he'd fallen for?

The truth clobbered him. He'd fallen for Kat Becker—hard. And how did he show it? By being a self-centered ass and shoving her away. Why had he discounted her? Since when were Kat's desires less important than his? After the

things he'd said to her, it would be a miracle if she wanted
to hear anything from him ever again.

Man. I've really messed this up, haven't I?

Chapter Twenty-Eight

The morning of the competition, Kat's nerves rattled like a pair of dice. Shawn and Dylan had taken on the roles of judge and jury. Three times they had her stand in front of the mic to sing. On the third rendition she bumbled a chord and forgot one of the words. For some reason, she couldn't sink herself into the music.

"Why're you so stiff? What's gotten into you? Loosen up." Shawn grabbed her arms and shook her.

Dylan cocked his head to the side. "You're putting your mouth too close to the mic. Every time you sing words that start with a 'p' or 't', it amplifies the puff of air too much."

She took a step back. "You guys are making me a wreck. I appreciate your help—I really do—but maybe I should just be myself."

"Okay, okay. You're right. I think we've overdone practice." Shawn ran a hand through his hair. "Let's call it a day. You don't want to go stale or be hoarse tonight."

She put down her guitar. "Thank you. I could use a chance to recharge. It's weird how jittery I feel about this.

I keep thinking how important the contest is, and how it could change my whole life." She shook her head. "All I want to do is write my songs and sing them on stage without all the side-hustle."

"I know. Why don't you just pretend it's another night at Pop's?" Shawn picked up her sheet music. "Then you'll do fine."

She noticed a slight tremble in his hand. "It's sweet of you to worry over me. I hope I don't let you down."

Dylan chuckled. "You might feel nervous, but it doesn't show. Shawn's the one who's been biting his nails. I don't doubt for a minute you'll do a great job." He stood and stretched. "Yesterday I heard from a friend who helps with setup for the competition. He told me there are twenty semifinalists who made it through to performance round. In my opinion, you'll blow them all out of the water."

"From your mouth to God's ear." She returned Dylan's grin. A girl couldn't get luckier. What a break to have Shawn and Dylan on her side.

"I also found out they have three judges lined up, and guess what? One of them is a superstar. Pete Casson!"

Kat nearly dropped her guitar. "Pete Casson? That's Trevor T. Ray's producer. He's the one I've been trying to get in touch with ever since I got here!"

Shawn whooped and threw Kat's sheet music. It fluttered to the floor. "This is great! Don't you see? I'm sure Trevor told Pete about you, and then Pete probably watched the video. You've got this one in the bag."

Her knees went soft, so she dropped into the sofa. "I would never have thought we'd meet in a situation like this."

Shawn recovered himself and picked up the papers he'd thrown. "But it's perfect. He'll hear what you have to offer in person and without any discussion. The odds keep getting better. Listen, why don't we go ahead and pack up your things? Dylan and I will drive you to the competition, and we'll take a seat front and center to cheer you on."

"Aww," she said. "My very own groupies. I love it!"

Charlie wove his way from Dylan's ankles to Shawn's and then to Kat's lap. "Too bad you can't go, mister," she said to the animal. "You're great moral support."

Shawn sat beside her and stroked Charlie's back. "Any leads on a place to stay yet?"

"Not really, but I've been too busy to look hard. A weird thing happened though. Your brother offered Charlie and me a place to stay in his spare bedroom." She deepened her voice. "Strictly platonic of course."

"I like the idea," Shawn said. "Take him up on it."

"I second the motion," Dylan added.

"I'm not sure it would be good for us to room together. He made it a point to remind me how much he hates the music scene. It isn't very encouraging when he's opposed to everything I want."

"That's just his way. My brother can be a mule, but don't give up on him. At some point he'll come around. He has for me, in more ways than I can count."

"It isn't the same thing at all. You're his brother. I'm a random person who bulldozed her way into his life. He has no reason to change his mind about me. Anyway, until he gets Ava out of his system, I don't think he'll ever be a fan of anything reminding him of her." She rose and put her guitar in its case. "How's Pop feeling?"

"He's doing fine. Ever since he came home, he's chomping at the bit to get back to work."

"I'm glad. After the competition is over, I'll bring him dinner. He's probably bored out of his mind."

Dylan nodded. "Pop's been a little discombobulated ever since the meeting."

Shawn slapped his palm to his forehead. "Damn. We got so wrapped up in rehearsing, I forgot to tell Kat what Pop's accountant said." He turned to her. "Since I couldn't be at the meeting, I got the full lowdown from Dan."

"A meeting? What are you talking about?" Kat clicked the latches shut on her guitar case.

"Dan met with the accountant. There'd been money missing from the restaurant. Pop was sinking deeper in debt trying to keep the doors open. The accountant discovered somebody had been cooking the books and pocketing cash…a lot of it."

Shock straightened her spine. "Who would do such a thing?"

"Jett, that's who. He was the manager. Pop didn't want to deal with the headaches anymore and let him handle everything. Jett took advantage of the opportunity. After Dan made a report, he found out Jett skipped town. The police issued a warrant for felony theft."

"Good Lord," she said. "I knew he was a jerk, but I didn't think he was a thief. I guess I don't have to worry about him turning anyone from Soaring Star against me." She'd been a touch apprehensive ever since she flattened his nose about what he might say to his connections—assuming he had any.

"Yeah, pretty crazy stuff. I wouldn't worry about it, though. Soaring Star was just another one of his lines. Anyhow, my brother took a leave of absence from work. He says it'll give him the time he needs to deal with all the fallout and take care of a few personal matters…whatever that means."

"I imagine he's got a lot on his plate." Never were truer words spoken. If she knew Mac's caretaker nature, the time off would give him the ability to do more than help Pop. He'd also be—yet again—dealing with Ava's troubles, a job he obviously had no desire to end.

The dilemma of staying with Mac until she found a place of her own moved from uncertainty to a decision. Who wanted to stay in a spare room with Ava lurking in the background, the subject of whispered conversations and surprise visits? No way. She'd find a place on her own. Nashville was a big city with plenty of rentals around. It couldn't be *that* hard to get the right one.

"I'm just glad to see he'll be away from the emergency room for a while. It'll do him good." Shawn nudged Dylan. "What do you think she should wear?"

"Nothing fancy. No sparkles or spangles. Some folks do it, but for a serious competition like this, it's best to keep it simple. Jeans, boots, and a shirt in white or some other bright color so you don't fade into a dark background."

"Okeydokey." Her mind ran through the outfits she owned. "I imagine there's something in my closet."

"All right. We'll see you in a few hours, toots. Chill if you can." Shawn kissed her on the cheek.

"Thanks for everything, guys. Later."

As soon as the door closed behind them, Charlie meowed.

"I know. You're hungry." She went to the kitchen and filled his dish. "I'd keep a bowl of kibble filled all the time for you, but then you'd get big as a mountain lion."

Charlie ignored her to focus on his meal. She left him and traipsed into the bedroom to peruse her closet. Jeans were a simple matter. She pulled out a silky white blouse and a bright pink one and shook her head. Rummaging a little more, she found a pale blue denim shirt, fitted at the chest but slightly flared at the hem, so she wouldn't have to tuck it in. Okay, not white or bright, but defi-nitely…comfortable. Winner.

A guitar riff ring tone sounded on her phone. She glanced at the caller ID and picked it up. "Hello, Mother."

"Hello, darling. Are you nervous?"

"About the competition? Not really." Kat squinted. "Where are you? I hear weird background noise."

"We're at the airport. We just landed."

"Really?" Kat smoothed a wrinkle from her jeans. "Where'd you go?"

"Your father and I are here. In Nashville."

"Huh?" It was all she could think to say.

"Since we know how important this is to you, we decided to come and watch."

"You decided…what?" Kat's brain had apparently lost the ability to process words.

"We want to hear you sing. We were due for a weekend away. Nashville seemed like a good place to go, so here we are."

Kat gulped. "Am I supposed to come pick you up?"

"Oh, no. We'll rent a car, get settled in our hotel, and see you tonight. I looked up all the information online, so we know exactly where the competition is."

"How nice," Kat lied. "It'll be good to see you again."

"That's not all, darling. I have more news. Your sister and her fiancé will be there too. We all want to see what you've accomplished."

"Uh, how come no one mentioned this to me before?"

"It was a last-minute decision. We wanted to surprise you."

"Mission accomplished." She took a breath to steady herself. "Okay. I need to get some things done. We'll talk later."

Kat ended the call as Charlie sauntered into the room, licking his whiskers. "They're all coming to see me. Just what I needed." Her face felt hot, and she touched her forehead. "Could we just dial back the pressure a tiny bit?"

She'd sung to a bunch of strangers many times. It rarely fazed her. Having her family in the audience to witness what happened? That was another issue altogether. Carolyn, the epitome of success in anything she did, would be there. What a huge embarrassment if Kat didn't put on a decent performance. And her parents. What would they say when the competition ended? It could either be a sincere round of congratulations or the dreaded "I told you so." She went to the bathroom for ibuprofen. The possibilities made her temples throb.

Thank goodness for Shawn and Dylan. They might be bossy, but at least she could count on them no matter what. Her fresh state of panic allowed a final longing thought to slide into her brain. An image of the steady and unflappable Dr. Dan McDonald. His warm rumble of a laugh. The boyish way his hair drooped onto his forehead. Deep crinkles at the corners of his brown eyes. Even thinking about him orchestrated a calming effect on her soul. If only he weren't so bogged down in his own history. Maybe…

Wait a minute. Mac might be adorable, but he had an axe to grind and enough baggage to fill every space of an airplane's overhead bin. She shook her head and shrugged. Wishful thinking didn't get anybody anywhere. "Get that guy out of your head right now," she ordered herself out loud.

Some things simply weren't meant to be.

Chapter Twenty-Nine

Kat sat in the back of Dylan's car, picking her cuticles while she revealed the news of her family's sneak attack. "Bang. Ouch. Lights out. This is all I need."

Dylan and Shawn exchanged glances, then went to work comforting her—bless them. First, they threw snatches of suggestions in an overt effort to keep her mind centered on her music. She replied in monosyllables, until Dylan took charge.

"Your family's heard you sing before, right?" he asked.

"Concerts at school and little things like that. Never at a bar. I'm not sure Mother's ever been in a bar. For all I know, she'll faint dead away if anyone gets tipsy and yells or acts up. Anything's possible."

"Don't think that way," Shawn warned. "No negativity. Do what I told you and treat tonight like another evening at Pop's."

"Easier said than done, my friend, but I'll try." She took a sip of bottled water and silently commanded her AWOL confidence to return. This wasn't a time for wimps. She couldn't call in a performance. She had to feel it.

Dylan rounded a corner, and she spied the venue ahead. The Tin Bell was housed in a good-sized building with weathered red brick that proved it had been around a while. And why not? It sat right in the middle of historic Music Row. Dylan steered the car into a side lot and parked.

Kat scanned the area. "I don't see many cars. I expected this place to be full to the max."

Dylan opened his door. "Don't forget we're early. They wouldn't take a reservation, and we wanted to nab a table up near the stage. Before the competition starts, I'd imagine someone will have a few words for the singers too."

"My parents tend to be late for everything." Kat hoisted her guitar from the vehicle. "I'll bet Carolyn and Rio will ride along with them."

"Works for me if they're late. They'll be stuck in back where you can't even see them. Maybe they won't be able to get in at all. Within the next half hour, this place most likely will be jumping." Shawn grabbed the bag with her music. "Now don't you feel better?"

"Yes and no. My family did come quite a distance for this. Their intentions were good, even if it doesn't feel that way."

"Zip it," Shawn said. "No more talking about them. From this point on, focus on your song and nothing else."

"You're right." She tried to clear her mind as they walked through the door.

Inside Tin Bell, there were a few dozen people, some of whom held guitar cases. She followed Shawn and Dylan to a small table, front and center with three chairs. The perfect location for her to make eye contact with friendly faces. They seated themselves and a server approached the table with a pleasant smile. "What can I get for you?"

The men each ordered a beer, and Kat asked for a glass of water. "I'm one of the singers," she announced. "Am I supposed to check in or anything?"

"You need to see Dawg." The waitress pointed at a man of slight build with a moustache, who apparently needed his fingers to communicate. He held a clipboard in one hand and waved the other around as he spoke to a tall fellow who carried a mandolin case.

"You ought to head over there," Dylan said. "If all the singers need to be briefed, he'd probably appreciate it if he didn't have to repeat what he has to say twenty times."

Kat left her guitar with Shawn and Dylan, smoothed her hair, and hurried over to Dawg. She waited politely as she could for a pause in the conversation to introduce herself. "Hi, I'm Kat Becker."

"Yep," Dawg said and put a checkmark by her name on the paper. "You're listed as nineteenth to sing, so remember your number. All the performers should sit as close to the front as they can. The procedure will go like this: I've got chairs set up over there"—he pointed to three folding chairs—"near the stage. To avoid any delays between numbers, when the first performer is on, performers two, three, and four should be seated on the chairs and ready—and so on down the line. Got it?"

"Okay." Kat and the tall man spoke the same word simultaneously, and Kat grinned at the mandolin player. He didn't respond, swiftly pulling his gaze away from hers. Apparently, he either had a bad case of nerves or didn't believe in fraternizing with the competition. *Oh, well.*

She waited for further instructions, but Dawg put his hand to his ear and began talking to an invisible person as he walked away. Ah. A Bluetooth headset. Mandolin Player solemnly dipped his chin at her. She waggled her fingers in response before heading back to the table.

"I'm contestant number nineteen. He told me what to do."

"What'd you say?" asked Shawn.

She raised her voice. "I said I'm number nineteen."

Shawn's question highlighted the enormous growth in noise level. In the few minutes she'd been with Dawg, the place had filled. Chairs scooted across the floor, glasses clinked, and the clamor of a bar jammed with people speaking at once surrounded them. She squinted her eyes and looked around but didn't see any sign of her family. Was this good news or bad?

In a much louder voice, Kat spoke again. "I wish I weren't practically the last singer."

"It's good to be last. They'll remember you," Shawn yelled back and gave her a thumbs-up.

It also means I get to spend more time being nervous. Kat took a sip of water and kept her thoughts to herself. *I'm not nervous. I am not nervous. Or am I?*

The waitress brought their order, but Kat's attention drew to a long table beside the stage where a woman and two men seated themselves. Dylan nudged Kat and spoke straight into her ear. "The judges. See the gray-haired guy on the end? That's Pete Casson."

Kat's postured straightened to get a better view of him. He appeared pleasant enough if looks counted for anything. *Good Lord willing, he'll love my song.*

Dawg went to the microphone and tapped it a few times, waiting for the commotion to fade before he spoke. "Welcome to the Soaring Star finals." He introduced each judge and the crowd welcomed them one-by-one. When he said Pete Casson's name, there were whoops and cheers from the crowd.

The only name familiar to Kat was Pete's, but someone would have to be a hermit not to have heard of him.

"Singer number one, please take the stage," Dawg called.

A woman in a sequined blouse with a dobro trooped to the platform. Three other people sat in the folding chairs—presumably singers two, three, and four. The woman introduced herself and started her vocal, but her voice wavered, and the spotlight made her pale face even more colorless. The tune she sang sounded okay, but it lacked a certain…zing. There wasn't any other word to describe it. She finished, and after polite applause, relinquished the stage to singer number two. Kat took occasional sips of her water and analyzed each performer in turn. She hated to admit it, but most of the songs were solid, although performers varied in skill. It occurred to her she was up against some mighty stiff competition.

By the time performer number fifteen sang, Kat had her guitar in her lap, ready to move to the line of folding chairs.

She'd tuned her instrument earlier, so she felt confident the strings hadn't gone flat. Then singer number sixteen took the stage, her cue to move into position. Before she could get up, someone touched her shoulder. She cringed. *Don't let it be Mother. Please.* She steeled herself to peek at who was behind her.

Mac?

She gripped her guitar tighter.

"This is for you," he whispered in her ear. His voice sent a scrumptious shiver down her spine. "Good luck."

Kat's eyes widened, and she knew they must shimmer with moisture. She blinked and took the single daisy from his hand. "Thanks," she managed to say. For a moment she wondered where to put the flower, then she tucked it into her hair, right behind her ear. "Please don't leave, Mac. Sit here."

When she rose, he claimed the seat she vacated.

Dan nodded his head at Shawn and Dylan. Dylan's face registered surprise, but Shawn wore a self-satisfied grin. Dan leaned close enough for his brother to hear him. "I brought Pop. He wanted to stay in the back, so he wouldn't make her nervous." After the comment, he took a moment to thank his lucky stars for the way Kat's gaze had softened when she saw him, and then bull's-eyed his attention on her. He'd arrived in time to see only a few of the other performers, but thought she ought to win this competition on appearance alone. She sat poised and calm—her head turned to watch the singer on stage. Even her curls were more subdued than usual.

Two performers later, Kat had reached the seat designating her as next in line. Dan felt beads of perspiration gather at his hairline and blotted them away. He hadn't felt so nervous since his first day as an intern. Kat stepped onto the stage, and his breath caught.

She leaned toward the microphone. "Hello, Nashville! My name is Kat Becker, and I'm here today to make a little music for you. I want to play a song I've been working on for a while now. It's called 'Along the Road.' I sure hope you like it."

She finger-picked an introduction, then sang along with chords she strummed. Her face transformed as she lost herself in the music, caressing each word lovingly. Her fingers flew across the strings in a way that appeared effortless, although Dan wasn't fool enough not to realize the amount of work that went into playing as well as she did. The guitar made a perfect complement to a story of mourning what had been left behind as well as hope for the future. He looked around the room. The crowd wasn't holding any side conversations. They were paying attention. She had them. Even Dan found his foot tapping to the chorus.

> *Along the road*
> *Head filled with schemes*
> *I found my heart*
> *As I chased a dream.*

Dan wasn't a music critic, but he knew what he liked. And he liked Kat's song, with its smooth bluesy-country sound. He couldn't wait to tell her.

Once she finished and the last notes died away, he joined in the resounding echo of applause. Kat beamed her thanks and waved. As she stood in the spotlight, Dan saw how being on stage revamped her from a sometimes— often?—funny girl into a woman with presence, grace, and maturity. She belonged in this business. He understood it as well as he knew the certainty of his own calling.

Instead of returning to the table, Kat exited the stage, turned, and melted into the darkness. Dan glanced at Shawn who said, "That's where the bathrooms are. This is intense. She probably needs a few minutes to herself."

When the twentieth singer finished, Dawg returned to the mike. "We'll take a short intermission while the judges make their decision. In the meantime, here's some Nashville music for y'all to enjoy." The sound system played a slow tune, and a few couples ventured onto the floor. Kat showed up at the table, looking a little sheepish as though she didn't know what to expect from them. Shawn pecked her cheek, and Dylan hugged her.

Dan got to his feet and grabbed her hand. Instead of commenting on her performance, he said, "Dance with me?"

Her cheeks turned pink, and her mouth quirked up. Shawn took the guitar from her hands with full-on approval stamped across his face. They joined the other couples on the floor. Dan's arm circled around her waist, and she leaned into him. He breathed in her sweet vanilla and citrus scent. Even in high-heeled boots, the top of her head barely reached his chin. With her slender body tucked solid against his, an urge distracted him from the music's beat. He nearly stumbled but recovered himself. She didn't hesitate, following his lead like they'd been dancing together for years. Why not? Music wasn't only in her life. It was in her soul. He closed his eyes as they moved to the tempo.

"You're a good dancer," she said. "I thought you might be."

Her comment opened his eyes. He'd almost forgotten they were in a room filled with people.

"So are you. Not to mention a pretty amazing singer. You did a fantastic job."

"Thanks," she whispered. "I didn't expect to see you here, but I'm glad you came."

"All the performers in Nashville couldn't have kept me away. Not tonight."

She lifted her chin to study his face. "Did I hear you right? Have you finished your war with the music world?"

He paused a moment. "What you said to me is true. The past belongs in the past. It's time for me to get over it."

"You mean it?" She bit her lip. "But what about Ava?"

"From what I understand, she's going back into rehab, but this time not on my dime. Most likely it'll be somewhere in Iowa near her mother. The social worker is in charge of making the arrangements. As for me, I've told Ava there's nothing more I can do for her and blocked her number in case she forgets. She won't be calling me again."

Amazement flickered across Kat's face for an instant. Then she smiled and rested her head against him. Her soft hair tickled his neck, but he wouldn't have moved away from her for a bank vault filled with cash.

The song wound into its closing notes. Dan wished the melody would never end. It felt far too nice holding her in his arms. When the music stopped, he didn't let her go. She stayed close to him as if she wasn't ready to break the connection either. He knew they couldn't stand alone on the floor forever, and finally stepped away, but he didn't let go of her hand.

"Okay, folks, take your seats." Dawg drawled into the mike. "Our judges have made a decision."

People scuttled back to their tables, and Dawg waited for them to quiet down.

Dan took the only unoccupied chair at Shawn and Dylan's table. He pulled Kat onto his lap. What else could they do? There wasn't a single empty chair in the place, and it wouldn't be polite for either of them to stand and block the view of the people behind them. She gifted him with a grin that could only be described as contagious and leaned back against his chest. Dan relished the sensation of heat between them.

A young woman in sequined cowboy boots handed Dawg a piece of paper. "Here we go, folks," he said. "The judges remarked on how much they enjoyed hearing these talented singers present their original songs tonight. It was a hard decision, but they've narrowed the field to three." Dawg held up the paper. "Here they are, in no particular order. When your name is called, please join me on stage."

He opened the envelope. "Erik Bernes." Applause followed as the man walked to the stage. Dawg read the next name. "Don Weston."

Kat turned her head, and Dan caught a glimpse of something in her eyes he'd never seen before. Naked fear. He gave her arm a squeeze of support.

"And our third finalist…Kat Becker."

She catapulted herself from Dan's lap, and he waited for the squeal of joy he felt sure would follow. Instead, she took a deep breath and straightened the hem of her blouse before joining the other contestants.

"Let's give our finalists a big round of applause."

The audience complied. Dan put two fingers in his mouth and let out an ear-piercing whistle.

Shawn laughed. "I haven't heard you do that since we were kids!" he shouted over the roar.

Dan laughed and whistled again.

Dawg's hand went up to command silence. "Ladies and gents, Here's the moment we've been waiting for. Which singer/songwriter will win Soaring Star and receive a recording contract under the Portal Productions label?"

Miss Cowboy Boots gave Dawg an envelope and he paused for a dramatic moment, while the three contestants fidgeted and most likely—Dan figured—sweated bullets under the hot lights.

Dawg opened the envelope. "The winner of this year's Soaring Star competition is…Don Weston!"

A thunder of applause followed while Dan's stomach tied into knots. Kat had worked so hard for this. It didn't seem fair. But she didn't show a trace of disappointment.

She laughed and hugged the guy who won, a mandolin player. Then she hugged the other finalist. Someone appeared with a camera, and a light flashed again and again each time the photographer snapped a shot.

Shawn released a loud breath. "Well, she did her best."

"She did," Dylan agreed aloud. "I thought her song beat out the others, but everyone knows judging is a subjective thing."

"I'm afraid what this might do to her." Dan fisted his hand, possessed by a swift defensive urge.

"Don't underestimate Kat. She's tougher than you think," Shawn replied.

Picture-taking seemed to go on forever. Once it finally ended, Kat returned to the table. Dan examined her face—in his opinion, a fixed mask of faux cheer.

She caught his gaze and pushed a stray curl away from her cheek. "They made the right choice. His song was more seasoned than mine. Maybe I don't have what it takes after all."

Dawg returned to the microphone to drone his closing comments. Dan whispered in her ear, "You made the top three. That's impressive in my view. Don't let this stop you. Never give up on what makes you happy."

Her eyes flared in surprise. She wet her lips, leaned down, and kissed him. The kiss filled his mind with an urgent need to take her somewhere far from the hubbub of too many people and too much noise.

When she broke away from his mouth, Dan realized Dawg had finished speaking. People milled around the room. A few spectators shot smiling glances toward their table, while Shawn and Dylan flew into comfort-talk mode. They were in the middle of Monday-morning quarterbacking her performance when Pop, looking rosier and more energetic than he'd been for some time, elbowed his way to the table. *Damn! I forgot all about the old man.*

Pop grabbed Kat into a bear hug. "You were great and don't let any fool say otherwise."

When he released her, Kat stepped back within the crook of Dan's arm. It lightened his heart to see her cut loose with a genuine laugh after a silly remark from Shawn. It occurred to him they ought to go somewhere for dinner to celebrate, when a small group of people burst through the crowd. An older couple and a younger one. The older couple marched straight in Kat's direction, with a blonde woman leading the way. She wore a fashionable dress and heels—completely out of place for the setting—her face a study in determination. Were they music critics? Rabid fans? Dan instinctively stepped forward to keep them from getting too close, but Kat took his arm.

"Mac," she said in a steady voice. "I'd like you to meet my family."

Chapter Thirty

After a limp wave in her parent's direction, Kat left Mac's side. She hugged her mother and then kissed her father's cheek. "It's good to see you both."

"Oh, darling, I'm sorry. I was so sure you'd win." Her mother's gloomy tone immediately set Kat's teeth on edge.

"Enough of that, Elise." Tom Becker knew how to make a point, especially when he had an audience. He launched into presenting a verbal affidavit to the jury. "Don't you worry about anything, Kitty-Kat. The contest was probably rigged. Those judges most likely had everything decided before anybody started to sing."

With an earnest wish her parents were ensconced as far from Nashville as possible, Kat silently moved to hug her sister's fiancé. Rio appeared to suppress a smile as he said softly, "You did great, little sis."

Carolyn's embrace included a whispered comment. "Mother wanted to see you at intermission, but since you were on the dance floor, I held her back." She rolled her eyes surreptitiously.

"Thanks," Kat whispered back.

In the awkward moment, Kat glanced around at a sea of mostly uncomfortable faces and remembered her manners. She supplied a proper introduction to everyone in the group. With an innate sense which astounded Kat, her mother immediately zeroed in on Mac. "Kathryn hasn't mentioned your name before. It appears you know each other rather well."

Mac didn't hesitate a beat before slipping his arm around Kat's waist. She silently blessed his support. "We do. Between preparing for the competition and helping at my dad's restaurant, Kat's been running herself ragged. Pop just got out of the hospital a few days ago. We couldn't have managed without her. I suppose it's our fault she hasn't had time to tell you much about her adventures here." His words flowed in a smoothly practiced way.

Her mother surveyed him with a spark of suspicion. "I see. And I suppose you work at your father's restaurant as well?"

It seemed more a statement than a question. Kat longed to clap a hand over her mother's mouth but settled for a tart retort. "No, as a matter of fact, Mac works at Vanderbilt Health Center. Y'all will be surprised to hear this, I'm sure, but he's a doctor."

Boing! Her mother's face morphed from suspicion to unbridled interest. She spared one quick glance at Kat to say, "You've picked up a twang, darling. You don't sound a bit like yourself." Then she returned her scrutiny to Mac. "Please. Tell us more about your work."

Thankfully, Daddy interrupted. "Not now, Elise. It's too noisy here to talk. I have a wonderful idea. Why don't we all go to dinner where we can be more comfortable? You pick the place and it's on us. We'd like to get to know our daughter's friends better."

What could go wrong here? Kat almost suggested Pop's but figured her dad had something much more upscale in mind.

Carolyn was the first to break the silence and smiled at Pop. "What about your restaurant? I'd love to go there. Would that be okay with everybody?"

The suggestion brought a grin of approval from Kat.

"Sure." Pop's chest swelled with pride. "But if we go to *my* restaurant, dinner will be *my* treat."

Her father held up a hand. "No, I insist."

"I insist louder," Pop replied, spearing her father with a narrow-eyed look.

"Tell you what," Rio interceded. "I'll herd our group to the restaurant, and we can easily settle the issue there. Kat, why don't you meet us after you wrap things up."

Struck anew with respect for her future brother-in-law, Kat said, "Good idea. The restaurant is called Pop's Place, and it isn't far. Plug it into your GPS."

Carolyn tugged her mother's arm, and Mother shot a furtive glance over her shoulder at Mac on the way out. Kat mentally transmitted good-luck vibes to her sister.

Mac nudged Shawn. "Will you guys take Pop? And can you handle Kat's things too? I'd like to drive her if she's willing."

She figured her grin answered Mac's question.

"Sure," Shawn said. "Dylan drove. Is that okay, Pop?"

"And why wouldn't it be?" Pop slapped Dylan on the back. "Come on, boys. Let's hurry. I want to tell my server who gets the bill."

"Okay, Pop." Shawn picked up Kat's guitar case.

The three left Kat and Mac standing at the table. Mac threaded his fingers through hers. "What a night."

"Amen to that," she said.

"Are you okay with being part of this get-together at Pop's?"

"I'm a little shell-shocked at the moment, but by the time we get there, I'll be fine."

"Look, we don't have to meet them if you don't want to. I'll take you wherever you want to go."

"Don't tempt me." She laughed ruefully. "All these weeks of buildup only for a letdown. Who knows what my parents will have to say about it? I'm not even sure yet how I feel."

Someone approached from behind her, and a baritone voice said, "I'll tell you how you should feel…proud."

She turned and inhaled a sharp breath. "Oh! Mr. Casson." She shook the hand he held out. "I've been trying to get in touch with you for ages. My name's Kat Becker."

"I know who you are. Sorry I haven't had time to return your messages. Trevor told me about hearing you sing. I only have a minute, but I wanted to tell you I watched your video, and I liked it. A lot."

"I guess I didn't do enough to impress you tonight though," she said.

"On the contrary. What you wrote is good, and you performed it well. I think your song has a lot of potential. What I'm advising you to do is work on it with someone who has a fair amount of experience. Someone who knows how to help you get to the core of your feelings. I'd suggest you look into Belmont as a place where you'll find songwriters who can teach you the best way to speak your truth and tell your own story."

"As a matter of fact, I'm enrolled to start at Belmont in a couple of weeks."

"Good deal. I do some adjunct teaching for them. Maybe I'll see you there. When you think your song is ready, call me."

She knew her cheeks must be glowing. It felt like someone had torched her face. "Thank you, Mr. Casson. I appreciate your suggestions."

"There's an old saying in Nashville," he said. "It all begins with a song. Find the right one, and you're on your way." He shook her hand again and then headed for a group of people clustered around the judging table.

Dan arched an eyebrow. "Who is he?"

"He was one of the judges. He also manages Trevor T. Ray. Pete Casson is major stuff. The real deal." She all but sizzled with satisfaction. "I thought things would go a lot different from the way they did tonight. Yesterday I was so sure I'd win a contract, I almost canceled registration at school. How dumb could I be?"

Mac took her hand, pulled her close, and kissed her so thoroughly she thought her knees might buckle.

Applause erupted around them and Mac ended the sexy lip-lock. They'd apparently entertained several onlookers who beamed their approval.

"Sorry, but I couldn't resist." His grin didn't indicate a smidgen of repentance. "Are you ready to go?"

"As for the kiss, no apology necessary, and I'm as ready to go as I'll ever be." A thought occurred to her, and she turned to stare at Mac. "Wait a minute. Here I am, making myself the center of everything. Shawn told me what happened with the accountant. It's awful."

"I'm sorry he brought it up. There wasn't any need to ruin your big night." He sighed. "Jett's been arrested. He'd been pilfering cash to be a big shot, buying fancy suits and Italian shoes, not to mention drinks and meals he gave away to impress pretty women. Scumbag kind of stuff."

"Geez," she said. "Will he go to jail?"

"I'm not sure. The good news is he has assets, so there's a chance Pop will get most, if not all, of his money back. We made a restitution request. We're also insisting Jett be required to attend sexual harassment counseling. His law-yer is hot to make a deal. He says his client would rather cooperate than do jail time."

"Well, thank goodness. At least that's one less worry for Pop." She gave him the side-eye. "Shawn says you took time off to get all this straightened out."

"I'll help until Shawn and Dylan step in. After discussing the idea with Pop, they've agreed to take over management duties at the restaurant. It'll be a great opportunity for them. They're already talking about bringing in new artists to perform. Who knows? They might be able to help launch a career or two. Pop's all for it, since he can come back on a part-time basis as soon as his doc clears him."

She took in what he said. "A perfect arrangement—and what stinkers they are for not mentioning this to me."

"We all decided to keep it quiet until a final decision was made." He ran a thumb across her knuckles. "There'll be big changes at the hospital too."

"What do you mean?"

"I'm leaving the ER next month for that research job."

"What?" She squealed so loud, people around them turned to stare.

"The time's come to take a chance and do what I want. Sound familiar?"

"Kismet. I told you so! Mac, I'm proud of you."

"I think you may turn me into a believer yet. By the way, has anyone ever mentioned you're an excellent muse?"

"Not until this minute." Her heart felt full enough to spill over. *Might as well voice the question now.* "This string of awesomeness has me curious about something. Is your spare room still up for grabs?"

"The room's available. But it's only fair to warn you, I can no longer guarantee the arrangement will be purely platonic." He watched her as if gauging her reaction. "If that's a problem, Charlie can stay with me while you settle into another place—hopefully nearby."

She puckered her mouth. "Settle into another place? No way. Wherever Charlie goes, I go."

Mac grabbed her arm and tucked it around his. "I was hoping you'd say that. Come on, let's have some wind therapy before we face the lions. The ride here made Pop feel better, so I imagine it'll shore you up too." He walked her outside. "Did I mention I've been considering a brief road trip before I start my new job?"

"It's adorable when you talk like you ever take a vacation."

"I'm not kidding. I'd like to get away for a few days."

"Well, then. What do you think about somebody tagging along?"

Laughter rumbled from deep in his chest. Mac offered her his warmest, sexiest smile. "I just might be interested."

He mounted the Roadmaster, and Kat climbed behind him, nestling against his back. Tenderness led her heart into a dazzling duet with the night creatures. She inhaled a world of possibilities, put her arms around his waist, and held on.

If you enjoyed Kat and Dan's story, there's more. Don't miss the next book in the Becker Family series featuring a new member of the family, one the Beckers never knew existed. Meet a young woman who holds the key to a family secret.

Pathway to Home—Coming soon!

Acknowledgments

Along the Road came into being out of my love for Nashville, a city I've visited many times. This lively location has it all—historical sites, great music, abundant activities, and tantalizing food. It's the perfect place for an artist, a story-spinner, or a dreamer to settle. From this notion grew the story of Kat Becker, representative of many who make the pilgrimage to find a future in Music City. I hope you enjoyed reading her story as much I enjoyed writing it.

The process of writing is indeed a solitary pursuit, but every writer relies on others to help hone and polish a manuscript. How lucky am I to have a strong network of family, friends, and fellow writers who are kind enough to support my work? I am grateful to have you in my corner.

To Coffee and Critique, you are the most eagle-eyed and encouraging critique group on earth. Sounding board, advisors, and attentive listeners when I need to vent, you make everything better in more ways than I can count. A special thanks to Alice Muschany, beta reader extraordinaire. You don't miss a thing! My village of writing friends makes the journey ever so much more fun.

Members of Saturday Writers, you inspire me with your ability to cheerlead, your interest in the ideas circling through my head, and your smiles of encouragement. Thanks for helping a wanna-be author grow into the writer I've become.

To Angie Wade at Joy Editing, thank you for your edits and suggestions. You keep me on track and find things I can't believe I missed.

To Jenny Quinlan at Historical Editorial, I am in love with your designs. Each one is better than the last. Thanks for sharing your talent and fine eye for detail in creating my book covers.

When it comes to the nuts and bolts of putting a book together, I'm thankful to have Jeanne Felfe on my side. I couldn't do it without you!

To my family, I'd be nowhere without your support. You mean the world to me.

And, as always, thanks to my readers. There are books, books, and more books available in today's world. You chose mine. I'm more grateful than I can say for your support and kind words.

A Note to Readers,

Thank you for reading *Along the Road*. I hope you'll be watching for the third installment of the Becker Family series—coming soon!

I love to connect with readers, and welcome your feedback. You can find me on the following social media platforms:

Website: PatWahler.com

Facebook: Pat Wahler, Author

Twitter: @PatWahlerAuthor

Instagram: patwahler

You can also find me on BookBub, Goodreads, and Pinterest

If you're like me, you discover a new book or author via a friend's recommendation, or after reading a review. Recommendations and reviews are important, as they help new readers discover books.

If you enjoyed this story, please leave a short review at your favorite retailer site. Your opinion is important to me and helps provide the encouragement I need to create the next book just for you!

Here's a link for your convenience:

books2read.com/u/4AzQGA

With warmest regards,

Pat